W9-CCY-437

Pamela led the way down the steps, down the narrow concrete path, and along the sidewalk, until they reached another concrete path. From this path, steps led up to another porch, smaller and with a plainer railing, onto which the back door opened.

Saying "I'll try again," Marlene hefted the gift basket and headed up the steps. As she pressed the doorbell, the rest of the group joined her on the porch one by one.

Marlene turned away after a few minutes and much enthusiastic pressing of the doorbell. "No answer," she murmured. "And I was sure ANGWY was clear about the date and time."

She shrugged, edged past the others, and started down the steps. Bettina, however, stepped closer to the door and tipped her head to peer at the doorframe. "I'm not sure it's closed all the way," she said and gave the door a tentative push.

The door swung open easily. After a shrug and a glance at the other women, Bettina raised a stylishly shod foot and stepped over the threshold.

"Tassie?" Her voice rang out with a cheerful lilt. "Hello? It's the ANGWY committee."

She disappeared inside, but a moment later she was back in the doorway. Her cheer had vanished, leaving her face a wan canvas that made her careful makeup appear garish.

Ignoring her heart's sudden lurch, Pamela took a few quick steps and joined her friend in the doorway. Bettina backed up against the door, anchoring it in a fully open position, and Pamela slipped past her into the kitchen.

A woman lay sprawled on the ancient linoleum, a slender blonde woman wearing a light cotton robe printed with small flowers in shades of blue and lilac . . .

Books by Peggy Ehrhart

Knit and Nibble Mysteries
MURDER, SHE KNIT
DIED IN THE WOOL
KNIT ONE, DIE TWO
SILENT KNIT, DEADLY KNIT
A FATAL YARN
KNIT OF THE LIVING DEAD
KNITTY GRITTY MURDER
DEATH OF A KNIT WIT
IRISH KNIT MURDER
KNITMARE ON BEECH STREET

Knit and Nibble Anthologies
CHRISTMAS CARD MURDER
(with Leslie Meier and Lee Hollis)

CHRISTMAS SCARF MURDER
(with Carlene O'Connor and Maddie Day)

IRISH MILKSHAKE MURDER
(with Carlene O'Connor and Liz Ireland)

Published by Kensington Publishing Corp.

A Knit & Nibble
Mystery

KNITMARE
on BEECH
STREET

PEGGY EHRHART

Kensington Publishing Corp.
www.kensingtonbooks.com

KENSINGTON BOOKS are published by

Kensington Publishing Corp.
119 West 40th Street
New York, NY 10018

Copyright © 2023 by Peggy Ehrhart

All rights reserved. No part of this book may be reproduced in any form or by any means without the prior written consent of the Publisher, excepting brief quotes used in reviews.

To the extent that the image or images on the cover of this book depict a person or persons, such person or persons are merely models, and are not intended to portray any character or characters featured in the book.

This book is a work of fiction. Names, characters, businesses, organizations, places, events, and incidents either are the product of the author's imagination or are used fictitiously. Any resemblance to actual persons, living or dead, events, or locales is entirely coincidental.

If you purchased this book without a cover you should be aware that this book is stolen property. It was reported as "unsold and destroyed" to the Publisher and neither the Author nor the Publisher has received any payment for this "stripped book."

All Kensington titles, imprints, and distributed lines are available at special quantity discounts for bulk purchases for sales promotion, premiums, fund-raising, educational, or institutional use.

Special book excerpts or customized printings can also be created to fit specific needs. For details, write or phone the office of the Kensington Sales Manager: Attn.: Sales Department. Kensington Publishing Corp., 119 West 40th Street, New York, NY 10018. Phone: 1-800-221-2647.

KENSINGTON and the KENSINGTON COZIES teapot logo Reg US Pat. & TM Off.

First Printing: December 2023
ISBN: 978-1-4967-3886-8

ISBN: 978-1-4967-3888-2 (ebook)

10 9 8 7 6 5 4 3 2 1

Printed in the United States of America

For all the knitters.

ACKNOWLEDGMENTS

Abundant thanks to my agent, Evan Marshall, and to my editor at Kensington Books, John Scognamiglio.

CHAPTER 1

Voorhees House did not face Beech Street. It had been built long before the Arborville neighborhood where it was located even was a neighborhood, and it had stood in solitary Victorian splendor oriented toward a rambling dirt road that no longer existed. Later, a developer had bought all the surrounding land, laid out modern streets named for trees (though his building project had involved the loss of many trees), and built the houses that were now its neighbors—all of which properly faced the new streets that their construction had necessitated.

Standing on the sidewalk that ran past Voorhees House, Pamela Paterson and Bettina Fraser were therefore contemplating the side of Voorhees House. The house was shabby now, but the clapboard siding, the fish-scale shingles, the turret, and the small stained-glass window testified to its former glory.

Bettina had no sooner spoken, saying, "They'll be here soon, I'm sure," than a car pulled up across the street and three women climbed out. "Such a thoughtful thing the ANGWY committee does," she added, "welcoming new arrivals to the neighborhood."

"I guess Arborville Newcomers' Group Welcomes You is as good a name as any for the committee," Pamela commented, "even if the acronym doesn't sound all that cordial." As associate editor of *Fiber Craft* magazine, Pamela was perhaps more attuned than most people to the subtleties of language. "Tassie Hunt, from what I've heard of her, doesn't really strike me as the suburban type though. I hope she doesn't find Arborville boring."

"She's a writer," Bettina pointed out. "Maybe she's looking for solitude."

Snatches of conversation reached them as the women, led by Marlene Pepper, straggled across the street.

"I still can't see why a young—well, young-ish—woman would want to move into this old place," Faye Lamb was insisting, as if reiterating a topic she had already explored on the drive over.

"Well, she *did* inherit it," Marlene said.

"She could sell it and buy something nice," Faye responded, "nice and modern, a townhouse even, where other people take care of the grounds. Look at these weeds, not to mention that the house itself is falling apart."

"Terrible eyesore," Libby Kimble agreed. "My mother, bless her soul—she's gone now—but our house is just around the corner, and she always took a detour rather than having to drive down Beech Street."

"Oh!" Faye reached for Libby's hand. "I *did* hear that your mother had passed. I'm so sorry!"

"Thank you!" Libby squeezed Faye's hand and then released it. "I'm doing okay."

They had arrived at the spot where Pamela and Bettina waited.

"Here we are," Marlene announced, lifting high a basket adorned with ribbon and bearing a tag that read "Welcome to Arborville." "No goodies though. She was adamant about that."

"She was? I didn't know." Libby wrinkled her forehead.

"Adamant." Bettina nodded. "She was thin, to judge by her book-jacket photo anyway. That's the price you pay. No goodies—though, Pamela, how you can be such a terrific cook and still be so slender will always be a mystery. Being tall helps, I suppose."

Bettina herself wasn't thin, or tall, but her interest in fashion was acute and her scarlet hair—a color she admitted was unknown in nature—added considerable panache to her ensembles. She had dressed for the June morning in a chartreuse linen sheath accessorized with kitten heels in bright yellow patent and a necklace and earrings of Murano glass beads in shades that evoked a kaleidoscope.

Two of the women who had joined them resembled Bettina in size and shape, though not in style, dressed as they were in comfortable cotton pants and shirts. Marlene Pepper, like Bettina, was in her fifties and Faye Lamb was perhaps a generation older. Libby Kimble was older too, but slender to the point of being almost frail, with pale skin and colorless hair. Light eyes looked out from behind glasses whose rims were colorless as well. Her outfit, like those of the other women, seemed chosen for comfort.

"So—we're all ready"—Marlene looked around brightly—"and I guess the front door is around here?"

She took a few steps to the right, murmuring, "Such an odd thing, a sideways house."

A narrow concrete path led from the sidewalk to a set of steps that seemed to have been added more recently to the end of the long porch—added, perhaps, when the new street plan left the house with its curious orientation. Marlene led the way, followed by Bettina and the others, with Pamela bringing up the rear.

The wooden porch floor was worn and creaky, and the railing, with its delicate spindles, was sadly faded. The door reminded Pamela of her own, with its oval window and graceful carved flourishes, though her house was not as old as this one.

Marlene aimed a finger at the doorbell and pressed, and a faint ring echoed behind the door. No hastening footsteps could be heard, however, even though Tassie had been quite aware that the committee was due that morning.

"Upstairs perhaps," Bettina observed, "and she didn't hear the bell. This house is huge."

Marlene rang again, pressing several times, and *ding ding ding* echoed inside. Still there was no response.

"Sometimes back doors have doorbells too," Pamela suggested.

She led the way down the steps, down the narrow concrete path, and along the sidewalk, until they reached another concrete path. From this path, steps led up to another porch, smaller and with a plainer railing, onto which the back door opened.

Saying "I'll try again," Marlene hefted the gift basket and headed up the steps. As she pressed the doorbell, the rest of the group joined her on the porch one by one, with Pamela again bringing up the rear.

Marlene turned away after a few minutes and much enthusiastic pressing of the doorbell. "No answer," she murmured. "And I was sure ANGWY was clear about the date and time."

She shrugged, edged past the others, and started down the steps. Bettina, however, stepped closer to the door and tipped her head to peer at the doorframe. "I'm not sure it's closed all the way," she said and gave the door a tentative push.

The door swung open easily. After a shrug and a glance at the other women, Bettina raised a stylishly shod foot and stepped over the threshold.

"Tassie?" Her voice rang out with a cheerful lilt. "Hello? It's the ANGWY committee."

She disappeared inside, but a moment later she was back in the doorway. Her cheer had vanished, leaving her face a wan canvas that made her careful makeup appear garish.

"Pamela?" she quavered, bobbing this way and that to locate Pamela at the back of the small group. "Pamela . . . you . . . we . . . need to . . ." She swallowed. "There's been . . ."

The other three women stepped aside, clearing a path to where Bettina stood. Ignoring her heart's sudden lurch, Pamela took a few quick steps and joined her friend in the doorway. Bettina backed up against the door, anchoring it in a fully open position, and Pamela slipped past her into the kitchen.

A woman lay sprawled on the ancient linoleum, a slender blond woman wearing a light cotton robe printed with small flowers in shades of blue and lilac. There was no blood, nor any sign of injury that Pamela could see.

She stood rooted to the spot for a long moment, her hand raised to her chest as if to guard against the possibility that her heart's intense leaping might actually propel it from her body.

"Is something wrong in there?" came a voice from the porch.

But before either Pamela or Bettina could answer, Marlene Pepper stepped into the kitchen. "Oh," she said. It was more a choking sound than a word. "Oh," she repeated. "I guess that's why Tassie didn't . . ."

Faye Lamb joined them then. She took in the scene with a glance and whimpered, "What should we do? I've never . . ." Her eyes roamed the room, with its worn counters and out-of-date appliances. Suddenly she gasped, a sharp intake of breath that seemed loud against the shocked silence. "She was poisoned," Faye breathed, aiming a trembling finger at a spot between the sink and the refrigerator.

That spot was occupied by a pie, blueberry to judge by the purplish syrup oozing from the haphazard slashes—steam vents—carved into the top crust.

"Nobody's eaten any," Bettina observed, still a bit tremulous. "It's a whole pie. She'd have to have eaten some to have been poisoned."

"And she doesn't eat sweets, anyway." Marlene had joined the conversation. "So . . ."

"Why is it here then?" Bettina left her position against the door, which stayed open nonetheless, and crossed the floor to examine the pie. She bent close, then raised her head. "It looks homemade," she declared.

"Someone must have brought the pie," Marlene said. "Tassie wasn't alone then." She scrutinized the body on the floor with the same intensity Bettina had directed at the pie. "No injuries though, not obvious anyway. She looks like she's asleep." As if it had just occurred to her, she added, "I guess we should call the police."

"Of course we should call the police!" Bettina seemed a bit recovered from her shock—and had perhaps concluded that she was the likely person to take charge, given that she reported on police doings (and all else that happened in Arborville) for the town's weekly newspaper.

She extracted her phone from the depths of her chic handbag—yellow patent, to match her shoes. Her carefully manicured fingers fluttered over its screen for a few seconds, then she looked up. "Done," she announced, with a decisive head shake that set the scarlet tendrils of her hair vibrating.

Faye Lamb, meanwhile, had strayed toward the doorway that led from the kitchen to the next room. "There wouldn't be any harm, would there, if we . . ." She left off, directed a hopeful glance at Bettina, and continued. ". . . if we sat down in there? I'm feeling a little shaky."

Indeed, above the collar of her neatly pressed shirt and framed by a tidy gray-brown bob, Faye's expression was bleak, and her hand grasped the doorframe with a grip that seemed desperate.

"I don't see the harm," Marlene said before Bettina could answer. She swept forward and slipped her free arm around Faye's waist. In her other hand she still carried the welcome basket.

Libby followed, and Bettina and Pamela. Within a minute or two, all five women had taken seats at the long table that dominated the room.

"Dining room, I guess," Marlene observed as she surveyed their new surroundings.

It was quite obviously the dining room, though rendered gloomy by the heavy velvet drapes that cloaked the bay windows. The long table, which could have accommodated a dozen people, was made of highly polished mahogany, as were the chairs that surrounded it. Their graceful curves and ornately carved backs echoed the table's design. Dark wooden moldings outlined the windows and doorframes and edged the walls at floor and ceiling. The walls were papered in a rich, deep burgundy enlivened with creamy arabesques shaped from delicate flower garlands. Up above, that motif was enlarged in a frieze that bordered the ceiling.

"Spooky." Faye shuddered. "I couldn't eat in a room like this. No wonder they say Voorhees House is haunted."

"Edith Voorhees survived here alone all those years without the ghosts getting her," Marlene said.

"I guess Tassie was a relative?" Faye glanced from Marlene to Bettina and back.

"Must have been." Bettina joined the conversation. "She can't have been Edith's daughter though—Edith Voorhees was ancient."

Ninety-six, to be precise. The *Arborville Advocate* had carried the obituary, written by Bettina, and then the house had sat empty for a year. Unconsciously, Pamela ran a finger over the table's surface and lifted the finger close to examine it in the gloom. No dust. Tassie, or more likely someone hired for the purpose, must have spent days making the house even somewhat habitable before she moved in. Pamela herself found the décor lovely—her own house was furnished with vintage treasures rescued from thrift shops and rummage sales—but the appeal to someone like Tassie, or at least like what she imagined Tassie to have been, was something of a mystery.

These ruminations were interrupted by a piercing siren. It subsided into a resentful yowl, indicating that a police car had slowed and then stopped somewhere nearby.

CHAPTER 2

Bettina was on her feet in an instant. She dashed through the doorway that led to the kitchen, leaving the other four women to regard each other in the gloom.

"What will they do?" Faye whispered.

"Look around," Marlene said, "and then ask questions."

They were silent then, but the air seemed heavy—weighed down by the women's unspoken thoughts, perhaps, or by the house's own particular history.

Bettina's voice broke the silence, her words reaching them from beyond the kitchen doorway. "She was lying on the floor just like this when we walked in." Responding to a question Pamela couldn't hear, Bettina went on, sounding a bit more excited. "No," she said. "I don't have a key. The door was unlatched, almost open really. I just gave it a little push. I didn't force it. And she was expecting us—or would have been . . . if she was still alive. The ANGWY committee was delivering a welcome basket."

Pamela rose and peeked through the doorway. Bettina had turned a distressing shade of pink, though the officers who had responded to the 911 call were among Arborville's least intimidating (not that anyone on Arborville's police force could actually be described as intimidating): Officer Sanchez, with her sweet heart-shaped face, and boyish Officer Anders.

Officer Sanchez, holding a small notepad and a pen, was focused on Bettina. Officer Anders had dropped to one knee next to Tassie's body and was peering closely at her face. He looked up and addressed Officer Sanchez. "Call Clayborn?" he inquired.

Officer Sanchez nodded. Then she caught sight of Pamela. "And the two of you are the committee?" she said.

"No." Bettina shook her head, setting her dangling earrings in motion. "We're not actually even *on* the committee. We just came along . . . well, I came because Tassie—the new resident—had sent the *Advocate* some material about her forthcoming book. She is . . . *was* . . . a writer." Bettina paused and took a deep breath. "The committee is in here." She took a step toward the doorway, and Pamela edged to the side as Bettina neared the threshold.

The committee members were on their feet, standing uncertainly near the doorway as if expecting to be asked to leave. But Officer Sanchez, who had followed Bettina into the room, waved them back.

"Be seated. Please be seated," she said, and watched while they all returned to their chairs, with Marlene and Faye and Libby exchanging nervous glances. "Detective Clayborn is on the way," Officer Sanchez explained when they were settled. "He'll talk to each of you individually."

She returned to the kitchen, and Pamela heard Officer Anders say something that sounded like, "Seems to be natural causes."

"Clayborn should take a look though, and he'll probably want the crime scene unit from the county," Officer Sanchez responded. "She does appear to have been a young, healthy woman."

They all stared at each other again, in a silence that was so intense it was like a physical presence. Five minutes passed, and then five more, before overlapping voices coming from the kitchen included a new, deeper, voice, suggesting that Detective Clayborn had arrived. After a brief conference with the officers, he stepped through the doorway and entered the dining room.

Dour as he was, he brought with him a welcome energy that lightened the atmosphere, though the expression on his homely face was as unremarkable as his nondescript sports jacket.

"I'm Detective Lucas Clayborn from the Arborville Police," he said, still on his feet and shifting his gaze slowly from one woman to another. A slight tightening around his eyes when he reached Pamela and Bettina was the only hint that, in their case, the introduction was unnecessary. Bettina, of course, talked to him frequently in connection with her reporting for the *Advocate*, and—curiously—this was not the first or even the second crime scene she and Pamela had stumbled upon. More curiously still, the clues that enabled the police to identify and arrest the town's evildoers were sometimes provided by Pamela's and Bettina's sleuthing.

"I'll be talking to each of you individually," Detective Clayborn went on. He extracted a small notepad and a pen from somewhere inside his sports jacket and

focused on Libby, who was sitting in the chair closest
to the head of the table. "Name?"

He flourished the pen, and she responded "Libby
Kimble" in a faint and tentative voice.

After he'd written down everyone's name, including Bettina's and Pamela's, he nodded sharply, as if to
himself, and gestured toward a doorway beyond the far
end of the table. From where she sat, Pamela's view
through the doorway was of forest-green walls, a swath
of burgundy velvet draping a window, and part of a
stiff-looking sofa upholstered in similar dark tones.

"This way, please, Ms. Kimble," he said, escorting
Libby through the doorway and closing the door behind them.

Pamela was the second-to-last person to be summoned through the doorway, leaving Bettina alone at
the long table. The room she entered had evidently
been the living room of the Voorhees House.

Seated on the sofa facing Detective Clayborn, who
was in a stiff chair upholstered in the same dark fabric,
she could see the entry with, to the left, the door whose
doorbell had been so ineffective in summoning the
house's occupant. To the right, stairs rose to the second
floor against a wood-paneled wall enlivened by a stained-
glass window that turned sunlight into dim rays of red,
blue, and gold.

The room was clean. As she'd surmised in the dining room, a great deal of effort must have gone into
making the house habitable before Tassie moved in,
given that its previous occupant—for decades—had
been an eccentric recluse, and the house had then sat
empty for a year. But it was very shabby. The carpet

was threadbare, the upholstery was worn, the drapes were faded, and the fireplace's marble mantel was chipped and stained.

The kitchen had clearly been updated at some point in the twentieth century—perhaps in the 1940s, when Edith would have come to the house as a young bride. But the other rooms Pamela had seen seemed almost to have retained the décor that furnished them when the house was new.

"Now then . . ." Detective Clayborn interrupted Pamela's musings. "What was your purpose in visiting Voorhees House this morning?"

Pamela repeated the explanation Bettina had given Officer Sanchez, about the committee's welcoming mission and Bettina's journalistic interest. And she added that she and Bettina were friends—at which Detective Clayborn seemed to suppress a resigned sigh—and Bettina had invited her to come along.

"No, I did not see the body right away," she answered in response to Detective Clayborn's next question. "Bettina was the first to enter the kitchen."

"Did you or anyone else touch or move anything after you entered the kitchen?" Detective Clayborn asked.

"No . . . no." Pamela shook her head. "Bettina looked at the pie . . ." Not sure whether Detective Clayborn had noticed the pie, she clarified. "The blueberry pie on the counter?" He nodded. "In fact, she looked very closely, but she didn't touch it."

"Was there some reason Ms. Fraser was particularly interested in the pie?"

"Well, it *was* a pie"—Pamela suppressed a smile as she pictured her and Bettina's mutual friend Holly Perkins adding, *Duh!*—"but actually," she went on, "the committee was wondering why a pie was there at all because Tassie had made it clear that she didn't welcome edible gifts, especially sweet ones."

Detective Clayborn bent toward his little notepad and wrote furiously for a minute.

"And then Ms. Fraser called nine-one-one, and you all went into the dining room?"

"Faye Lamb was feeling shaky, and there weren't enough chairs in the kitchen," Pamela said. "We thought it would be okay—better than having her faint."

Detective Clayborn tipped his head in a businesslike nod, his homely face expressionless. "That's all." He nodded again. "Please ask Ms. Fraser to join me in here."

Officer Anders was stationed in the kitchen near where Tassie Hunt still lay on the floor in her summery cotton robe. He gestured for Pamela to make a wide circle around the body and then opened the back door and ushered her onto the porch. She would wait for Bettina, of course—they had come together in Bettina's car.

But when she reached the street, she realized she would not be waiting alone. Marlene was perched on a folding chair on the sidewalk. The chair, Pamela learned, had been thoughtfully provided by a neighbor.

"Very nice woman." Marlene pointed toward the house to the right of Voorhees House. "Of course, she *was* awfully interested in what was going on." Marlene waved at a small, older woman sitting on that house's front porch.

And, as if to reward that interest, a huge silver van turned onto Beech Street. On its side was the logo of the county sheriff's department. The van slowed as it neared Voorhees House.

"Libby and Faye are at Libby's house," Marlene said. "They walked. Like she said, Libby lives just around the corner on Catalpa. She's making coffee and tea, and we're all invited to join them there when Detective Clayborn is through with Bettina. Libby and Faye are both very rattled."

Pamela was longing to get back to her own comfortable house, but Marlene stood up, as if to present her case from a more commanding position. "Please do come." She grasped Pamela's hand. "I know Bettina will be willing—she's such a sympathetic soul."

Someone must have pitched in with yard work during the time that Voorhees House was vacant, Pamela reflected as they waited for Bettina. In contrast to the manicured yards elsewhere on the block, the swath of land between Voorhees House and the sidewalk was still a jumble of perennial foliage interspersed with tall stalks of wild grass, but not as wild as if it had been completely untended all that time.

"Here she is!" Marlene pointed toward where Bettina had edged aside to let two people in the white jumpsuits of the crime scene unit pass en route to the back porch. In a few moments, she had joined them on the sidewalk.

"What did he ask you?" Marlene inquired, climbing to her feet again and grasping Bettina's hand. "He told me he'd have to impound the welcome basket. I suppose he'll take that blueberry pie too."

For her part, Pamela studied her friend's face, concluding after a long stare that Bettina looked exactly like her usual self and therefore must not have received a scolding from Detective Clayborn. Granted, they had all entered the house without permission, but the door had been unlocked—and finding the body sooner rather than later would certainly be of value in case the medical examiner discovered that Tassie had not died of natural causes.

In short order, Bettina agreed that refreshments at Libby's house would be a welcome solace after that morning's adventure. The borrowed chair was returned to the neighbor, who was quite awed by the fact that a van from the sheriff's crime scene unit was parked right on her very block, and Bettina led Pamela and Marlene to where her faithful Toyota waited at the curb. Before turning her key in the ignition, she took out her phone for a quick call to her husband, Wilfred, advising him she'd be home a bit later than planned.

The journey to Libby's house was short. Her house, in fact, backed up to the other side of Voorhees House. Like all the houses on Beech Street, except for Voorhees House, the houses on Catalpa Street were tidy structures of brick and stone, with sharply peaked roofs and half-timbered gables that created a charming storybook effect. That effect was enhanced by the front door, rounded at the top and constructed of wide wooden planks, with dark metal hardware that looked hand-forged (though it probably was not).

The inside of Libby's house was charming too, in an old-fashioned way. The cozy living room was furnished with a dusty-pink sofa and a matching armchair, upholstered in a soft-textured pile fabric. Lamp tables at either end of the sofa held matching lamps with bases that evoked Chinese urns, an oval coffee table flanked the sofa, an antique desk occupied one wall, and a long, narrow table under a window was crowded with framed photos, family photos seemingly.

There were many many photos, older photos in back and newer photos in front, successive generations edging out their elders on the tabletop as they had edged out their elders in life. Photos in the front row memorialized a wedding, a graduation, a prom, a child with a dog, and a sunny day at the shore. Parts of older photos could be glimpsed through spaces between the front-row frames. One of those showed another wedding—this one from an era when formal photos seemed all the more formal for their sedate black-and-white tones. Another, also in black and white, captured the serene gaze of a baby in a long, knitted christening gown. And in still another, color this time, three little boys in graduated sizes but matching suits posed with a department-store Santa.

"I love your house!" Bettina exclaimed to Libby, who had greeted them at the door. Sounds of clinking china coming from somewhere farther back in the house suggested that Faye had pitched in with refreshments.

"I grew up here," Libby said, "then I moved back in to care for my mother after I was widowed. Now that she's gone, I've inherited it, and I'm back in my old bedroom. Sometimes I wake up surprised that so much time has passed."

Faye popped into the room from a doorway that opened into a hall. "Is anyone besides Libby a tea drinker?" she inquired.

Nodding as three people responded in unison with "No," she disappeared again.

"Please make yourselves comfortable," Libby urged, gesturing in a random way that Pamela interpreted to mean they were being steered toward the sofa. Once they were seated, with Marlene in the middle, Libby turned and headed toward the hall.

Soon a familiar and tantalizing aroma signaled the arrival of refreshments, and Libby stepped into the room bearing a tray laden with steaming cups of coffee, delicate china cups nestled on saucers. "I *am* a tea drinker," she said, "but I keep coffee on hand for guests, and I have one of those fancy coffeemakers now."

"The coffeemaker's name is Faye Lamb," came a voice from somewhere behind Libby. In a moment Faye appeared, peeking over Libby's shoulder. "Sugar and cream are on the way, ladies," she added. "And a special treat—Libby's homemade muffins."

After a few minutes of bustle, involving more trips to the kitchen and the delivery of cream and sugar, spoons, napkins, a platter of muffins, and small china plates to accommodate the muffins, all five women were seated, with beverage of choice at hand. Faye had settled into the armchair that matched the sofa, and Libby was perched at the far end of the coffee table on an attractive straight-backed wooden chair fetched from its position at the antique desk.

As Bettina focused on calibrating the precise amount of sugar and cream that would transform the dark brew in her mug into the sweet mocha concoction she favored, Faye served the muffins. Transferring them from the platter to small plates, she set one in front of each of the three women sitting on the sofa and stood up to deliver one to Libby.

They sipped and nibbled in silence, except for Bettina noting about the muffins that lemon and poppy seeds made a very good combination. After a bit, Libby set her mug down with a contented sigh and said, "I do feel a bit calmer now." She tilted her head back, and behind her glasses her eyes fluttered shut. She opened them again to add, "What a shock that was this morning."

"It would have been bad enough," Marlene observed, "but then the police made such a big thing out of it. I certainly couldn't see any evidence that a crime had been committed. Sometimes people just . . . *die*."

Pamela nodded. "I thought I heard one of the officers say it looked like Tassie's death was due to natural causes. They have to make sure though . . ."

"They do." Bettina joined the conversation after first conveying a last tidbit of muffin to her mouth. "Tassie Hunt was young, and she was certainly fit. If an elderly person, especially one who's been under a doctor's care for a serious illness, dies in a situation like that—dead on their kitchen floor with no sign of foul play—it's usually clear what carried them off and there's no need for an autopsy. But in this case, Tassie wasn't elderly and she wasn't ill, as far as we know. The medical examiner who does the autopsies works for the county sheriff, so they sent the van, and the whole CSI crew, though I didn't notice that anyone was photographing the scene or dusting for fingerprints."

"An autopsy makes sense." Marlene's cup paused halfway to her mouth. "They could discover she had a stroke or an aneurysm—even a heart attack. And I'm sure her family would want an explanation."

"My cousin had a brain aneurysm," Faye murmured. "It *almost* killed him."

The sound of heavy feet on the stairs leading down from the second floor distracted them then. The feet continued toward the doorway that opened into the hall, and a tall young man ducked his head into the room.

"Hey, Grandma," he said. "Were the police doing something around the corner?"

It was only a short distance from where Libby was sitting to the doorway where the tall young man stood. She hopped to her feet and covered the distance in a few quick steps. Taking his arm, she led him into the hall, from which came the low hum of an unintelligible conversation. After a minute, the low hum was replaced by the sound of the front door opening and closing, and she returned to her perch on the straight-backed chair.

"My grandson," she said with a fond smile. "He's staying with me while his parents are off gallivanting in Europe. He was hurrying out to his job at the mall or I would have introduced you."

"He's quite the accomplished young man." Faye tilted her head toward the sofa to address the three women lined up there. "High school valedictorian and an athlete besides."

"Really? How impressive!" Bettina was always quick to respond when she sensed that a compliment was being sought. Her brightly painted lips curved into a smile, and her eyelashes fluttered. "What is his sport?"

"Wrestling." Libby took over from Faye. "He'll be going to Millford University in Vermont on a wrestling scholarship this fall."

"That is indeed impressive." Bettina's smile widened. "And I'm sure readers of the *Advocate* would be interested in his story. People always like to read about the accomplishments of Arborville's young people."

"He'd be happy to talk to you." Libby looked quite

pleased. "I'll check on his work schedule and let you know when he'll be around."

"More coffee, anyone?" Faye asked, leaning forward to study the contents of their cups.

Pamela's "I'm fine" overlapped with Bettina's "No thanks" and Marlene's "Maybe just a splash." Reminded of her coffee, Pamela took another sip and then focused on the lemon and poppy-seed muffin. It was rich and buttery, made with fresh-squeezed lemon juice, she suspected. The tang of lemon juice and the slight nuttiness of the poppy seeds offset the muffin's sweetness, though plenty of sugar had gone into its making, she was sure.

The topic of Libby's grandson and his accomplishments had provided a welcome segue from the adventure that had brought them all to Libby's house. As Faye replenished Marlene's coffee and her own, as well as Libby's tea, the conversation flowed into more quotidian channels.

Marlene, who was chair of the community garden program, enthused about the effect the particularly wet May had had on the crops, with the squash vines already producing magnificent blossoms. Bettina contributed that Wilfred had brought back rhubarb and asparagus from his recent trip to the Newfield farmers market. And Pamela, whose principal crops were herbs in pots on her back porch and tomatoes in one small sunny spot afforded by her otherwise shady yard, reported that she had already noticed blossoms on the tomato plant advertised as early bearing.

Half an hour passed in this pleasant way until, announcing herself as very much comforted and refreshed, Marlene climbed to her feet and eased her way past Bettina's knees. Pamela, Bettina, and Faye rose too, and Libby saw them all to the door. Once outside, people dispersed to their respective cars, and soon Bettina's faithful Toyota was heading down the hill that led to Arborville Avenue. From that corner, it proceeded to Orchard, where Pamela and Bettina lived halfway down the block in houses that faced each other across the street.

CHAPTER 3

As Bettina pulled into her driveway and parked the Toyota next to Wilfred's ancient but lovingly cared-for Mercedes, the front door of her house opened. A bulky man in bib overalls stepped out, followed by a large and shaggy dog and a small young woman with dark, curly hair.

"Dear, dear wife!" the man, who was Bettina's husband Wilfred, cried, extending his arms and hurrying down the walk that connected the driveway to the house's front porch. "We were starting to get worried! I know you phoned, but you didn't say why you'd be delayed, and then so much time passed . . ."

He reached Bettina's side and pulled her into an embrace, her bright scarlet head nuzzled against the denim of the overalls he had adopted as his everyday uniform when he retired. The shaggy dog, so large it reached nearly to his waist, sidled up to his thigh. He loosened his grip on his wife to let a hand rest comfortingly on its back.

Meanwhile, the young woman, who was Pamela's daughter Penny, had darted around to the other side of the car, where Pamela had just lowered her feet to the asphalt of the driveway.

"Where have you been?" Penny inquired, a worried crease momentarily disturbing her smooth forehead.

"Bettina went along with the ANGWY committee when they paid a welcome call on the new resident of Voorhees House," Pamela said, climbing to her feet. "She invited me to come too."

"I know about that part." The worried crease reappeared. "You said you'd be back in an hour. It's been more like three."

Before Pamela could answer, Wilfred's voice reached them. "Dead?" He reared back and the shaggy dog gave a subdued yelp. "What happened?" He bent forward to study his wife's face, his own genial features twisting with concern.

"Tassie Hunt was lying on the kitchen floor, dressed as if ready for bed," Bettina said. "There was no sign she was injured or anything, and when the police came, it sounded like they thought she had just . . . died . . . there, on her own."

"*Mo-om!*" This came from Penny. "Why are you always around when things like this happen?"

"Nothing happened." Pamela wrapped an arm around Penny's slender shoulders and squeezed. "But we had to call the police, of course, and they wanted to talk to everyone . . ."

"And"—Bettina took up the story, addressing Penny over the roof of the Toyota—"the ANGWY women were upset, and Libby Kimble wanted everyone to come to her house to calm down with coffee and muffins—though she actually drinks tea." She paused, then added parenthetically, shifting her gaze to Wilfred, "Lemon-poppy-seed muffins."

Penny sighed. "Well, I'm just glad you're both back." She sighed again and turned toward the street. "I have plans for the day."

After quick goodbyes to Bettina and Wilfred, Pamela followed her daughter back to their own house.

The Frasers' house was the oldest on the street, a Dutch Colonial built and inhabited by the proprietors of the apple orchard that had given Orchard Street its name. Later, the apple trees had been replaced by more houses, houses that themselves were now old. Pamela's house, a wood-frame house with a wide and deep porch and clapboard siding, dated from the early 1900s. She and her architect husband, newly wed then, had bought it as a fixer-upper and worked and worked on it together. They had barely completed their labors when he was killed in a tragic work-site accident, but Pamela had stayed on in the house, with Penny, who was just a small child then. She had wanted Penny's life to remain as much the same as possible, and she herself felt her husband's presence as she moved through the refurbished rooms where they had labored together.

"I was getting worried," Penny explained as they approached their front walk, "so I crossed the street to ask Wilfred if he'd heard anything, and he had, but you could have thought to call me."

"You told me you were going to the mall with Lorie," Pamela said. "I didn't know you'd be sitting at home waiting for me."

"I *am* going to the mall." Penny bounded up the porch steps. "I'm going to grab my purse and my phone, and I'm not going to tell you when I'll be back."

A few minutes later, Penny was on her way, but even with her daughter gone, Pamela was not alone in her house. A ginger-colored cat was delicately sniffing her mistress's shoes, as if seeking, in her own way, an update on Pamela's morning adventures. Soon a lustrous black cat joined them, padding in from the kitchen, happy to see her mistress but uninterested in her shoes. From the top platform of the cat climber in the living room, an elegant Siamese cat watched the proceedings briefly and then went back to grooming herself.

The lemon-poppy-seed muffin had been filling, if not particularly sustaining. Though lunchtime had come and gone, Pamela didn't feel inclined to eat. Perhaps she'd been more troubled by the morning's events than she'd let on to Penny. A body on a kitchen floor, natural causes or not, was a shocking sight, and her mind was still unsettled. But a remedy awaited.

Pamela's work was a great distraction, both in the content of the articles submitted to *Fiber Craft* and in the focus her editing work required, a focus that often put her into a meditative state not unlike the effect of knitting. And since she worked from home, her office was only a flight of stairs away.

At her desk, in the pleasant upstairs room that looked out on her backyard, Pamela allowed her computer mouse to range freely on its mouse pad until its wanderings awoke her monitor. She scanned the two emails that had arrived since she'd checked her inbox that morning—a note from her alma mater about an upcoming reunion and a reminder from the power company that summer storms can cause power outages—and then she clicked on the message from her boss at *Fiber Craft*, Celine Bramley.

Short titles for three attachments were lined up across the top, each accompanied by the Word logo: "Woven Together," "Silk Road," "Mother of Invention." The message itself instructed that the articles were to be copyedited and returned by the following Monday. She opened the first, whose full title was "Woven Together: Ancestral Rug-Making Skills Enrich Contemporary Carpet Design in Oaxaca."

A few pages into the article, Pamela's stomach reminded her that she'd never had a proper lunch. After a quick meat-loaf sandwich, she returned to her office and immersed herself in her editing work until Penny's voice floated up the stairs. It was nearly six p.m., though her office windows were still bright behind their curtains. Penny was back from the mall, and it was dinnertime, for both cats and humans.

Marcy Brewer, the *County Register*'s ace reporter, had outdone herself. The next morning, Pamela fetched the *Register* from the end of her driveway, extracted it from its flimsy plastic sleeve, and unfolded it on her kitchen table to reveal a headline that inquired in bold-face type, "DID SHE DIE OF FRIGHT?" The accompanying photograph showed the exterior of Voorhees House, shot in such a way as to make it look like a haunted-house attraction at an amusement park.

The comforts of coffee and toast would be necessary, Pamela decided, as an accompaniment to reading the article itself. And the kettle was whistling to remind her that the water she had set to boil on the stove before collecting the newspaper was now ready for its coffee-brewing task.

Accordingly, she quickly measured fresh coffee

beans into the grinder and fitted a paper filter into her carafe's plastic filter cone. She pressed down on the grinder's cover to launch the clattering and whirring that would transform the beans into fragrant grounds, tipped the grinder over the filter cone, and followed up with the steaming, bubbling water. As the water dripped through the grounds into the carafe below, she slipped a slice of whole-grain bread into the toaster.

A few minutes later, she was seated at the little table, coffee at hand in a wedding-china cup and buttered toast on a wedding-china plate, ready to ponder the *Register*'s treatment of the scene she, Bettina, and the ANGWY committee had stumbled upon the previous morning.

Stressing that the police had found no sign of foul play, Marcy Brewer played up the house's spooky history as the home of an aged recluse. And she included testimony from neighbors who had noticed weird noises and unexplained lights during the year the house was empty after Edith Voorhees's death. Referring to Tassie's recent book debunking spiritualism, *A Sucker Born Every Minute*, Marcy Brewer suggested that perhaps she had been particularly eager to take possession of the house she had inherited to demonstrate that she was not afraid of ghosts and that any supposed hauntings had rational explanations.

Pamela reached the end of the article just in time to look up and greet Penny, who had appeared in the kitchen doorway still in her pajamas and with the ginger-colored cat in her arms. The cat, whose name was actually Ginger, was Pamela's second feline adoptee. The first was the lustrous black cat, Catrina, who had showed up on Pamela's front porch as a woebegone stray a few years earlier. Catrina had given birth to

Ginger and five additional kittens after an unplanned dalliance with a dashing ginger tomcat. The third cat, the elegant Siamese whose name was Precious, had come into Pamela's life as a result of her previous owner's death.

"She needs her breakfast," Penny said, lowering Ginger gently to the floor. "I see the others have already eaten," she added, nodding toward the corner where two bowls containing only the faintest traces of cat food testified to Catrina's and Precious's appetites.

She took a half-full can of cat food from the refrigerator and a clean bowl from the cupboard, and soon Ginger was savoring a healthy scoop of seafood medley.

Marcy Brewer's article had continued to an inner page of the *Register*, where a smaller headline read, "PUZZLE IN VOORHEES 'HAUNTED HOUSE' DEATH." Penny had been on her way to the stove, where a carafe still half-full of coffee waited, but she paused en route and leaned over Pamela's shoulder.

"Does it mention you and Bettina?" she asked.

Pamela swiveled her head to make eye contact with her daughter. Penny's pretty lips had curved into an unhappy close-mouthed smile that carried a hint of disapproval.

"Only in passing," Pamela responded. "But Marcy Brewer *did* track Marlene Pepper down for a quote."

Penny was still leaning over Pamela's shoulder. "Nothing like this has ever happened to the ANGWY committee before, according to committee member Marlene Pepper, " she read aloud, suppressing a laugh at the end. "Well, I hope not!" she exclaimed and continued on toward the stove.

Pamela was about to put Part 1 of the *Register* aside

in favor of Lifestyle, when she was interrupted by the doorbell's chime. She hopped to her feet and stepped into the entry. Bettina, whose scarlet hair made her recognizable through the lace that curtained the oval window in the front door, was waiting on the porch.

Her first words after she crossed the threshold were, "Crumb cake." She displayed a white bakery box secured with a crisscross of string and headed for the kitchen.

"No need for toast, Miss Penny," Pamela heard her say.

Pamela entered the kitchen to find the bakery box on the table, the flap turned back to reveal a very generous portion of the Co-Op Grocery's crumb cake. Penny was at the stove, watching the carafe for the small bubbles that would indicate the leftover coffee was approaching drinkable temperature, and Bettina was pouring heavy cream into the cut-glass cream pitcher that matched Pamela's thrift-shop sugar bowl. Pamela herself set out two more wedding-china cup and saucer sets and two more wedding-china plates.

A few minutes later, they were all gathered around the little table, Pamela on a chair fetched from the dining room. Each plate held a square of crumb cake, moist and yellow and topped with a rumpled layer of buttery-floury-sugary crumb deposited in careless profusion. Encircled by the rose-garlanded rim of her coffee cup, Pamela's coffee, black and steaming, awaited. Bettina and Penny, whose tastes were less spartan, had sugared and creamed their coffee to a paler shade.

"So . . . you're off on your big adventure!" Bettina set her cup down after an exploratory sip and focused all her cheerful attention on Penny.

Penny's eyes widened, and she nodded. To Pamela,

her daughter looked too young for any big adventures at all—especially sitting at the breakfast table in her pajamas with her features still softened by sleep. But she was out of college now, and she and her Arborville friend, Aaron Carlisle, were leaving the following week to spend a month building a school in Guatemala.

"Wilfred and I can't let you go without a going-away party." Bettina leaned across the table to grab Penny's free hand—the other was holding a fork. "So I hope you and Aaron, and Pamela, of course"—she shifted her gaze to Pamela and then focused on Penny again—"will come for a barbecue Saturday night."

"Of course! Of course!" Penny squeezed Bettina's hand. "I'd love to, and I know Aaron would love to. He's never met you, but now he will."

"And Pamela"—Bettina turned to Pamela—"that handsome boyfriend of yours is welcome too."

Pamela's "He's not really—" overlapped with Penny's "Mom, I didn't know—" and they both stopped and stared at each other.

"He's nice, Mom," Penny said. "I like him, but is it . . . serious?"

"So eligible," Bettina murmured, as if to herself.

"No!" Pamela had picked up her fork, but she returned it to her plate with a clunk. She shook her head, a spasmodic motion as if to reshuffle her thoughts. "I mean, yes, Pete *is* eligible, if a person was looking for that sort of thing, but it's not serious. He's nice, and I like him too, and that's it."

"So, he's coming to the barbecue?" Bettina's expectant smile made it clear what answer the question demanded.

"He doesn't really know Aaron . . ." Pamela's lips shaped a regretful half-smile.

"Neither do Wilfred and I," Bettina noted. "But we're hosting the barbecue anyway, because you and Penny are our dear friends."

"There's not that much point in Pete coming, though." Pamela's voice was firm.

"I know Wilfred would like to see him. Wilfred likes him."

"*I* like him."

"So, why not invite him?" Bettina urged. "Just ask him. See what he says."

Pamela occupied herself with her crumb cake while she gathered her thoughts. She teased off a corner with her fork, a corner that included a generous bite of the topping, and conveyed it to her mouth. It didn't disappoint. The fine-textured cake, with its slight hint of lemon, offered the perfect contrast to the buttery topping with the consistency—almost—of unbaked cookie dough.

Bettina, fork poised over her own portion of crumb cake, was watching her.

"Okay." Pamela sighed. "I'll ask him."

The barbecue invitation and its attendant business out of the way, Bettina relaxed and turned her attention to Penny, with inquiries about the school-building project and Aaron's connection with the volunteer group sponsoring it, and even Penny's wardrobe plans for the adventure.

When the plates were empty but for a few crumbs, and only dribbles remained in the porcelain depths of the coffee cups, Penny pushed her chair back and stood up. Bettina watched her with a fond smile.

"On your way, then?"

Penny nodded, and her dark curls bounced. Leaning on the table to give herself an extra push, Bettina stood up too. She took a few quick steps, stretched her arms out, and pulled Penny into a hug. Then Bettina watched Penny disappear through the kitchen doorway and slipped back into her chair.

CHAPTER 4

"I've been with Clayborn," she said, picking up her empty cup. "Is there more coffee?"

"Enough for a few swallows." Pamela shrugged. "But you can have it."

On her feet again, Bettina headed for the stove, carrying her cup.

Being an inveterate fashionista, Bettina dressed every day as if even crossing the street to have coffee with her friend called for a carefully coordinated outfit. But on days that included errands associated with her job as a reporter for the *Advocate*, she put extra care into her toilette.

For the meeting with Detective Clayborn, she had taken a pink-and-white checked shirtwaist from her closet, its flared skirt pressed to crisp perfection, and accessorized it with white ankle-strap sandals. The shirtwaist's open collar revealed a string of oversize white beads, and the same white beads bobbed at her ears.

The *Register* had been transferred to the counter to make room for the coffee and crumb cake, but Bettina nodded toward where it lay, folded but with the bold headline visible.

"No word from the medical examiner yet," she said, "so Clayborn had nothing to tell me that was different from what he told Marcy Brewer for her article." She tapped the side of the carafe to check whether the coffee—dregs that it was—had reached the proper temperature. She decided that it had, slipped her hand into an oven mitt, and tipped the carafe over her cup.

"I must say though"—she paused for a disapproving tongue-click—"when I report on Tassie's death for the *Advocate*, I don't plan to play up the sensational the way Marcy did."

She reclaimed her seat at the table and endeavored, with the aid of abundant sugar and cream, to render the unpromising potion in her cup drinkable.

"No word on the pie yet, either." The hand bearing the coffee cup paused halfway to Bettina's lips. "I guess they feel they have to check, whether it's poison or whatever, since they took the trouble of collecting it. But how a pie that no one has eaten yet could be implicated in a death is beyond me."

They chatted about other things for a bit, and then Bettina went on her way, after extracting a promise from Pamela that she would *really* invite Pete to the going-away barbecue. Pamela climbed the stairs to her bedroom, where she made her bed, lining up her collection of vintage lace pillows against the brass headboard as a final touch. The jeans she had worn the previous day were folded neatly on a chair. She pulled them on and added one of the casual blouses she pre-

ferred when the weather was too warm for a sweater.
In the bathroom, she ran a comb through her dark hair,
which hung straight to her shoulders, unlike Penny's
curls, inherited from her father.

Back out in the hall, she nearly collided with Penny,
who had just emerged from her bedroom. Penny had
changed from her pajamas into an outfit incorporating
one of her thrift-shop finds: a flared skirt in a 1950s
print combining pink, turquoise, and gray.

"Do you have plans for the day?" Pamela asked.

"I do," Penny said. "Dinner too, at Aaron's. We have
a lot to talk about." She proceeded to the stairs and
started down, but turned when she reached the landing.
"He can come Saturday night," she called back. "I'll
be sure to let Bettina know."

Pamela's next stop was her office, where she spent
an hour double-checking her editing work on "Woven
Together: Ancestral Rug-Making Skills Enrich Contemporary Carpet Design in Oaxaca." Closing the file,
she murmured, "One down and two to go." Instead of
opening the file labeled "Silk Road," however, she
rolled her chair away from her desk and stood up.

The articles weren't due back for nearly a week and,
based on her early-morning foray to the curb for the
newspaper, this June day was too beautiful to spend indoors. The fact that her pantry was nearly bare meant
that a visit to the Co-Op Grocery was in order, and thus
a walk could also serve a useful purpose.

After a quick lunch of scrambled eggs with cheese,
Pamela fetched one of the notepads that various char-
ities kept her well supplied with. The shopping list
couldn't be too long, since the errand would be done
on foot, but she'd been pondering an interesting sum-

mery lunch to make for Pete's visit the following day,
and a chicken could provide her and Penny with several days' worth of dinners.

"Cooked shrimp," she wrote, followed by "Organic
chicken, celery, green onions, red bell pepper." She
filled out the list with the staples, like cat food and
whole-grain bread, that she replenished every week.
And, responding to a sudden inspiration, she added,
"Lots of lemons." Then, canvas grocery bags in hand,
she set off up Orchard Street. The houses she passed
on the way to the corner were not unlike her own—old
houses, wood-frame, with shingles or clapboard siding. Some of her neighbors paid more attention to their
yards than she did, some paid less, but every yard offered soothing greenery, and most offered bursts of
summery color: beds lively with orange or yellow
daylilies, roses climbing on trellises or outlining broad
porches, hydrangeas with their puzzling jumbles of
blue and pink blooms on the same bush, even humble
little impatiens, willing to put forth their delicate flowers in the shadiest spots.

At the corner, a stately brick apartment building
faced Arborville Avenue. It offered both the treat of
discarded treasures set out for trash day—Pamela had
taken home live plants among other rescues—and the
peril of an encounter with the building's long-winded
super, Mr. Gilly. Today he'd latched onto another conversation partner and was happy to acknowledge Pamela with a genial wave.

Arborville's commercial district lay five blocks to
the north along Arborville Avenue. Narrow storefronts,
some with awnings, offered nearly all the goods and
services that anyone could need—though people ventured to neighboring Timberley when in search of

fancy yarn or custom floral arrangements, and to the mall when greater selection was desired. But everyone agreed that when it came to shopping for food, a person could do no better than Arborville's own Co-Op Grocery.

An automatic door was the Co-Op's only concession to modernity. The aisles were narrow, and the wooden floors creaked, but the produce was abundant and various, the meat was sourced from local farms, at the fish counter fish so fresh they seemed alive stared at one from beds of crushed ice, the cheese selection was international, and the bakery's crumb cake was only one of many superlative offerings.

The first stop was the produce section, where Pamela added celery, green onion, and a red bell pepper to her shopping cart, along with tomatoes and cucumbers. At the fish counter, she requested a pound of the cooked and shelled shrimp, then watched as the fish man's clear-plastic–gloved hand gathered a few handfuls of what to her always called to mind large pink commas. Bagged and weighed, the shrimp joined the produce in her cart.

Proceeding to the meat department, Pamela chose a good-sized organic chicken, then veered off into the aisle where shelves held pet food in such varied flavors that they rivaled entrées one could imagine for humans. Her selections included fish and chicken, as well as liver, and some combinations only a cat could like, such as chicken-salmon medley.

The cheese counter offered a bewildering array of choices, in a display that ranged from tiny logs of pure white goat cheese to huge wedges of Gouda—deep gold within and red wax without—and hole-riddled Swiss, blue-veined Roquefort like soft-textured marble, and so many many more . . . that, dazzled by such variety, Pamela generally came away with half a pound of Vermont cheddar.

That was the case today, and at the bakery counter she chose a loaf of whole-grain bread, sliced and bagged, though the bakery counter too dazzled with its variety.

Back at home, Pamela put her groceries away, returned her canvas grocery bags to the closet, and climbed the stairs to her office, where she skimmed "The Silk Road Wasn't Just About Silk" before embarking on her copyediting task. The article wasn't one that she had evaluated, and so she was completely unfamiliar with its contents.

She already knew that the Silk Road was a long— very long—trade route that had connected the Far East with Europe for centuries. She hadn't known that it traced all the way back to the Chinese Han Empire, established in 206 BC, or that it only became known as the Silk Road when a German geographer named it that in 1877.

Silk, of course, was a commodity transported on the Silk Road, and it lent itself to being carried thousands of miles in an era without modern transportation, given that it was extremely light and extremely valuable. But the Silk Road facilitated the trading of other commodities too, even horses, and not everything that traveled along the Silk Road started in China and ended up in Europe. Trading happened all along the way, and many commodities traveled from west to east, like Roman glassware valued by the Asian elite.

Pamela had just scrolled back to the article's beginning to settle into her copyediting task when a light tapping drew her attention to her office door. It opened a crack to reveal a sliver of Penny's face.

"I'm leaving now," Penny whispered, as if in response to the library-like atmosphere of Pamela's office.

"So early?" Pamela swiveled her chair around to face the doorway.

"It's after six," Penny said.

"Oh!" Pamela blinked a few times. Jade, spices of course, and even Siberian furs had traveled the Silk Road, and Pamela, caught up in imagining the pleasure these luxury items must have brought to those wealthy enough to afford them, had lost track of the time.

"Okay," she added. "Have fun! Say hi to Aaron."

Swiveling back around, she closed the file. Knit and Nibble was meeting at Nell's, Bettina had offered to drive, and she would be at the door soon. Nell's aversion to sugar meant that when it was her turn to host Knit and Nibble, the refreshments veered more in the direction of health than decadence, but a quick cheese sandwich before leaving would probably be a good idea anyway.

The Bascombs' front door was reached via stone steps that zigzagged up through lushly planted azaleas and rhododendrons. The rugged setting suited their house, which was built from natural stone on a steep hill and situated in the section of Arborville that people called the Palisades. The road that led to the Bascombs' house continued on to the summit of that hill, offering a view of the Hudson River from the cliffs the river had carved out eons ago.

It was Harold Bascomb who greeted Pamela and Bettina, waving them into the entry with a smile and a half bow.

"Roland preceded you," he said, and the smile enlarged, "though he ran back out to make sure he was parked on the side of the street that's legal on Tuesdays."

Harold turned to close the door, but pulled it farther open instead, and Roland DeCamp stepped across the threshold. "It's fine on your side tonight," he announced, "just as you said. But I'm glad I checked. Now I can concentrate on my knitting without being distracted."

"Of course." Harold nodded, and his soothing tone evoked the doctor he had been before retiring. He was a rangy and vigorous man in his eighties now.

As the three of them stepped toward the wide arch that separated the entry from the Bascombs' living room, a female voice reached them from the long hallway off to the side.

"Welcome, welcome, welcome," Nell Bascomb sang out as she reached the end of the hallway. "Please sit down and make yourselves comfortable." Nell, too, wore her years lightly. Her faded blue eyes peered out from nests of wrinkles and her hair was a corona of white, but she was as slender as she had been in her youth and livelier than many people half her age.

The Bascombs' living room echoed Nell's invitation wordlessly. Beneath a high, beamed ceiling, a pair of loveseats upholstered in faded chintz flanked a natural stone fireplace with a broad hearth. Between the loveseats was a large wooden coffee table. Inside the fireplace, an arrangement of dried flowers was a summery stand-in for the logs that provided cozy fires in the chilly months. A long sofa that faced the fireplace provided plenty of additional seating.

Seated on the sofa, Roland was already hard at work on his knitting project, needles crisscrossing busily and the skein of bright turquoise yarn at his side contrasting with the sober pinstripe of his fastidiously tailored suit. The elegant leather briefcase that he used in place of a knitting bag reposed on the carpet at his feet. Roland was a corporate lawyer whose doctor had suggested that his blood-pressure numbers would benefit from a relaxing hobby like knitting, and he'd been a member of the Knit and Nibble group since its founding.

Pamela and Bettina took places side by side on one of the loveseats. Nell had remained in the entry, and now she was greeting the remaining two members of the group, Holly Perkins and Karen Dowling. They were the youngest members, by far, both in their early thirties. Otherwise, they could not have been more different. Holly was dark-haired and outgoing while Karen was blond and shy, but their friendship was based on the fact that both, along with their husbands, inhabited houses that had once been fixer-uppers. They had met and bonded while studying paint samples at Arborville's hardware store.

Nell ushered Holly and Karen into the living room, settled the two of them on the other loveseat, and then lowered herself onto the sofa next to Roland.

Harold had lingered at the edge of the entry. He surveyed the group with a genial smile for a moment or two and then said, "I'll leave you to your knitting."

"Oh, please—not quite yet." Holly spoke up from the loveseat, accompanying the words with one of her dimple-inducing smiles. She raised a pretty hand, complete with glittering manicure, and beckoned Harold to draw nearer.

Holly was hard to resist, and Harold was happy to obey. He crossed the carpet, slipped past the coffee table, and perched on the hearth.

"I'm all ears," he announced, gazing expectantly at Holly.

"Marcy Brewer implied that Tassie Hunt died of fright," she said as Karen's placid features registered alarm. "Can that really happen?"

"Indeed." Harold folded his hands in a professorial gesture. "It's rare, of course, but a large spike in adrenaline can cause an abnormal heart rhythm which, in turn, interferes with the heart's ability to pump blood to the rest of the body. And so—"

He was interrupted by a sound like a cross between moan and a growl. It came from Nell and was so startling that Roland lowered his needles to his lap and turned to stare at his neighbor on the sofa.

"We do not need to talk about Tassie Hunt." Nell's chilly gaze landed first on Harold, shifted to Holly, and even took in Karen, though she was blameless. Then it skimmed from Karen past Holly and Harold to reach the loveseat that held Pamela and Bettina, in case they'd been harboring an impulse to bring up the recent event at Voorhees House. Roland had returned to his knitting and, anyway, had often made it clear that he came to knit and not to chat, no matter what the topic.

Harold rose from the hearth and scurried out of the room. Except for Roland, no one else had so much as opened their knitting bags, and much busyness now ensued in the silence that followed Nell's admonition.

At the moment, Pamela was between knitting projects. She'd finished her last major project some time ago, a crewneck pullover in tawny brown with the fun detail of a large black cat on the front. Since then she'd been browsing through her collection of knitting magazines and devoting her knitting time to helping Nell with one of her do-good projects, knitted toys for the children who accompanied their mothers to the women's shelter in Haversack.

The current animal was donkeys. Nell had demonstrated the technique and given Pamela the pattern, and Pamela had been turning out one or more a week, enjoying the chance to use up odds and ends of yarn left from other projects. Neither Nell nor the children who received Nell's knitted toys were concerned with verisimilitude, and the partly finished creature that Pamela extracted from her knitting bag was a bright marigold-yellow. Glancing toward the sofa, Pamela noticed that Nell's in-progress donkey was pale green.

She settled into her work, happy for the continued silence. The donkey pattern involved strategic increasing and decreasing, which made it possible to knit the head and legs as extensions of the body rather than separate pieces. But concentration was required, lest a lapse in attention result in a donkey-giraffe hybrid, for example. Next to her, Bettina was pondering the next step in her project.

The silence, however, was not so welcome to all. Holly's fingers were in motion, guiding the crisscross dance of her needles and looping and twisting the strand of deep-purple yarn that connected the few inches of work that hung from her needles to the fat skein that lay at her side. But her expressive eyes were dividing their glance between her own active hands and those of her fellow knitters.

Suddenly she spoke up. "That will be an amazing color on you!" she exclaimed.

Who was she talking to? The donkey beginning to form on Pamela's needles was obviously not a wearable object, and Bettina's project had been discussed and admired at several previous meetings. It was a pullover sweater in royal blue intended as a Christmas present for one of her sons, Wilfred Jr., with a similar one to follow for the other son, Warren. Nell never made clothes for herself, and the tiny dress taking shape on Karen's needles was clearly meant for a doll.

When there was no response, from anyone, Holly went on. "The turquoise! Wherever did you find that luscious yarn, Roland?"

Roland's expression as he focused on his work was so intense as to border on grim. Without looking up or altering the steady rhythm of his busy needles, he responded, "Online, of course. I have more important things to do with my time than go shopping."

"I couldn't buy yarn online," Bettina murmured. "I have to see it in person and touch it."

"I do too!" Holly's effusive tone and her wide smile welcomed Bettina as a kindred spirit. She turned her attention back to Roland. "You've picked a beautiful color though. So cheerful, and the sweater—I guess it's a sweater—should be done in plenty of time for you to wear it when the weather turns cooler."

"It's not for me." Roland's expression became grimmer, but his hands kept moving. "It's for my father-in-law, and he picked out the color. And now I need to concentrate."

Bettina's hands, however, had stopped moving, and

she had lowered her needles, with the few rows of ribbing she had completed for an in-progress sleeve, to
her lap.

"I really could never buy yarn online," she said, as
if she'd been pondering the concept further. "Going to
the yarn store is part of the fun."

"I agree." Holly nodded, rippling her dark waves.
Holly's brunette hair set off her vibrant complexion to
great advantage, an effect made all the more striking
by a deep-purple streak that echoed the color of the
yarn she was working with.

She turned toward Nell. "Don't you agree?"

Nell responded with a fond glance and a gentle
laugh. "I do," she said. "I do—though I haven't bought
yarn in ages. I have a lifetime of odds and ends left from
projects, and luckily, donkeys don't take very much—
though now that I think of it, a two-tone or even three-
tone donkey could be fun when I get down to the very
last bits." She surveyed the progress on the current
donkey, which so far had half a head and front leg.
(The donkeys were knit in two mirror-image halves,
with a third piece, like a gusset, forming the stomach.)
"I have so much though—bins full—that I suspect I'll
be gone long before it's used up."

"No! No!" Holly seemed genuinely horrified. "Don't
even think such a thing! What would Knit and Nibble
be without dear Nell?"

It was hard to know, then, whether the silence that
fell was a sad acknowledgment of mortality or simply
an indication that justice had been done to the topic
under discussion. Pamela was happy to focus on her
knitting, distracted only by the sounds of Bettina
rustling through the pages of the booklet that contained
the pattern for the in-progress sweater.

After a time, Holly and Karen began to converse in quiet murmurs, occasional audible words suggesting they were finalizing plans for an upcoming visit to a carpet outlet in Haversack. Pamela knit on, approaching the point at which she would start to form the donkey's back leg.

But then a sudden flurry of activity drew her attention to the sofa. Roland had ceased knitting in mid-row, set his work aside, and was consulting the impressive watch that normally lurked beneath his faultlessly starched shirt cuff. He'd pushed the cuff back and was staring at the watch face, whispering to himself, "Fifty-six, fifty-seven, fifty-eight, fifty-nine . . ." He looked up and intoned, "Eight o'clock sharp. Time for our break."

CHAPTER 5

Nell's husband had apparently been watching the clock too. No sooner had Roland spoken than Harold Bascomb appeared at the end of the hallway that led to the kitchen.

"Coffee is perking," he announced, "and the tea-kettle is whistling."

No sooner had he spoken than the seductive aroma of coffee, faint but perceptible, reached Pamela's nostrils. But even more seductive than the aroma of coffee was the sight of the cake Harold was bearing. Smiling a mischievous smile, he tiptoed across the carpet and eased along the edge of the hearth to deposit it on the coffee table.

"Oh . . . my . . . goodness!" Bettina murmured, and Pamela felt the loveseat tremble as her friend shivered with excitement.

"Harold!" Holly spoke from the other loveseat. "You are awesome! And *this* . . . Does it have a name?"

Even Roland looked impressed. Harold remained on his feet, surveying the group.

"Black Forest cake," Harold said. "I didn't actually *make* it . . . I knew Nell was planning to whip up a batch of her broccoli bars for tonight, but I just happened to be in Kringlekamack and I realized I was right near the German bakery . . ." His voice trailed off, but he added a wink.

Over the many decades she and Harold had been married, Nell had had ample opportunity to perfect the look she now directed at her husband: brows contracted and lips in a tight line that struggled against a crooked, close-mouthed smile.

The Black Forest cake was tall and splendid. Thickly encrusted chocolate shavings nearly hid the whipped cream that covered the sides. More whipped cream lay in thick drifts on the top, encircled by a ring of deep red cherries interspersed with more chocolate shavings.

"We're going to need plates," Bettina declared, springing to her feet with an ease that surprised Pamela, who often had to lend a hand when Bettina rose from a sitting position.

Holly followed Bettina and Harold to the kitchen, and soon Bettina returned with a stack of small plates, as well as forks and spoons and napkins. Harold arrived bearing a tray holding five cups of coffee, and Holly brought up the rear with another tray holding two cups of tea and Nell's cream and sugar set.

Once the coffee and tea had been distributed, Harold stared at the cake for a moment.

"We're going to need a knife," he said to himself, and headed back toward the kitchen.

The serving of the cake was undertaken with appropriate ceremony. With a tongue-in-cheek flourish, Harold raised the knife in the air, studied the cake thoughtfully, and then sliced it exactly in half, careful to position the knife in the spaces between the cherries. He turned the platter ninety degrees and sliced again, quartering the cake.

"Nell, my dear"—he turned to his wife—"can you eat half of one of these quarters?"

"Of course not, Harold." The long-practiced expression returned, with the close-mouthed smile perhaps gaining a bit of ground. "Just a sliver, please."

Harold made a great show of nudging off a slice that was less than half a quarter but considerably more than a sliver. He eased it onto a plate, set the plate aside, and proceeded to slice and transfer the slices to plates as Bettina arranged the cake-laden plates at intervals around the coffee table.

Nell's china was as old as Nell's kitchen, which had remained untouched since the 1950s—when the house's original kitchen had been updated with what were then the latest modern conveniences and in the most fashionable colors. The china pattern featured abstract wildflowers and sheaves of wheat, once bright coral and deep gold, but faded now.

The table had become quite crowded, and Pamela moved her cup and saucer, which also featured wildflowers and wheat, a bit closer to her plate. The liquid contained in the cup was dark and aromatic, with a slight hint of bitterness coming through. Nell herself was a tea drinker, but Harold loved coffee, which he brewed in an ancient aluminum percolator.

The cake's interior had been revealed once it was served. The chocolate shavings on the outside proved to be a preview of the inside. The cake itself was chocolate sponge, baked as two layers perhaps, but with the layers then sliced horizontally to make four. Between the layers was whipped cream, offering a dramatic contrast of light with dark.

But the whipped cream was streaked in places with deep red, a thick reddish syrup, and on closer inspection the chocolate sponge appeared to be soaked with that syrup. The deep red cherries that ringed the top proved to be a preview of the inside too. Sliced cherries in the same deep red had been intermingled with the whipped cream between the layers of chocolate sponge.

Even before she tasted the cake, Pamela suspected, from the murmurs of pleasure arising around the table, that the experience of eating it lived up to the promise of its appearance. And indeed, the taste did not disappoint.

The chocolate sponge was rich and intense and truly chocolaty, despite the sweet, fruity effect of the cherries and cherry syrup and something else that was . . . alcoholic in an almost nose-tingling way. Cherry brandy, she decided. And with all that going on, the simple whipped cream, only barely sweetened, was the perfect complement.

"Amazing, absolutely amazing! And delicious!" Holly's murmur resolved itself into speech. Radiant even under normal circumstances, she was now fairly glowing with pleasure, as she regarded Harold with something like awe.

"I didn't actually *make* it . . ." Harold himself was almost blushing, so alluring was Holly's enthusiasm.

"You picked it out though." This came from Bettina. "You drove all the way to Kringlekamack . . ."

Nell interrupted with a good-natured laugh. "He 'just happened' to be there. Remember?"

"Well, whatever . . . it's divine." Bettina teased off another forkful and lifted it to her lips.

Pamela added her compliments, as did Karen and Roland, and even Nell, who said, "I don't think my broccoli bars would have gotten the same reaction. So thank you, sweetheart, for just happening to be in Kringlekamack."

The vision of Nell, with her white hair and lined face, certainly didn't match the vision of the exuberant Holly. But Harold beamed at his wife from his perch on the hearth and raised a forkful of cake in a toast.

Soon the plates were empty, but there was still coffee to be sipped, and tea. Absent the distraction of the sublime cake, people's thoughts turned to the quotidian. Vacation plans were discussed, which led Nell to recall that Penny would be leaving for Guatemala soon. Karen exclaimed how brave it was of Penny to embark on such an adventure.

"She'll be fine, I'm sure," Pamela said, though she had been struggling to convince herself of that very thing ever since the Guatemala plan was broached.

"Some of those countries can be quite dangerous." Roland's tone implied that the statement was a settled fact.

"If we wanted to avoid every possible danger, we'd just stay home all the time," Nell commented. "And we can't do that."

"No, we can't." Harold spoke up. "Nell and I had some remarkable travel adventures in our youth." He glanced across the room to where Nell was sitting on the sofa. "Remember that summer hitchhiking around Europe . . . ?"

"You two hitchhiked around Europe?" Holly's head swiveled from sofa to hearth and back. "Awesome!"

"The world was safer then," Bettina observed. She studied Nell's face, and then Harold's. "Wasn't it?"

Nell shrugged. "We survived. I'm not sure I'd do it now."

Pamela had been enjoying the remains of her coffee, but she set her cup down. The flavor had changed, and she wasn't sure whether it was because she had reached the bitter dregs—perked coffee could be intense at the best of times—or whether this conversation had shaken her confidence that Penny would return safely from her trip.

Now Bettina was studying her face, though in profile. Pamela wasn't sure what her friend saw there, but she was grateful when Bettina introduced a new topic.

"And what are you making with that gorgeous yarn, Miss Holly?" Bettina inquired, leaning forward so vigorously that the loveseat creaked.

"Oh, this?" Holly had set her project aside when she'd jumped up to help serve the refreshments, but now she picked up a fat skein of deep-purple yarn. "An eggplant! I'm making an eggplant." With her other hand she picked up her needles and displayed the few inches of knitting suspended from them.

"It's kind of hard to tell at this point," she went on, "but you increase and increase and so it becomes sort of rounded, then you decrease to make that eggplant shape. And you sew up a seam in what becomes the back and you stuff it with fiberfill."

"What will you do with it?" Roland had already resumed his steady work, but apparently the concept of a knitted eggplant was sufficiently novel as to distract him from his industry.

"A pillow, of course." Holly flashed him a merry, dimpled smile. "There's a blog, and the woman thinks of the most amazing things to do with yarn."

She extended her needles and surveyed the beginnings of the eggplant, looking as pleased as if the completed vegetable already dangled before her.

"It gets a stem too, of course—dark green—and those funny little leafy things that eggplants have at the top."

Harold, meanwhile, had begun to stack the empty plates. That task completed, he piled the silverware on top and headed for the kitchen with his burden. Karen slipped from her spot next to Holly on the loveseat and followed him with a few cups and saucers.

Soon all signs of the evening's nibble had been cleared away, Karen had settled back into her seat, and Harold had retreated to his den.

"I never thought of doing that," Nell said, as if to herself. The group had been working in silence for some minutes, and the comment seemed detached from any context.

Responding to a few puzzled stares, Nell added, "Knitting vegetables, I mean."

Holly laughed. "Animals . . . vegetables . . ."

"Minerals?" Karen suggested in her gentle voice.

"A rock pillow?" Bettina joined in. "It wouldn't seem very cozy."

On that note, heads bent once more toward busy needles. A quiet conversation sprang up between Holly and Karen as they chatted about household projects, and Bettina murmured to herself as she consulted the pattern for her project.

Pamela consulted her pattern too, double-checking how many rows remained before the back leg was complete. She was so focused on her task that she nearly jumped when Bettina's voice reached her.

"Roland is packing up," Bettina said. "It's nine p.m."

Indeed, everyone was packing up. Karen and Holly were even already on their feet. Roland lowered the lid of his briefcase with a solid *clunk* and snapped the tongue of its latch into place. Pamela hastily tucked her yarn and her work back into her knitting bag.

After cheerful goodbyes that spilled from Nell's entry out onto her porch, a small procession of knitters made its way down the stone steps that threaded through the lush azaleas and rhododendrons. The procession halted when it reached the sidewalk, and Roland peeled off, heading toward the white Porsche that waited just a few yards away.

Pamela recognized Holly's orange VW Beetle a few car-lengths beyond, but Holly and Karen lingered as Roland climbed into his car and, with a wave, pulled away. It seemed that one or the other, probably Holly, was feeling inclined to chat—and that turned out to be the case.

"I can't stop thinking about that Voorhees House story," Holly said. Sunset had come and gone, but darkness was not yet complete, and her intent gaze compelled attention in the waning light. "Do *you* think she died of fright?"

Bettina shrugged. "I thought Marcy Brewer was just looking for a sensational angle when I read her article in the *Register*, but now, after what Harold said, I'm not sure."

"It was weird, I thought, that somebody like Tassie, and single, would want to live in a big old place like that, even if she did inherit it," Holly went on.

"She could have sold it," Karen chimed in, "and

bought something smaller and newer. I love my old house, but Dave and I have Lily, and maybe there will be more children, and anyway, our house isn't nearly as old as Voorhees House. And it's certainly not spooky." She shuddered.

"So"—Holly was still gazing at Bettina—"maybe Tassie did move in there as a kind of publicity stunt, to promote her new book, *A Sucker Born . . .*" She frowned, and her voice trailed off.

"*Every Minute,*" Bettina supplied. She nodded thoughtfully. "Press releases? With photos? Tassie posing in her Addams Family Victorian living room as if daring the house to do its worst."

Caught up in the idea, Pamela contributed an imagined headline: "Noted Debunker Challenges Ancient House's Restless Ghosts."

"Do you think there *are* ghosts in Voorhees House?" Holly shifted her gaze to Pamela.

Pamela didn't really believe in ghosts, but she tried not to be scornful when the topic of noncorporeal beings came up. For one thing, some people—even people she liked—held quite firm to the idea of a spirit world. Arguing with them would be mean, and pointless.

And then, also, what if Tassie really had been challenging restless ghosts to make their presence felt? And what if they had? Perhaps it was best not to provoke them by denying their existence.

So, when she responded, it was to cite another detail from Marcy Brewer's article: neighbors' claims that the house had not actually been empty after Edith Voorhees's death—at least if one was to judge by the weird noises they had heard and unexplained lights they had seen.

"Spooky," Holly commented.

"We'll know more," Bettina said, "not about the ghosts, but about what really caused Tassie's death. Even though there were no signs of foul play, her body is with the medical examiner now."

Holly nodded. "And I know Arborville's awesome weekly newspaper will keep us all completely up-to-date on the story as it unfolds."

And with that, she and Karen turned away and headed toward the orange Beetle.

Coming from almost anyone else, Holly's parting comment could only have been sarcasm. As a weekly, the *Advocate* was not in a position to keep anyone up-to-date on anything—except maybe the doings at the community garden or the library's read-aloud program.

Both its detractors (those who left it uncollected in their driveways until rain seeped into its plastic wrapper and turned it into papier-mâché) and its admirers described it as containing "all the news that fits." But Holly's enthusiasms were genuine, if effusive, and she was an unashamed Arborville booster.

Pamela and Bettina didn't speak again until they were seated in Bettina's faithful Toyota and heading down the hill toward Arborville Avenue.

"Penny will be fine," Bettina said suddenly, her voice loud in the car's dim interior. "She's not going alone, and they'll be working with a group in Guatemala, won't they? Two people can't build a school all by themselves."

"I know," Pamela responded.

"It's natural to worry, but she's known Aaron for a long time, and he seems like a responsible young man."

They were approaching the corner where they'd

make their turn. The sky to the west was dark now, and cars moved slowly through the intersection, nearly invisible but for the headlights that preceded them.

"He does seem responsible," Pamela said. "And very generous, to give his time to the school-building project."

"Penny is giving her time to the school-building project too," Bettina pointed out. She braked, waiting for a lull in the traffic. "Or do you think she's mostly doing it so she can spend a month in an exotic place with Aaron?"

"I don't know." Pamela felt herself frown. "I don't know if her feelings for him are . . . romantic."

Bettina swung the steering wheel to the left and glided onto Arborville Avenue. "Why don't you ask her?" she inquired once she was again on the move and heading south.

"I don't know." In the darkness, Pamela shrugged. "It seems nosy, and I don't know if she'd tell the truth anyway." She shrugged again. "You ask people personal things like that all the time."

Pamela knew this well. She had more than once been on the receiving end of Bettina's good-hearted probing.

"Some people tell me the truth." Bettina laughed. "But some people get mad. One person in particular comes to mind."

"I know." Pamela joined in the laughter. "And I think I know who that 'one person in particular' might be."

They were silent, except for lingering chuckles, for the rest of the short drive to the corner of Orchard. After they made that turn and as they were approaching the spot where their houses faced each other across the street, Pamela spoke again.

"I'll tell you something now," she volunteered, "even without you asking."

"Oh?" Bettina swiveled abruptly to face Pamela.

"I'll tell you who's coming to lunch tomorrow, but you have to watch where you're driving."

Pamela waited, smiling to herself, until Bettina pulled into Pamela's driveway and twisted her key in the ignition to silence the car's engine.

"Okay"—Bettina faced her once again—"who?"

"Pete Paterson."

"*Pete Paterson!*" Bettina clapped her hands.

"I told you I liked him," Pamela said. "That doesn't mean it's *romantic*."

"Do you think it could become . . . *romantic*?"

"You're doing it!" Seeking an outlet for her amazement, Pamela slapped the Toyota's dashboard. "Asking things!"

She couldn't see Bettina's expression, but the small voice that emerged from the darkness, murmuring, "I can't help it," sounded hurt.

Suddenly contrite, Pamela added, "If it does, you'll be the first to know." She reached for Bettina's hand and gave it a squeeze. "I promise."

The fact that Pamela and Pete Paterson both had the same last name and the same first initial was the coincidence that had led to their meeting. He was a local handyman who had abandoned a lucrative Wall Street career to pursue work that he found more fulfilling. A misdirected phone call from a caller who wanted P Paterson to repair a set of screens had led eventually to Pamela's hiring Pete for the same task.

CHAPTER 6

Wednesday morning, after the rituals of cat food, human breakfast, and newspaper were out of the way, and Pamela had tidied her room and dressed, she returned to the kitchen. There, she set a pot of water boiling—covered, because she believed water came to a boil faster in a covered pot—then measured out a cup of elbow macaroni. Stepping out onto the back porch, she harvested several sprigs of fresh parsley from the planter where she grew her herbs. Back inside, she took from the refrigerator her recent purchases of celery, green onions, and red bell pepper and set them on the counter near her cutting board.

"A watched pot never boils" was one of Wilfred's favorite sayings, but sometimes a cook just couldn't resist. Pamela edged over to the stove and lifted the lid she'd placed on the pot of water. A few bubbles were making their way, hesitantly, up the sides of the pot. She replaced the lid and distracted herself by washing the bell pepper and slicing it in half with her sharpest knife.

A few minutes later, the pepper's stem and all the pale seeds and the fibrous ribs they clung to had been removed and placed in the compost bin. Energetic chopping had transformed the pepper itself into something resembling a heap of confetti, bright red against the white cutting board. She scraped it into a bowl.

A low, rumbling sound drew Pamela's attention to the pot of water on the stove. Steam was escaping around the edges of the lid, and she lifted the lid to find the water boiling as vigorously as one might wish, with its surface in turmoil as huge bubbles rose and burst. She poured the macaroni in, stirred it around with a wooden spoon, and set the pot lid aside.

While the macaroni cooked, she washed and sliced a few ribs of celery and did the same with a few green onions. They joined the chopped pepper in the bowl, where the shades of green, both dark and pale, mingled with the bright red in a festive medley.

Macaroni cooks fast. With the vegetables prepared, Pamela turned her attention back to the contents of the pot. She used a spoon to capture one of the little noodle curls as they swirled in the boiling water, blew on it, and then tipped it into her mouth. It was just right, not chewy in a rubbery way, but not too soft.

She took a large strainer from the cupboard, turned the burner off, and carried the bubbling pot to the sink. Holding the strainer in her left hand and the pot in her right, she poured the contents of the pot through the strainer. Clouds of steam momentarily obscured the result, but when the steam cleared, she shook the strainer a few times to make sure the macaroni was thoroughly drained and then tipped the strainer over a large bowl.

The macaroni would sit and cool until it was time to assemble the salad, but to make sure the individual noodles didn't stick together, she added a dollop of olive oil and used the wooden spoon to make sure each noodle was coated.

Nothing was left to do on the salad until right before it was to be served, and Pete wasn't arriving until noon. But the day was looking so nice that Pamela thought eating lunch on the porch would be more pleasant than eating inside, either at the kitchen table or in the dining room. So she put the bowl of chopped vegetables in the refrigerator and stepped outside to inspect the condition of the porch furniture.

Two metal chairs, like French café chairs, flanked a round metal table. A fine layer of dust had settled on the table's dark-brown surface, and on the chairs, since the last time she and Bettina had taken advantage of the early summer weather by enjoying their coffee and crumb cake in the outdoors.

Pamela headed back inside to fetch a sponge and a bucket of water, pausing en route to smile at Catrina, who was napping in the sunny spot that appeared on the entry carpet on days when the sun was out.

The smile reappeared as she stepped through the kitchen doorway and encountered Penny.

"On your way out?" she inquired of her daughter. Penny's outfit seemed calculated for an activity more exciting than lounging around in her room communicating with friends on her phone. She was wearing one of her vintage finds, a sundress with a close-fitting bodice and a gathered skirt that set off her pretty figure. The dress was fashioned from crisp cotton in a print that featured old-fashioned sailboats against a background of pale aqua.

"In a bit," Penny responded. She had been standing at the counter, near where the bowl of cooked macaroni waited. "Are you making something interesting?"

Pamela described the macaroni salad she planned, with the shrimp adding enough protein to make the salad a summery lunch on its own and the chopped vegetables adding piquancy, crunch, and color. A dressing that combined mayonnaise, vinegar, and Dijon mustard would give the combo an added boost.

"Sounds good," Penny said.

Pamela had been heading for the laundry room to collect her plastic bucket and the sponge she used for heavy cleaning, and now she continued on her way toward the doorway that led to the back hall. But Penny showed no inclination to move and continued studying the bowl of cooked macaroni.

"What time is he coming?" she inquired just as Pamela reached the doorway.

"About noon," Pamela responded without turning.

In the laundry room, she collected bucket and sponge from the utility closet and retraced her steps to the kitchen. Penny was still studying the macaroni.

Without looking up, she said, "Do you think you could get serious about him, Mom?"

"Uh—" The question required more than a response tossed off in transit to the front porch. In addition, Pamela needed to pause at the sink and run some warm water into the bucket. But for now, she dropped the sponge into the bucket and lowered the bucket to the floor.

Penny left off pondering the macaroni and turned toward her mother, her face wearing an expression that was hard to interpret. Her blue eyes were piercing in their gaze, and her normally smooth forehead was marred by the hint of a furrow.

Pamela knew that Penny joined Bettina in wishing that Pamela would at long last open herself to a new romantic attachment. The intense expression suggested that Pamela's answer was important—but what answer was Penny hoping for?

"Would you want me to?" she asked after what seemed a very long time.

Penny shrugged. "He seems nice . . ."

Mother and daughter stared at each other, Pamela struggling lest her own expression rival Penny's in its intensity. Penny was small, a head shorter than Pamela, and Pamela was aware that she herself could look quite intimidating. Bettina, with her inborn cheer and mobile features, seemed preternaturally gifted when it came to drawing people out, encouraging them to say what they wanted to say.

So, she waited, lips slightly parted, eyes expectant, for Penny to finish the sentence that had trailed off.

Penny shrugged again, then she nodded toward the kitchen window and the house beyond. "I always thought you might end up with him."

That house was the house of Richard Larkin, Pamela's next-door neighbor. He'd shown a marked interest in Pamela nearly as soon as he moved in, newly single after a divorce—and Penny had befriended his grown daughters. But Pamela had hesitated to respond, and he had become re-involved with an old girlfriend. Now he was unattached again.

"I think it would have happened by now." Pamela felt her lips tighten into a rueful smile. "But it hasn't . . ."

"Okay." Penny seemed satisfied, though Pamela's

original question remained unanswered. She took a few steps toward the entry.

"Penny . . ." Pamela took a deep breath. The ice had been broken, so why not . . .

Penny paused and turned. The piercing gaze and the furrowed forehead had reappeared. Had Pamela uttered Penny's name in such portentous tones as to imply she was about to reveal some long-hidden secret? Pamela struggled to conjure up a smile.

"I could ask you the same thing about Aaron," she said.

"Why don't you?" Penny's face relaxed. "I don't mind."

"Well . . ." The smile became more genuine.

Penny saved her the trouble of continuing. "Do I think I could get serious about Aaron? I could—but not yet. He's staying in Guatemala after the school project ends. He wants to live there and work there, teaching English, maybe forever. I want to make my own plans about my own life."

Penny left a few minutes later, after explaining that she and Aaron were off to visit some friends of his who were leaving soon for their own summer adventure. Pamela accompanied her daughter to the door and then returned to the kitchen to take up the chore involving the bucket and sponge where she had left off.

Once the table and chairs were suitably clean, she dumped the water into the shrubbery and stowed the bucket and sponge. Upstairs in her office, she reimmersed herself in "The Silk Road Wasn't Just About Silk."

The writer brought to vivid life the worlds inhabited

by those through whose territories the Silk Road passed. The descriptions of the luxury items and the lives they enhanced were so compelling that Pamela completely lost track of the time. Were it not for the doorbell's chime, a repeated and insistent chime—as if the visitor had begun to despair of finding anyone home—she would have been unaware that noon had arrived and her luncheon guest was standing on the front porch.

She hurried down the stairs to let him in and excused herself to hurry back up to her office, where she saved and closed the Word file that contained the article. On the way down again, she paused on the landing to study Pete Paterson from this unaccustomed angle.

Penny's question—*"Do you think you could get serious about him, Mom?"*—had retreated to the back of her mind as she focused on the many wares traded by the merchants who traveled the Silk Road. Now the question advanced to the foreground.

Pete Paterson was certainly eligible. He was unattached and of a suitable age. He liked the same things she did, notably old houses and old things in general. His Wall Street career had allowed travel and experiences that lent him an easy sophistication, but he was happy now to be living an uneventful life and working with his hands.

Looks weren't everything. In fact, they weren't much of anything. Bettina, whose Wilfred was ruddy of face and portly of girth, considered herself the most happily married woman on earth—and rightly so, in Pamela's estimation. Pete Paterson was, however, quite handsome.

He was tall and fit, with thick brown hair and regular features. The jeans and denim shirts he wore for his everyday work were so flattering that Pamela sometimes wondered whether he'd had them specially tailored.

"Hello again!" He caught sight of her on the landing and stepped toward the stairs as she continued her descent. "You must have really been lost in your work. I was beginning to wonder if I had the wrong day."

On first meeting Pete a few months ago, Pamela had noted a kind of Roland-like intensity about him, complicated by the melancholy cast to his eyes. His smile, though, transformed his face, relaxing the tension and cheering the melancholy. He was smiling now.

"Not the wrong day at all." Pamela returned the smile. "Come on in the kitchen while I put the finishing touches on our meal."

"You're still okay?" He leaned closer as if inspecting her. "No lingering nightmares about Monday?"

Pete had called Pamela after seeing the *Register* article reporting Tassie's death, and she had assured him that she was fine.

"Still okay," she confirmed again.

Catrina had vacated the entry as her sunny spot vanished with the sun's climb toward noon, but Ginger was standing on the entry chair gazing through the window at a squirrel on the driveway. Pete detoured to give her a head-scratch, then followed Pamela through the doorway.

The first thing he noticed was the Co-Op lemons piled in a favorite bowl on the counter, their vivid hue bright against the antique wood.

"I'm planning lemonade with those," Pamela said. She'd already fetched her seldom-used mechanical juicer down from an upper shelf. It was a sturdy chrome thing, already old when she bought it long ago.

"Today?" Pete asked.

"Do you like it?"

"You have a lemonade porch."

Pamela knew that real estate listings sometimes described deep, wraparound porches like hers as "lemonade porches." She found the term sad in an odd way, since most people hardly ever even sat on their porches anymore, let alone sipped lemonade on them. Once upon a time, when her house was built, perhaps people had watched their neighbors instead of television, and lemonade instead of soda had been the chosen beverage.

"We're eating lunch outside," Pamela said and transferred the cooked shrimp and the bowl of vegetables from the refrigerator to the counter.

"I'll be the lemonade guy, then." Pete slipped a knife from the wooden block that housed Pamela's knife collection and stationed himself at a spot on the counter well away from where Pamela's salad ingredients waited.

A few minutes later, Pete had been supplied with a cutting board, a cup to catch the juice as it dripped through the juicer, a supply of sugar, and a long wooden spoon.

"And . . . we'll need . . ." Pamela stepped into the dining room and returned carrying a tall pitcher, clear glass with a delicate filigree border etched near the rim. It had been a thrift-shop find, with matching glasses, and she stepped out again to fetch two of those.

"The sugar just sinks to the bottom," Pete said, "unless you dissolve it in boiling water first." Pamela supplied him with a small saucepan, and he moved to the stove to complete that operation. While the syrup cooled, he worked on the lemons, methodically cutting each in half, positioning the halves under the gleaming dome of the juicer, and pulling the lever that crushed them against the ribbed dome below.

Meanwhile Pamela combined mayonnaise and apple cider vinegar in a small bowl and added salt, pepper, and powdered mustard, blending until the mixture was smooth and pale yellow, from the mustard, throughout. She took a large bowl in a bright Fiesta-ware orange from the cupboard and tipped in the cooked macaroni. After stirring to make sure the olive oil had successfully kept the pasta curls from sticking to each other, she added the chopped vegetables and the cooked shrimp, cut into bite-sized pieces.

As they worked, they chatted about Penny's upcoming adventure. Pete, it turned out, had vacationed in Costa Rica some years earlier.

"Beautiful," he said. "More focused on tourism than Guatemala, perhaps, but that part of the world is definitely worth visiting."

Soon the salad was complete, the pasta and the delicate pink shrimp enlivened with the red and green of the chopped vegetables and parsley, and set off by the deep orange bowl. All that remained was to combine the syrup and lemon juice in the pitcher and add water and lots of ice. The glasses destined to receive the lemonade got a few cubes too.

The table on the porch was just large enough to accommodate two plates, two glasses, and the salad bowl and lemonade pitcher. Once seated, Pamela and Pete were silent for a moment, enjoying the expanse of summer greenery all around and the slight breeze the porch seemed designed to invite. The view included Pete's sleek silver pickup truck parked at the curb.

Pamela served generous helpings of the salad while

Pete poured lemonade into the glasses. Then she picked up her fork and with a "*Bon appétit*" that echoed Wilfred's customary signal that it was time to eat, captured a nubbin of shrimp and a few pasta curls and conveyed them to her mouth.

The salad was perfect for a summer day. The macaroni provided a backdrop for the sweet, fresh shrimp. The celery and green onions added crunch and tang, and the red bell pepper was sweet too, in its own way. All was delicately bathed in the dressing, which hinted at mayonnaise without being heavy, while the mayonnaise soothed the notes of vinegar and mustard.

"This is delicious," Pete said after his first taste. "I'm not sure my lemonade is in the same league."

"Let's see." Pamela set her fork down and reached for the frosty glass. The ice cubes tinkled invitingly as she lifted it to her lips and, once tasted, the chilly liquid proved to balance sweet and tart most appealingly. The effect elicited a smile and a nod.

"Perfect lemonade for a lemonade porch," she declared.

They ate and drank in silence for a bit, refilling glasses at one point and adding a few scoops of salad to their plates. As the pace of eating slowed, Pete raised his eyes from his food and focused on Pamela.

"I wasn't sure if I should mention this—"

Pamela felt a sudden pang. What could be coming?

She must have looked startled because he leaned forward and frowned slightly, as if studying her. He looked so concerned that she smiled.

"Now you *have* to mention it," she said, "whatever it is. Or I'll forever be curious."

"Tassie Hunt contacted me before she died, about doing some work on Voorhees House." Pete shrugged and raised an eyebrow as if to imply he still wasn't sure if he should mention it. "She told me she'd inherited it through her mother, Mildred, who is now dead. Joe Voorhees was the brother of Jack Voorhees, Edith's husband, and he was Tassie's grandfather." He frowned slightly again. "You might not want to think or talk about Voorhees House in any way. I know you're not a gossiper."

"I'm not," Pamela said, "but I *have* recovered from encountering Tassie's body on Monday morning. What did she want to do to the house?"

"She wasn't sure yet. She'd already had workers come in to do some cleanup and make it habitable."

"'No job too big or too small.'" Pamela quoted the motto she'd once noticed on Pete's estimate pad.

"I know I say that"—Pete laughed—"but there's big, and then there's *big*. I'm not the guy for a major remodel. She showed me around though. All but one bedroom were piled with decades' worth of stuff, and we didn't even go into the attic."

Quite a bit of salad remained in the orange bowl, but they'd just about finished off the lemonade.

"Do you want more salad?" Pamela asked.

"I couldn't eat another bite." Pete started to rise. "And I've got an appointment to look at a fence that needs repairing, but I can't leave you with these dishes."

He stacked the plates and put the silverware on top, and Pamela led the way back into the house carrying the salad bowl. After each had made another trip back and forth, the table was clear.

Pete moved around the kitchen with easy grace, stooping to slip the plates into the dishwasher after rinsing them at the sink. He contemplated the pitcher and glasses for a moment before inquiring about washing them by hand since they were obviously vintage.

"It's okay," Pamela assured him. "I wash my wedding china in the dishwasher."

"I enjoy this," Pete murmured, as if talking to himself. Then he turned to Pamela, who was standing near the refrigerator transferring the leftover salad into a plastic container. "Before I quit Wall Street, I was too busy making money to do anything useful . . ." He laughed, but his eyes remained melancholy.

A few minutes later, they were back on Pamela's porch again, and Pete was thanking her for the lunch invitation. "We'll do Hyler's together soon," he added. "Where the Arborville elite meet to eat."

"The elite and everybody else," Pamela said. "But speaking of invitations . . ." She described the barbecue the Frasers were hosting that Saturday evening. "And Bettina would love it if you would come," she concluded, "and so would I, of course."

"Saturday!" His lips shaped an unhappy smile. "I can't do Saturday because it's my son's birthday, and I'm taking him and my daughter out to dinner. Otherwise . . . a barbecue at the Frasers' sounds great!"

He lifted his wrist to check the watch lurking beneath the cuff of his denim shirt. "I'm off," he announced. "Off to talk to a guy about a fence." And he descended the steps and headed toward where his pickup truck waited at the curb.

CHAPTER 7

En route upstairs to her office, Pamela had barely reached the landing when the doorbell chimed. Had Pete forgotten something? she wondered. But she turned, and even from that distance she recognized her caller as Bettina, her scarlet hair vivid through the lace that curtained the oval window in the front door.

She made her way back down the half flight of stairs, feeling strangely grateful that Pete's departure hadn't overlapped with Bettina's arrival. The instant he was gone, Pamela was sure, Bettina would have requested a detailed report on all that had been said and done. But now she had been spared that.

Except she hadn't. No sooner had Bettina set one foot, shod in a navy-blue pump that matched her dress, across the threshold than she seized Pamela's hand and tilted her head to gaze earnestly into Pamela's eyes.

"So—how was the lunch?" she inquired. Bettina had been covering a luncheon event at the senior center and was dressed for the occasion in a navy-and-white polka-dot sheath, featuring a peplum and short puffy sleeves.

"It was nice," Pamela said. "Very nice. I made macaroni salad with shrimp in it, and he made lemonade, and we ate on the porch."

"And . . . ?"

"It's a lemonade porch. He pointed that out."

Bettina was still clutching Pamela's hand and gazing into her eyes. "That's all?"

"Well . . ." Pamela retracted her hand. "He didn't get down on one knee and declare his undying love, if that's what you're angling for."

Bettina's head bobbed forward until her face was hidden by a tousled mass of scarlet waves. "I wasn't angling," she said in a small voice. "I know you think I'm nosy, but I'm just interested in your welfare." She looked up hesitantly. "It's not good to be alone when you're old."

Her eyes grew large, and she raised her fingers, tipped with bright pink polish, to her mouth. "I didn't mean it! I didn't mean it!" she whispered. "You're not old, not nearly as old as me and Wilfred, and . . ." She paused and gulped. "I was just thinking about the future. People—anyone, *everyone*—should always plan for the future."

At this point Pamela was laughing, hard. When she was able to control herself, she said, "Coincidentally, Penny asked me about my feelings for Pete Paterson this very morning."

"I won't ask what you told her"—Bettina shook her head mournfully—"because you'll get mad at me."

"And I asked her about her feelings for Aaron."

"Can I ask what she told you about that?"

"I suppose." Pamela put an arm around Bettina's

shoulders and took a few steps toward the kitchen doorway. "Come on in and sit down. There's some macaroni salad left. We drank all the lemonade, but I can make coffee."

"Not necessary," Bettina said. "There was plenty of food at the luncheon and plenty of coffee."

Seated at the kitchen table with Bettina across from her, Pamela described the conversation she'd had with Penny.

When she had finished, Bettina nodded approvingly. "Women used to follow men all over the place," she observed. "And then they wondered why they never had an interesting career or money of their own. Penny's smart. She takes after you."

It was hard to know what to answer, so Pamela remained silent. Bettina seemed to interpret the silence to mean that the discussion had reached a natural conclusion. As if to add further punctuation, Ginger strolled in and sniffed at Bettina's shoes.

"I actually dropped by for a reason," Bettina commented after offering Ginger an opportunity to investigate her fingers as well. "Then we got sidetracked into talking about Pete and . . . things . . ."

Pamela refrained from pointing out that the very first words Bettina had uttered upon stepping through the door had been about Pete and . . . things. Instead she conjured up a smile and said, "You know you're always welcome, even without a reason."

"Are you busy tomorrow morning?" Bettina had suddenly undergone a subtle transformation. The question was asked in a voice that Pamela recognized as belonging to Bettina's reporter persona. So Pamela was not surprised when Bettina's next words were, "I have an assignment for the *Advocate*."

Without waiting for an answer, she went on to explain. The neighbor on one side of Voorhees House, Winifred Colley, had called the *Advocate* to say there were once more signs of haunting next door, like lights going on and off and weird noises, and she thought the *Advocate* should investigate. She noted that a popular website, New Jersey Confidential, had already done a post on Voorhees House and its spooky reputation.

"Personally," Bettina added, "I think a supposedly haunted house is a dubious feature for Arborville to play up. It doesn't fit at all with the image our little town should project, but my editor wants me to do the story. I'm going to start by interviewing Winifred Colley tomorrow morning. Do you want to come?"

"Sure." Pamela nodded. She had plenty of time to finish her work for the magazine before it was due, and she was curious to meet a person who claimed first-hand experience with a haunting, if only as a next-door neighbor.

They chatted a bit more, about various town goings-on, including the senior center event that Bettina had just come from.

"It was outdoors," Bettina said, "in that park across from the rec center. Did I tell you that?"

"No, but it was a perfect day to be outdoors."

"I certainly wouldn't have worn these shoes if I'd known I'd be tramping around in the grass." Bettina extended a foot to survey one of her chic navy-blue pumps and leaned over to pick a bit of leaf off the toe. "But yes, it was a perfect day, and I hope this weather lasts through Saturday evening."

"By the way"—Pamela held up a finger—"I did invite Pete to the barbecue."

Bettina's bright lips parted in an expectant smile.

"*But*"—Pamela grimaced, anticipating Bettina's disappointment—"he already had plans. It's his son's birthday, and he's taking both his children out to dinner."

"Oh . . . well." Bettina's head drooped, and she sighed. But so habitual was her cheer that in a moment she was smiling. "The summer has barely started," she declared, springing to her feet with a boost from the table. "In fact, officially it's not even summer yet, not for a few more weeks. There will be more barbecues, lots more barbecues for him to be invited to. Maybe he'd even like to bring his children . . ."

"Bettina! Bettina!" Pamela lifted both hands with fingers outspread, then lowered them again in a gesture that suggested restraining a large, expanding object. "Let's just concentrate on . . ."

On what? She wasn't sure.

"Anyway, I have to get going." Bettina took a few steps toward the entry. "I want to write up the article on the seniors' event while it's still fresh in my mind."

After Bettina had gone, Pamela took up where she had left off, climbing the stairs to her office and settling in front of her computer. No email messages required immediate responses, and soon she was immersed once again in the article on the Silk Road. After a few hours of work, she clicked "Save," closed the Word file, and leaned back in her chair.

Two articles were finished. The one that remained, whose full title proved to be "The Mother of Invention: Wartime Privation and French Women's Fashion Strategies," promised to be at least as engrossing as the previous ones had been—but it was getting on toward dinnertime and a chicken was waiting to be roasted.

As Pamela entered the kitchen, she was surprised to

discover that Penny was home. She'd changed out of the sundress into shorts and a T-shirt and was, at the moment, opening a can of cat food. Three very interested cats were observing her progress.

"This one is chicken liver with gravy," Penny said when she saw that Pamela had joined them. "Does Precious like liver?"

"Usually she likes fish better." Pamela crossed to the cupboard where she stored the cat food and plucked out a can with a leaping salmon on the label. "And, anyway, she prefers to eat out of her own bowl, so she might as well have something different."

Pamela opened the can of salmon while Penny scooped generous servings of chicken liver with gravy into one of the large bowls that Catrina and Ginger often shared. As soon as the bowl had been lowered to the floor, both cats scurried toward it. Bodies taut and tails extended against the black and white tiles, they addressed themselves to the contents of the bowl as excitedly as if they were wild creatures and the bowl contained the results of a successful hunt.

"Are you here for dinner?" Pamela inquired, turning her attention to her daughter after Precious had received her own bowl.

"Is it okay?"

"Of course." Pamela laughed. "I'm delighted to have your company."

"I'll be gone for a month, so while I'm still here . . ."

Though she left the sentence unfinished, the implication was clear, and Pamela yielded to impulse and gave Penny a quick hug.

"So," Penny said as she detached herself, "was that a whole chicken I noticed in the refrigerator?"

Pamela nodded.

"Can we roast it with the rosemary like you used to do sometimes?"

The next morning, Bettina rang the doorbell just as Pamela finished rinsing her breakfast dishes. She called goodbye to Penny, collected her purse, and stepped out onto the porch.

Bettina was dressed for the splendid June day in wide-legged linen pants, pistachio-green, and a crisp cotton shirt that mingled shades of green in an abstract print. Bold jade earrings and a matching necklace completed the look.

"I checked AccessArborville last night to see if anyone was weighing in on the haunting phenomena at Voorhees House," she commented as they crossed the street to where her faithful Toyota waited in the driveway.

"Was anyone?" Pamela inquired.

"Not so far." Bettina opened the passenger-side door for Pamela and then circled the car to let herself in.

Once she was settled behind the steering wheel, she went on. "But Libby Kimble is very active on the listserv—" She paused to insert her key in the ignition.

"She's one of the ANGWY people," Pamela interjected.

"Yes." Bettina nodded, and the jade earrings swung back and forth. "She was part of the welcome committee on Monday morning. That was her house we went to after . . . uh, afterward."

She twisted the key, and the engine came to life with a guttural purr.

"Anyway," she continued, "Libby seems to have recovered from the experience. In fact, she's gotten a lot of attention online with her reports on being part of the group that discovered Tassie's body."

"It's a good thing Nell doesn't pay attention to AccessArborville." Pamela shuddered. "She'd be horrified."

They were silent then, as Bettina backed out of the driveway. Once they were well on their way, cruising past verdant lawns and flower beds near their peak of loveliness, Bettina spoke again. This time, though, the topic was Bettina's daughter-in-law, Maxie.

Maxie was one-half of the "Arborville children," as Bettina referred to her son, Wilfred Jr., and his wife, since Wilfred Jr. had stayed in Arborville and lived nearby with his young family. The other son, Warren, and his wife were the "Boston children."

Wilfred Jr. and his wife had two sons, but they had recently revealed that they were expecting a third child.

"And that would be wonderful enough," Bettina had told Pamela at the time. "But what if . . . what if . . . they have a little *girl*!"

Warren and Greta did have a little girl, but they had made it clear to Bettina from the start that the child was not going to be actually raised as a *girl*—but rather as a *person*—and that girly gifts of all sorts were forbidden.

"But in the case of Maxie—" Bettina said now, "if the baby turns out to be a girl, I know Maxie will let me buy her dresses and dolls and—" She squealed and clapped her hands. Pamela suppressed her own squeal as the Toyota veered toward the curb.

"Anyway," Bettina said after she had regained control of the car, "Maxie is about to have that test where you find out the sex of your baby."

Pamela agreed that it would be wonderful if Bettina's wish was granted and she could rejoice in the prospect of a granddaughter for the remainder of Maxie's pregnancy.

By now they had reached Arborville's commercial district and were driving slowly past the small cluster of storefronts. In no time at all, though, the shops and banks and nail salons had been left behind, and they'd reached the cross street that led up the hill to the neighborhood where Voorhees House had once stood in solitary splendor.

A few minutes later, they arrived at their destination, and Bettina steered her Toyota to the curb in front of Winifred Colley's house. Voorhees House next door seemed gloomy even in the morning sunlight, and the contrast with Winifred Colley's house was striking. Winifred's house was the same style as Libby Kimble's, with half-timbered gables and a sharply peaked roof, like a storybook house.

The front door opened before Pamela and Bettina were even halfway up the walk.

"I was watching from the window," a tiny, elderly woman explained from the threshold. Her voice was high-pitched, and she spoke quickly, almost breathlessly. "I saw you drive up, and I said to myself, that has to be Bettina, here right on time."

She focused on Pamela. "And you're her friend Pamela. She told me she was bringing her friend, and I said, by all means, bring your friend."

She stepped aside and waved them through the doorway.

"I'm Win, by the way. Just call me Win—everybody calls me Win."

Win not only spoke fast. She also moved fast, darting behind them to close the door, and then scurrying around to lead the way into the living room. There was something birdlike about her, Pamela thought, with her small, pointed nose and so tiny and quick.

The first impression of the living room was . . . pillows. Needlepoint pillows, with carefully worked designs featuring everything from dogs and cats, to flowers—of course—to vegetables, seashells, and even a horse. They were everywhere, piled several layers deep on the sofa and crowding all the chairs, save for one particularly comfortable-looking armchair, where an in-progress needlepoint project waited on the cushion.

"You have a lovely house," Bettina said, glancing around. The living room walls were an appealing shade of blue, quite pale, and the sofa—what was visible of it beneath all the pillows—was upholstered in a darker blue. The carpet blended blue and rose in a graceful Asian design.

"I came here as a bride," Win responded, "ages ago. Edith, next door, was already next door, of course, already a widow, and a complete recluse. Her late husband, Jack, was the grandson of the Voorhees who built the house, way back in 1887. There was another grandson, Jack's brother, but Jack ended up with the house because he was the oldest, I guess."

With a sudden, unexpected movement, she grabbed Bettina's arm with one hand and Pamela's with the other.

"Look! Come here!" She pulled them both toward the armchair with the in-progress needlepoint project on the cushion. It faced a large window, and she tugged at them until they were facing the window.

"Edith sat there day in and day out, except when it

was cold or raining. See!" She pointed with a spidery finger. "This window faces the front porch of Voorhees House."

It was true. The window offered a perfect view of almost the whole porch.

Win glanced away from the window to focus on Bettina. "Voorhees House is sideways, you know. So weird. Anyway, she was knitting. Knitting, knitting, knitting, all the time. Wouldn't it get boring?"

Pamela forbore remarking that apparently making needlepoint pillows didn't get boring.

"We're both knitters," she volunteered instead. "But not all the time. Definitely not all the time."

"And we're quite sociable about it," Bettina added. "Not reclusive at all. In fact we're in a knitting club." She paused. "But you didn't invite me here to talk about knitting." She paused again. "I think you said something about a haunting . . . next door . . ."

Win had released their arms, but now she seized them again.

"I certainly did," she said, and began to tug them toward an open door through which Pamela could see a dining room table surrounded by chairs. As Win tugged, she continued speaking, in that same breathless, high-pitched voice.

"I'm sure the readers of the *Advocate*, of which I'm one—" She halted suddenly, causing Bettina to nearly collide with her. "I love your writing, by the way," she interjected.

"Anyway, I'm sure the readers of the *Advocate* will be interested in what I've observed, and I've made some coffee because there's a lot to go over—" They'd reached the doorway. Win let go of Pamela and stepped through, pulling Bettina after her, then waited as Pamela followed.

"Sit," she said, gesturing at the table. "I'll get the coffee."

Three china mugs had already been set out, and the mug at the head of the table was accompanied by a thick spiral notebook.

Win disappeared for a few minutes, returning with a tray bearing a tall thermos-type carafe, a cream and sugar set that matched the mugs, and three spoons and napkins. Once the coffee had been poured, she picked up the notebook and opened it.

Bettina had begun the ritual by which she transformed the dark brew produced by the action of boiling water on ground coffee beans into the pale, sweet libation she preferred. Win watched silently, her head tilted and her eyes alert, like an attentive bird.

Once Bettina had completed her task, taken a sip, and set the mug down with a pleased expression, Win nodded.

"Let's get to work now," she said, "and, Bettina, you'll want to record this on your phone."

Another delay ensued while Bettina fetched her phone from the handbag she had left in the living room.

Win studied the open notebook for a moment and said, "This goes all the way back to when it started." She raised her eyes from the page and glanced from Bettina to Pamela, like a teacher making sure her students were fully engaged. Focusing on Bettina, she added, "Edith had just died, and the house was empty—of corporeal beings, that is. But the very first night"—she looked down and read off a date—"I saw lights.

No cars coming or going though—so nobody *human* was inside.

"Then the next night—that was a Tuesday—I heard a sound." She tipped her head back and closed her eyes. From her half-parted lips came a plaintive, hooting moan, rather like a train whistle. She repeated it a few times for good measure. "And I saw lights again too, of course," she added.

Win read off several more dates and specified which had featured lights—"mostly in the attic but not always," which had featured sounds, and which had featured both. She turned to the next page of the notebook and continued, clearly pleased with the industry and initiative revealed by her project.

Quite a few pages later, she looked up from the notebook and said, "At this point—around the beginning of May—I heard something new." She tipped her head back and closed her eyes again. Opening her mouth so wide that her nose wrinkled, and exposing her teeth, she produced a sound that reminded Pamela of a hissing cat.

She bent back to the page and continued reading off dates, each date followed by a comment about what she had heard—sometimes illustrated by a hoot or a hiss—and observed.

Pamela and Bettina were facing each other across the table. Pamela had been struggling to suppress a smile as she watched Bettina's eyes grow larger and larger and her chest heave with prolonged sighs. Now she felt the corners of her mouth begin to turn up despite her best efforts.

"So interesting!" Bettina exclaimed suddenly. "You've done an amazing job here. Really amazing." She fingered her phone, which was sitting on the table before her. "I think I've got plenty of information now, and the coffee was delicious, so now we'll . . ." She started to rise and Pamela stirred as well.

Win reared up and straightened her spine against her chair back. "But I'm only at September now," she protested, seeming genuinely amazed that they would want to leave before Bettina got the full story.

"Maybe you could jump ahead?" Bettina's mobile features arranged themselves into an expression that combined hope and encouragement.

"The sounds started to change in October," Win said. Her tone of voice was almost accusatory. "Sometimes there was a *wheee—ooo—aaa—wahh wheee—ooo—aaa—wahh*." The syllables seemed to emerge from her nose.

"Yes." Bettina nodded thoughtfully. "That is distinctive. I'm glad you mentioned that one."

Pamela wasn't sure, but it seemed that Bettina winked at her. Then Bettina leaned toward Win and held up both hands as if to command silence.

"*So* glad you mentioned it. However, I believe you said the sounds, and the lights, stopped when Tassie moved in."

"The sounds, yes," Win chirped. "Not all the lights, obviously, because someone—a human someone—was living there now, but the weird lights stopped, the lights in weird places at weird times."

Her fingers hovered over the notebook as if she was longing to take up where she had left off, but she continued to focus on Bettina.

"Tassie was one of those ghost-buster people," she said suddenly. "She wrote that book, and maybe she scared the ghosts away. Just temporarily though, obviously."

She leaned toward Bettina, as motionless as a bird on high alert. "Do *you* think she died of fright?" she inquired, and seemed to hold her breath the moment the words had been uttered.

"Uh . . ." Bettina had made her skepticism about Win's report of haunting clear to Pamela, and she had agreed to do the interview and write the article under duress.

"People *can* die of fright," she responded, perhaps grateful for Harold Bascomb's clear, if brief, explanation at the Knit and Nibble meeting. "And," she went on, "the fright could probably be caused as much by something they *thought* they saw as by something they really saw . . ."

"Oh, she really saw it." Win nodded, in a motion that suggested pecking, given her small, pointed nose. "Or *them*. And no sooner did they have the house to themselves again, but they came back to stay. I'm sure of that."

She bent toward the notebook and began flipping through the pages, her fingers fluttering so rapidly they became a blur.

"And here we are!" Her fingers stilled, and she raised her head triumphantly. "Last Tuesday night."

Her head dipped toward the page, nearly the last page in the notebook. Pamela wondered whether she had another in reserve to continue the journal.

"Sounds! At midnight! The sounds woke me up, and I grabbed this notebook. The sounds were like *waheeohh waheeohh*." The sound was almost donkey-like, a soprano donkey perhaps. "And lights in the attic again, but flitting around on the other floors too."

Bettina—valiantly, Pamela thought—managed to

look fascinated. "That would have been the night right after the . . . death," she said.

"The ghosts didn't waste any time—and they were very active almost all night, moving around and making noise until three a.m." Win glanced back down at the page open before her. "No sign of vehicles coming or going—I made sure of that. So, it wasn't a case of people moving around in there."

"And then the same thing last night?" Bettina asked.

"No." Win's hands retreated from the notebook into her lap.

"No?" Bettina seemed genuinely surprised. Her head twitched, setting the jade earrings into motion.

"Or rather . . ." Win seemed to shrivel. "I don't know. I was so tired from the night before that I might have just slept through it." She shriveled further, and her voice became a high-pitched whisper. "I guess I'm not a very good detective after all."

"Oh, no . . ." Bettina reached out a comforting hand, carefully manicured. "You've been . . ." She gestured toward the notebook. "This is really remarkable, and"—she fingered her phone—"I have plenty of material. I'm sure readers of the *Advocate* will be enthralled."

Pamela spoke up then. "I wonder," she said and paused because both Win and Bettina seemed startled, perhaps because she'd been so quiet up till that moment. But Win's mention of vehicles, or rather lack of vehicles, had tickled her curiosity.

"Did you notice any unfamiliar vehicles coming around last Sunday night?" she asked. "Like someone paying a call at Voorhees House?"

Win shrugged. "I wasn't really watching for vehicles, and I hadn't been paying that much attention to the house for a while because, like I said, the ghosts went away when Tassie moved in. But no . . ." As if controlled by a drawstring, her lips tightened into a knot. "No, I don't think so."

Pamela started to rise, and Bettina collected her phone and followed suit.

"You're sure you wouldn't like more coffee?" Win remained seated and reached for the carafe.

"We're fine, really," Bettina insisted. "The coffee was lovely, and thank you again for all the information."

Win was on her feet now, and Bettina grasped both her hands, squeezed them, and repeated her thanks. "It's too late for the article to be in tomorrow's *Advocate*," she added, "but look for it next Friday."

CHAPTER 8

As Pamela and Bettina walked toward where the Toyota waited at the curb, Bettina turned to Pamela. "Why did you ask her whether she noticed any unfamiliar vehicles Sunday night?" she inquired. "It doesn't seem that Tassie was murdered."

"I don't know," Pamela responded, realizing she genuinely didn't know. "It just popped out."

They were nearing the car, but Bettina veered to the right before they reached it. She made her way along the sidewalk until she reached the disordered swath of vegetation that edged the foundation of Voorhees House.

Pamela watched Bettina for a moment, then she noticed a man standing in the street near a car up ahead. The car was parked in front of the house that was neighbor to Voorhees House on the side opposite Win. The car's trunk gaped open, and within was a bulky parcel that filled the trunk with little room to spare.

"How are you today?" Bettina called in her cheeriest voice.

The man glanced at her, hopped toward the back of the car, and slammed the trunk closed.

"I'm Bettina Fraser from the *Arborville Advocate*," she added when she was a few yards from the car. "Do you have a minute?"

"Spud Birdsall," the man replied cordially enough. "Glad to meet you. Hang on."

He turned away and loped down the driveway, which was surfaced with pavers, rather than asphalt, in a grayish color. Parts of the driveway were wet and noticeably lighter than the rest, as if he'd been washing it. In fact, resting near an especially puddly area was a device like a giant water pistol with a long snout. A hose reached from it to a faucet on the side of the house, which was another pleasant, storybook house like Win's.

His destination was the garage. Its interior was shadowy, but the space seemed crowded with a jumble of furniture, boxes, stacks of newspaper, gardening equipment, and much else. He reached up, grabbed the bottom edge of the door, and lowered it with a thud.

That task accomplished, he turned and loped back to where they were standing. Spud Birdsall was a tall man, and burly, in his mid-forties perhaps, with thinning blond hair and the easily sunburned complexion that blond people often have. The sun and his driveway exertions had rendered him sweaty and quite pink.

"You're from the *Advocate*?" He bent down to peer at Bettina in a pleasantly inquisitive way. "My wife never misses an issue." He straightened back up and folded his arms across his broad T-shirt-clad chest. "What can I do for you?" He paused for a moment and nodded toward Voorhees House. "I didn't know her, if that's what you're wondering."

"No," Bettina said. "No, not at all." She gazed up at him in a manner that seemed designed to flatter his height. "I'm wondering if you've seen any sign of the ghosts."

"Ghosts?"

"Win Colley?" Bettina fluttered her eyelashes. "The neighbor on the other side of Voorhees House?"

"Oh!" Spud took a step back, slapped his belly with both hands, and laughed a hearty laugh. "That haunting business! Give me a break! It's an old house—so what?"

"Win Colley says she's seen mysterious lights and heard weird sounds—especially during the time the house was empty after Edith Voorhees died, but also last Tuesday night, when it was empty again after Tassie Hunt was found dead."

Spud bent toward Bettina again with eyes wide and a teasing expression on his face. "Did she die of fright?" he inquired in mock-portentous tones.

"I personally don't believe so." Bettina responded as seriously as if his question had been asked in earnest. "But," she went on, "my editor believes our readers will be interested in Win's story."

"Well . . ." Spud fingered his chin. "I do have to admit I saw lights sometimes while the house was empty—and there were no cars coming and going, so . . ." He shrugged. "They gave my wife the willies. She paid more attention, to tell you the truth—I've always been more of a common-sense kind of guy. Anyway, I think I could hold my own against a ghost."

He folded his arms across his chest again. "What could one do to you? That is, assuming you didn't die of fright?"

Bettina's admiring smile suggested she was convinced that Spud, indeed, could hold his own against a ghost. But when she spoke, it was to say, "I'd love to talk to your wife."

"Oh, yes . . ." Spud glanced here and there. Finally, he settled on staring at the car whose trunk he had recently closed. "She's not at home just now."

"Another time, then?" Bettina's voice was confident. "Maybe tomorrow?"

"Uh . . . I'm not sure. Her schedule is . . . not very predictable . . ." He was still staring at the car.

"Could I call this evening? Talk to her on the phone?"

"No, no." Spud shook his head. "That wouldn't be good. She will definitely be out tonight." He transferred his gaze from the car to the driveway. "And I should get back to work. This driveway won't wash itself."

He turned away and began to lope toward where the giant water pistol with the long snout rested on the pavers. Pamela and Bettina started down the sidewalk, but as they passed the side of Voorhees House, Win Colley emerged from among the disordered shrubbery.

"She hasn't been around for several days," Win announced without preamble. "I can see why you'd want to talk to her—she's very observant, like me. Notices things, though I don't think she ever wrote anything down, about Voorhees House, that is. I'm sure she wrote lots of other things down—grocery lists and the like. She's very organized. He's not."

Win fell in step with them and continued talking.

"He's been busy though, lately. Very busy, especially the power-washing. Going over and over the driveway ever since last weekend. But I haven't seen his wife around since"—she paused, and a quick frown came and went—"well, since last Friday. Then all the washing started."

They had reached the car, and Bettina probed in her handbag for her keys. Win watched her, bright eyes alert.

"You'll call me if you need any more information," she chirped in her eager, breathless voice, phrasing the utterance like a statement rather than a question.

"Of course, of course." Car keys clutched in one hand, Bettina reached out to stroke Win's arm with the other. "And thank you so much!"

"Or we could go back inside." Win seemed encouraged by the gesture. "I was looking through my notebook after you left, and there's lots that I didn't tell you about, different sounds, especially. I could make more coffee . . ."

"No, no. Really!" Bettina summoned an appreciative smile. "You've been so helpful, and I'll be sure to get in touch if I realize there's anything I . . ."

She slipped her key into the lock on the passenger side and twisted it. Pamela quickly opened the door, hopped inside, and pulled the door closed.

"Look at the time!" Pamela heard Bettina exclaim. The car window was closed, and Bettina's voice was muffled, but she illustrated the statement by lifting her wrist to consult her watch.

A few minutes later, they were on their way.

"My goodness!" Bettina sighed as she steered the Toyota along Beech Street. "That woman can certainly talk. Interesting, though, about the lights and the sounds—and no vehicles coming and going to suggest anyone was visiting the house."

"Will you really do an article?" Pamela asked.

Bettina shrugged. "My editor wants one." They'd

reached the corner where Beech Street crossed the road that meandered down the hill to Arborville Avenue. Bettina made the turn and continued speaking. "It's too bad I couldn't talk to Spud's wife though. More than one source is always a good idea. I could quote him though—saying he thinks he could hold his own against a ghost. That was kind of funny."

What could a ghost actually do to you? Pamela wondered. Movie ghosts were always sort of transparent. If ghosts were really like that, they couldn't grab you or smother you or anything. So, why were some people—some of the people who believed in them, that is—afraid of them? Her thoughts continued in this curious manner until Bettina's voice broke through to announce that they were home.

When she entered her house, Pamela found a note from Penny saying she was at Lorie's but would be back in time for dinner. After a quick lunch of lentil soup from a can, she climbed the stairs to her office, where she found Ginger stretched out atop her keyboard. She slipped into her chair and offered the cat a spot on her lap, but Ginger hopped to the floor instead and pawed at the door, which Pamela had closed behind her.

Once Ginger had gone on her way, Pamela allowed her mouse to roam its pad until her monitor's screen brightened. She found nothing pressing when she checked her email and settled down to work on the last article still to be copyedited from the batch that was due Monday.

Soon she was engrossed in "The Mother of Invention: Wartime Privation and French Women's Fashion Strategies." The wartime privation proved to be that caused by the German occupation of France during

World War II. The article was illustrated with historic photographs drawn in some cases from the media, in others from archives the author had consulted. The photographs depicted women looking as chic as only Frenchwomen could, but the text explained that the ensembles represented a determination to remain stylish no matter what the circumstances.

The elegant turbanlike hats, for example, might be created from bits of ribbon, fabric scraps, and even newspaper. The high-heeled shoes that flattered a shapely pair of legs might have been resoled countless times. And the simple but tasteful dress or suit might be the wearer's only garment, but varied from day to day by the addition of a collar, cuffs, a scarf, or a belt, again cobbled together from scraps and odds and ends.

The author was a French academic whose English was excellent, if occasionally un-idiomatic, and she tended to struggle with prepositions and the difference between "made" and "did." But the corrections were easily made, and after one last admiring look at the scenes of women preserving their fashion identity in trying times, Pamela saved the file and closed it.

With a few hours yet remaining until dinnertime, Pamela took her knitting onto the front porch, where she completed the donkey half currently in progress and launched the other half, which would be its mirror image.

"Did you think it sounded okay?" Bettina asked upon entering Pamela's kitchen the next morning.

That week's *Advocate* lay on the kitchen table, atop that day's *Register*. Pamela intuited that Bettina was referring to the article headlined "Author Tassie Hunt's

Residence in Voorhees House Cut Short by Death" and identified as written by Bettina Fraser.

"It's fine," Pamela said. "Clear, informative."

"I didn't want to pander to those 'Did she die of fright?' people. Marcy Brewer can be undignified if she wishes, but the *Advocate* is aimed at a higher class of reader."

Pamela turned away to hide a smile, picturing the forlorn copies of the *Advocate* that sat unclaimed for days in driveways all over Arborville.

"The ghosts will be next week," Bettina went on, "and I don't know what I'm going to say about that topic. It will be hard not to pander."

That business out of the way, Bettina advanced to the table, where she deposited a white bakery box. A crisscross of string and a firmly tied bow held it closed.

"The coffee was just dripping when you rang the bell," Pamela said, "and I hadn't even started the toast."

"Cherry Danish." Bettina tugged at the string ends, the bow yielded, and the string slipped away. She folded back the flap that hid the contents. "We'll need plates."

From the open box came a tantalizing hint of yeasty, fruity sweetness that mingled with the bracing, yet exotic aroma of the coffee.

Bettina darted around the little kitchen, collecting plates, cups, and saucers from the cupboard where Pamela kept her wedding china, filling the cut-glass cream pitcher from the carton in the refrigerator, and settling it and the matching sugar bowl on the table. Pamela contributed silverware and napkins, and within a few minutes, she and Bettina were seated at the table, each with a cup of steaming coffee and a cherry Danish at hand.

But before Bettina had even added the first spoonful of sugar to her coffee, they were joined by someone else in quest of breakfast. Penny stood in the doorway that led to the entry, clad in a light cotton nightgown and with her dark curls in tangled disarray.

"Good morning, Miss Penny!" Bettina exclaimed. "I didn't expect to see you up this early."

"I could go back to bed." Penny's pretty lips struggled to suppress a teasing smile. "I'm not tired though. Mom and I spent a quiet evening here, watching the nature channel."

"Your mom will miss you while you're in Guatemala."

"I was away from home when I was in college."

"That was different," Pamela murmured. "Somehow."

Bettina took over. "Boston is much closer."

Penny advanced toward the table, surveyed the tempting fare set out on the plates, and peered into the bakery box. "There's another one of those," she said.

"So there is." Bettina laughed. "Get yourself a chair and join us."

By the time Penny had slipped through the doorway that led to the dining room and returned with an extra chair, Bettina had fetched another wedding-china cup, saucer, and plate, as well as another napkin, fork, and spoon. She filled the cup with coffee as Pamela transferred the third cherry Danish from the box to the plate.

For a few moments, both Bettina and Penny devoted themselves to sugaring and creaming their coffee. While they were occupied, Pamela was happy to sip her own in the pleasantly bitter state that she preferred. Bettina followed with a sip of her sweet brew, leaving a bright imprint of fuchsia lipstick on her cup's rim. The cherry Danish, however, pleased everyone just as it was. Glazed pastry, yeasty and a bit chewy, encircled a goodly dollop of deep red cherries, slightly sour but bathed in a thick sweet syrup.

Several bites of Danish and several sips of coffee were consumed before anyone spoke again. When conversation resumed, it focused at first on the excellence of the Danish, the superiority of cherry Danish to all other sorts of Danish, and the great good fortune the residents of Arborville enjoyed owing to the Co-Op Grocery's bakery department.

Those topics exhausted and coffee cups refilled all around, Bettina addressed Penny as they both commenced the sugaring and creaming ritual once again.

"Now, Miss Penny," she said, "what clothes are you packing for your adventure?"

Bettina herself was wearing her version of a casual outfit chosen for a summer day with nothing special on the agenda: calf-length pants in a striking shade of fuchsia, topped by a blouse whose fabric featured exotic blooms in the same fuchsia shade, surrounded by luxuriant green leaves. Her eager expression made clear the vicarious pleasure she expected from the details of Penny's travel wardrobe.

"Jeans?" Penny looked up from stirring her coffee.

"Of course." Bettina nodded. "For the construction work. And what else?"

"T-shirts?"

"And . . ." Bettina fluttered her fingers in an encouraging gesture.

"A jacket."

"That's all?" Bettina seemed stunned.

"I'm only taking a carry-on," Penny said. "There isn't room for a lot, and we're going to be—"

She broke off as Bettina frowned.

". . . working," she concluded.

But Bettina was staring toward the doorway. "I think I hear my phone," she murmured, "and I'd just ignore it, except that Maxie, you know, is having that test and . . . I'm not sure when . . . but she said soon . . ."

Leaning on the table to boost herself to her feet—shod today in green wedge-heeled espadrilles that matched the luxuriant leaves on her blouse—she rose from the chair and hurried through the doorway that led to the entry.

A moment later, Pamela heard her say, "Oh, my goodness!" A silence followed, then she added, "No, I can't imagine . . . under the circumstances, yes. You did the right thing to call." After a longer silence, she followed up with, "Yes, yes! Of course I'll come."

She was greeted by two worried faces when she reentered the kitchen. Pamela had quietly filled Penny in on the nature of the test Bettina had referred to.

"Is everything okay?" they asked in unison.

"I'm not sure," Bettina said. "A strange man has appeared."

"A strange man?" This time only Pamela spoke.

"Wearing funny clothes."

Pamela hopped to her feet. "Bettina . . ." She hesitated. "What are you talking about? Was that Maxie on the phone? Or Wilfred Jr.? What does a strange man wearing funny clothes have to do with the baby Maxie is expecting?"

Bettina blinked. "The baby Maxie is expecting?"

Pamela felt an irritated wrinkle form between her

brows, but she tried to keep her voice matter-of-fact, and she even smiled. "When you went to take the call, you said you thought it might be Maxie, or someone, about the test."

"Oh!" Bettina laughed. "I got distracted. That was Win Colley, the woman who lives next to Voorhees House. She's got another story for me."

"About a strange man wearing funny clothes," Pamela said. She sat back down and reached for her cup, but Penny still seemed more interested in Bettina's phone call than in her own coffee.

Bettina joined them at the table and slipped into her chair. "He's taking pictures of the house, using a funny camera. Win talked to him, and he told her he thinks the house needs to be rescued."

"From what?" Penny inquired.

"She wasn't sure. She said he was confusing to listen to, but nonetheless, she thinks readers of the *Advocate* will be interested in what he's doing and that I should come over there quick before he leaves." At that moment, Bettina noticed the nearly full cup of coffee, sugared and creamed to perfection, which she'd abandoned when she got up to take her call. She lifted the cup to her lips and took a long swallow.

"Do *you* think readers of the *Advocate* will be interested?" Pamela asked.

"I could work it into the ghost article."

"The ghost article?" Penny seemed alarmed. "*Did* she die of fright?"

"Of course not, and there are no ghosts haunting Voorhees House, despite what the neighbors might say." Bettina leaned forward and peeked into the bakery box, but no more Danish had magically appeared.

"So, when do we leave?" Penny stood up. "I have to get dressed, of course, but I won't be a minute."

"I guess I should get dressed too." Pamela followed Penny through the kitchen doorway with Bettina bringing up the rear.

While Penny and Pamela continued on to the stairs, Bettina perched on the entry chair with her phone to let Wilfred know her plans.

CHAPTER 9

The strange man was indeed strange, but charmingly so. He was wearing slim dark trousers and a slim dark coat in a cutaway style, open to reveal a brocade vest patterned with stylized golden vines. The vest was complemented by a cravat of lustrous gold satin knotted between the points of a well-starched collar and anchored by an ornate diamond pin.

The camera was a cumbersome thing, a boxy device fitted with an accordion-pleated leather sleeve that culminated in a brass-mounted lens. It was balanced atop a tripod constructed from slender strips of highly varnished wood.

The man was young, and quite dashing in his unusual ensemble, with black hair well-groomed but just long enough to look purposely old-fashioned.

As he watched Bettina, Pamela, and Penny climb out of the Toyota, his well-formed lips quivered in the beginnings of a smile.

"Ah—reinforcements!" he exclaimed once it was

clear that he was their objective. "I surmise that Mrs. Colley has informed you of my presence. I assure you, as I did her, that there is no nefarious purpose to my undertaking."

"Nefarious?" Bettina offered a flirtatious glance from beneath a delicately shadowed eyelid. "Fascinating, more like."

She advanced and extended a hand. He bowed, but then extended his own hand in response. The gesture revealed an expanse of starched shirt cuff and an elegant cufflink.

"Bettina Fraser from the *Arborville Advocate*," Bettina said as she grasped his hand. "And these are my associates, Pamela Paterson and Penny Paterson."

More handshakes all around followed, as well as a name: Edmund McClintock.

"A very worthwhile project." Bettina nodded toward the camera. "This is undoubtedly one of the oldest houses in Arborville, and it definitely has stories to tell."

"Did she die of fright?" It was hard to know from Edmund's expression, quite deadpan, whether he was asking the question seriously or alluding to Marcy Brewer's article.

"It's possible, but unlikely." Penny spoke up. Had she been Googling? Pamela wondered, or—curious as Holly had been—consulting Harold Bascomb?

"You're not here to photograph the ghosts, are you?" Bettina asked.

"No." Edmund laughed. "Though the Victorians wouldn't have pooh-poohed the idea. Spirit photography was one of their pastimes. I'm here to memorialize this magnificent house before they completely destroy it . . . completely destroy it, as I'm sure they will. Modernizing! Ugh!" He snorted, and then began speaking again, faster and faster. "I can't tell you how many historic houses all over the county have been lost forever, remuddled by people who'd rather have six bathrooms and ten closets and open-plan kitchens—never mind that then you have a view of dirty dishes piled by the sink as you sit on your living room sofa, and everything is painted white or gray with marble counters— rather than . . . rather than appreciate the craftsmanship that went into . . . into—"

He stopped, and it seemed to Pamela that he was on the verge of tears, but he blinked and shook his head a few times, then went on.

"Or worse yet . . . worse yet—it's a tear-down, and then it's gone forever and they build a McMansion in its place."

Bettina had retreated as he spoke. Now she inched forward and said, "But Tassie Hunt is . . ."

"Dead. I know that." Edmond's face took on a stern expression that complemented his formal clothes, somewhat like an expression that might have been captured in a portrait taken when his camera was new.

"She'd been talking to a contractor or an architect or somebody before she died. How do I know that? Never mind. Never mind. But she was probably contemplating something . . . *nefarious* . . . and another piece of history is gone forever."

"But now . . ." Bettina ventured cautiously, "now that she's gone . . ."

"There's another one of them." Edmund's tone was ominous. "Another marauder. Her paramour was around on and off while she was living here, and he's going to take possession in a few days and will probably launch the destruction."

"Tassie Hunt had a . . . paramour?" Pamela and Bettina spoke in chorus.

"Chad Donahue," Edmund said. "Don't ask me how I know that. But you'd think one death would have made it clear that this house is not to be tampered with . . . definitely not to be tampered with."

He slipped a hand beneath the lapel of his coat. The hand emerged holding a flat silver case from which he extracted a card. With a slight bow, he extended it toward Bettina, saying, "I'd be delighted to go on record in the *Advocate* with my views, dear lady. Please accept my card."

"Oh, I can just scan it with my phone." Bettina clicked her handbag open and started to reach inside.

"Phone?" He shuddered. "No. Please . . . take it."

Bettina acquiesced with a smile. As she tucked the card away, Pamela got a glimpse of it: on thick ivory cardstock, an elaborate wreath of interwoven curlicues framed a few lines of elegantly engraved text.

As they walked back to where the faithful Toyota waited, Pamela glanced toward the window from which Win Colley had said she could see Edith sitting on her porch knitting. The morning was bright, and the interior of Win's house was shadowy, so it was hard to know whether Win was keeping tabs on them or not, waiting to rush out and accost them. But Pamela was happy once the Toyota was in motion.

As if she'd been reading Pamela's mind, Bettina broke the silence a few moments later, murmuring, "Thank goodness we didn't have to talk to that nutty woman again."

"Are you going to put Edmund in your article?" Pamela asked.

"I'm not sure." Bettina slowed as they approached the corner where she would make her turn.

"I think he does believe in the ghosts." Penny spoke up from the back seat. "I liked him, though, and he was cute. Sort of a steampunk look."

"Steampunk?" Bettina asked.

"It's a thing," Penny said. "Victorian clothes, steam— as in the age of steam engines, but there's a science-fiction aspect. They have conventions and like that."

"Do they believe in ghosts?" Bettina followed up.

"Not necessarily. Maybe not at all. I don't think that's part of it."

"Then why did you say . . . ?"

"That I thought he believed in them?" Penny waited, but when there was no response, she went on. "Because of what he said right before he offered you his card: 'But you'd think one death would have made it clear that this house is not to be tampered with.' He thinks the ghosts are protecting the house because they like it the way it is."

It was with a new appreciation of the ordinary that Pamela opened the Toyota's passenger-side door and stepped out onto the Frasers' driveway. Nothing about the Frasers' house, or her own just across the street, hinted at the supernatural, and the sight of Wilfred in his bib overalls guiding the timorous Woofus along the sidewalk enhanced her satisfaction with the familiar scene.

Bettina made her way to the end of the driveway and watched as they approached.

"Dear wife," Wilfred called as he passed the house

next door, a house of neat brick softened by a luxuriant climbing rose.

"We've had the most curious adventure," Bettina said when he was close enough that she could speak at a normal volume.

She extracted Edmund's card from her handbag and extended it toward Wilfred. Woofus held back, straining at his leash and casting wary glances at Pamela and Penny, but Wilfred advanced to embrace his wife and take the card from her hand.

Wilfred looked up after a moment. "Edmund McClintock?"

"Do you know him?" Bettina asked. "He's very . . . historical."

Wilfred was a fixture in Arborville's historical society.

"He looks like a character out of Charles Dickens," Penny explained, "or somebody who's into steampunk. He was taking pictures of Voorhees House with an ancient camera to preserve the memory of it—because he's afraid it's going to be all redone and it won't look Victorian anymore, or maybe even torn down."

"Photographing it sounds like a worthy project." Wilfred nodded. "And Voorhees House certainly should be protected, but no, he's never shown up at a meeting of the historical society—maybe because our interest is more the Revolutionary Era."

They chatted a bit more, with Bettina mentioning that Edmund seemed to be in the camp of those who thought Voorhees House was haunted and Wilfred noting that the Victorians had probably been just as irrational as most people before or since.

"Come over at about six tomorrow," Wilfred said as

they parted ways. "The weather looks to be fine, and we'll be grilling in the backyard."

"What can I bring?" Pamela asked. "How about ice cream?"

"I've got that covered." Wilfred smiled. "I'm making some."

Pamela and Penny made their way across the street to their own house, and Woofus ceased straining at his leash and greeted Bettina by licking her hand.

Saturday morning brought a surprise caller. Pamela and Penny were lingering over coffee and the morning paper when the doorbell chimed.

"Bettina, maybe?" Pamela looked up from a gardening article about constructing raised beds with wood salvaged from fruit crates.

"I'll get it." Penny hurried toward the entry.

Pamela heard the door open and then a surprised squeal. When Penny returned to the kitchen, she was accompanied by another young woman, a bit older than Penny, much taller, and with tousled blond hair that cascaded past her shoulders. She was wearing a casual shift in a fabric whose loose weave and bright paisley print gave it a bohemian flair. And she was carrying a small black kitten.

"Why, Sybil Larkin!" Pamela rose. "How long have you been in town?"

No sooner had Pamela spoken than two other cats joined them. Catrina and Ginger crept through the doorway, prowled briefly around the young blond woman's sandal-clad feet, and then settled back onto their haunches gazing upward. Catrina added a soulful meow for good measure.

"Since last night," said the young woman, who was indeed Richard Larkin's daughter, Sybil. "My dad left for Maine first thing this morning to spend the week volunteering with the Recycle, Renew group. I'm house-sitting—and cat-sitting."

She stooped to the floor and set the kitten down—gingerly. The kitten's amber eyes were very large in its small face, and its coat was still fuzzy with kitten fur.

"What name did your father decide on?" Pamela asked. Some months earlier Richard had let it be known that he was looking to adopt a kitten, and soon afterward Pamela had happened to meet a woman whose cat was on the verge of giving birth. The birth had taken place, and the litter had included this kitten.

"Frank," Sibyl said, "or, more formally, Frank Lloyd Wright."

Catrina and Ginger had both backed away as Sibyl stooped. Now Catrina ventured forward, creeping low to the ground and with her tail twitching abruptly back and forth. Ginger watched from a distance.

Frank extended his neck and peered at Catrina, who continued her advance. As she got closer, a ridge of hair rose along his backbone, and his tiny mouth opened in a ragged hiss. Despite that, Catrina ventured closer, extending her own neck until she was nearly nose to nose with him.

Frank jerked back and huddled against Sibyl's leg, wrapping his tail around his extremities as if to protect them.

"Maybe they've had enough exposure to each other for now," Sibyl suggested. "I've read that it can take a while for cats to get acquainted. These guys are going to be neighbors, and friends, I hope—not that any of them are outdoor cats, but . . ."

But? Was Sibyl imagining that someday Pamela and Richard might combine households—and cats? Pamela wasn't aware that she had reacted to Sibyl's statement until Penny said, "What's wrong, Mom?"

"Nothing! Nothing!" She raised a hand to her forehead lest a frown was lurking there.

Sibyl was about to scoop Frank up when he skittered forward. Catrina had begun to sniff the spot on the floor from which he had retreated earlier. She looked up and watched as he advanced, then she took a few tentative steps toward him. Neither retreated until they were once again nose to nose, nuzzling each other in the most delicate, probing way.

Ginger crept forward now, vigilant and low to the ground, but soon she and Catrina exchanged places, and she and Frank embarked on the delicate process of probing and sniffing.

The humans were enjoying this glimpse into the rituals of feline social interaction. Pamela knew, of course, that cats also sniffed humans, unfamiliar humans introduced into their households, and even their own humans if their humans returned from somewhere bearing on their shoes or elsewhere olfactory evidence of an interesting adventure. She wondered, suddenly, if cats ever found it odd that humans never sniffed them.

After several minutes, Catrina and Ginger appeared satisfied that they knew all they needed to know about this new creature, and they wandered back through the kitchen doorway as Frank settled into a resting position near Sibyl's feet.

"I guess it's time to take this little guy back home," Sibyl said as she bent over to scoop the kitten up with one hand. "He's had enough excitement for one day." Cuddling him against her chest, she turned to Penny and added, "Come on over if you're not busy. I can make us some lunch later, and we can catch up on things."

Then the kitchen was empty but for Pamela, who felt a bit at loose ends. She and Penny and Aaron weren't due across the street for the going-away barbecue until six, and it wasn't even lunchtime yet. The work for the magazine, due on Monday morning, was all finished. The pantry was getting bare, but Bettina and Wilfred would be providing that evening's dinner.

She could make a list though, for a trip to the Co-Op the next morning. And she could take a walk, maybe down the hill to the nature preserve. And there was laundry to be done, and vacuuming and dusting. Full of purpose once more, Pamela fetched one of the notepads that charitable organizations so thoughtfully kept her provided with and settled down at the kitchen table.

"Crab," she wrote at the top. She would make crab cakes as a special going-away meal for Penny Sunday night. The Co-Op fish counter offered cans of fresh crab meat, kept chilled on ice.

CHAPTER 10

Even if the Frasers hadn't made it clear in advance that the evening's meal would be prepared on their backyard grill, the aroma of a charcoal fire that greeted Pamela's nostrils when she stepped outside would have announced that fact. Aaron Carlisle had rung the doorbell, Pamela and Penny had joined him on the porch, and now all three of them were heading down Pamela's front walk under a summer sky, cloudless and still bright blue at six p.m.

"They just live across the street, like I told you," Penny was explaining to Aaron.

She had taken the lead, with Aaron at her side, and Pamela was lagging a few yards behind. She remembered when Penny met Aaron a few Christmases earlier. He'd seemed alarmingly glamorous then, with dark good looks that involved sculpted cheekbones, arresting blue eyes, and a mouth that verged on the sensuous.

Penny had seemed totally smitten, in a way that

made Pamela fear her daughter was heading for her first broken heart. But then winter break had ended, and Penny had returned to Boston, and the romance—if that was what it had been—had mellowed into a casual friendship. Now the connection seemed once more based on something other than friendship, but deeper, Pamela hoped, than the dazzling effect of Aaron's undeniable good looks.

Bettina emerged from around the side of the Frasers' garage just as Penny and Aaron reached the driveway.

"Welcome, welcome!" she exclaimed, extending her arms as if proposing to gather them both up into a hug. She was looking festive in a red-and-white checked sundress with a fitted bodice and a flouncy skirt. On her feet were white wedge-heeled espadrilles with ankle ties, and a necklace of large white beads set off the dress's plunging neckline.

Penny's dress was equally festive: a thrift-shop find, bright yellow, with a parade of large red roosters accenting the skirt's hemline.

The hug did not materialize, perhaps because Bettina had yet to be introduced to Aaron. That detail was rapidly accomplished, and Aaron extended a hand and professed himself delighted to meet "Ms. Fraser."

"Oh! *Bettina*, please!" Bettina grabbed the hand in both of her own.

Wilfred had appeared at her shoulder, garbed in one of the heavy-duty aprons he reserved for his barbecuing exploits.

"And I'm Wilfred," he said, seizing Aaron's hand as soon as Bettina released it. "Come on back." His expansive gesture took in the whole group, and he added, "We've got plenty of cold beer, and there are chips and dip."

The Frasers' backyard featured a wide patio that in warm weather was nearly an extension of their spacious kitchen, separated from it by only sliding glass doors. A broad lawn stretched from the edge of the patio to the fence at the back of the property, and abundant drifts of shrubbery, as well as a venerable maple tree, added to the verdant effect. Geraniums in glazed ceramic pots contributed a touch of color to the scene.

The barbecue grill, from which wisps of smoke were rising, sat on the grass some distance from the patio. On the patio was a large table spread with a flowered cloth in shades of red, pink, and coral and surrounded by five chairs. A basket of potato chips awaited, as well as a bowl of dip.

"Who's for a beer?" Wilfred asked once everyone had gathered near the table.

Interpreting nods and smiles as assent, he slid one of the glass doors open and disappeared into the kitchen. While he was gone, Bettina launched the obvious conversation topic. Directing one of her most encouraging smiles at Aaron, she remarked, "So . . . you're off to Guatemala."

Aaron, who was quite self-possessed, needed little encouragement to describe the project he and Penny were about to undertake. Discarded plastic bottles, it seemed, could be filled with sand and used in place of bricks to construct sturdy, insulated walls. A group of volunteers from New Jersey would work with members of the community in a small Guatemalan village to replace the existing school with a larger and more weatherproof structure.

"That sounds fascinating," Bettina cooed. An admiring gaze underlined her words.

Pamela, meanwhile, was watching her daughter. Did

the gaze that Penny was directing at Aaron reflect her satisfaction with the worthy project they were both about to undertake, or her personal reaction to Aaron himself? No matter. Aaron seemed a worthy object for Penny's affections.

Wilfred reappeared then, carrying a tray that held five tall glasses already starting to collect beads of moisture as the summer air condensed on their cold surfaces. The beer they held was a rich amber color, topped by an inch of creamy foam.

"A school built from discarded plastic bottles!" Wilfred exclaimed after he had set the tray down on the table and handed glasses of beer all around.

"Killing two birds with one stone, you might say," Aaron remarked.

"I was just going to say it." Wilfred, who had an old saying for nearly every occasion, raised his glass in a toast.

Both laughed, and the next few minutes were devoted to sipping beer and sampling the chips and dip. It was the classic onion dip, Wilfred explained, like his mother had made way back when he was young: onion soup mix in a foil packet mixed with sour cream.

The potato chips were ripple chips, sturdy enough to scoop a generous portion of the dip without breaking, and the effect was satisfyingly creamy and rich and salty and crunchy, with an oniony tang unlike anything that could have been achieved with fresh onions. Sometimes classics were classic for a reason, Pamela decided as she refreshed her tongue with a bracing swallow of the cold beer and reached for another chip.

When people spoke again, it was to praise the chips and the dip and the beer as perfect for a summer barbecue. Then Bettina focused on Penny, inquiring about travel plans. Penny explained that the last leg of the journey would involve a daylong bus ride, and Aaron chimed in with further details.

But Wilfred had questions too, for Aaron, and soon the two men had migrated across the lawn, chatting all the way. They paused when they reached the barbecue grill, and Wilfred bent over to examine the coals. He made a few adjustments with a pair of tongs, and they returned to the patio—but not for long.

Apparently, their conversation had returned to the concept of using sand-filled bottles to build schools and then veered into the topic of building things in general.

"Coals will be ready for the burgers in about ten minutes," Wilfred announced. "Meanwhile," he added as he stepped toward the sliding glass doors, slid one open, and beckoned to Aaron, "come on down to my basement workshop. I've got a dollhouse in progress."

"Dollhouse?" Pamela inquired when they were gone.

Bettina smiled. "For the baby Maxie's expecting, in case it's a girl." She lifted the hand that wasn't holding her beer and crossed two fingers, tipped with nails painted to match the bright red checks of her dress. "Of course, it will be a while before she can actually play with it. And if it's not a girl, he'll give the dollhouse to Nell for the women's shelter."

After a brief pause, during which she seemed to contemplate the likely—at least fifty percent—possibility that she would soon have a granddaughter to spoil, she resumed her hostess duties and turned to Penny.

"I'm so glad we got to meet Aaron at last," she said, "and I hope we can all get together again when you get back from the trip. I'm sure you'll have stories and photos . . ."

But before Penny could answer, she went on, speaking to Pamela. ". . . but it's too bad Pete couldn't make it tonight."

"He doesn't really know Penny and Aaron." Pamela offered an apologetic smile. "We went over all that, and I'm only just getting to know him. It's not like we're a *couple* and have to go everywhere together."

"You do like him though." The utterance was more a statement than a question. "And you can't string an interested man along forever. Experience has proven that."

Penny had begun to edge away, as if sensing that her mother would just as soon respond to Bettina without an audience—especially an audience composed of her daughter. After studying the pots of geraniums for a few moments, she glanced toward the glass doors between the patio and the kitchen.

"They're back from the basement, and they're getting ready to bring the food out," she exclaimed in a voice tinged with relief at being offered an excuse to be somewhere else. "I'll give them a hand."

The door slid open, and Aaron stepped through, carrying a large platter. Arranged on the platter were six raw hamburger patties, glistening and pink. Penny slipped into the kitchen as he left.

"Lots more to carry, I'm sure." Pamela headed for the open door. In her hurry to get away from Bettina, she nearly collided with Wilfred, who was on his way out, followed by Woofus.

She watched as Wilfred caught up with Aaron and pointed toward the grill. "Have you ever thought of building a full-size thing," Pamela heard Aaron inquire, "like a school perhaps? Using sand-filled bottles?"

They set off across the lawn with Woofus loping alongside. She couldn't hear Wilfred's response, but he paused to give Woofus a reassuring pat, suggesting that he wasn't committing—at least right then—to an adventure that would take him away from his wife and pets.

Pamela joined Penny in the kitchen, and Bettina followed soon after, carrying the remains of the chips and dip. The plates and flatware and napkins they would need had already been staged on the high counter that separated the cooking area of the kitchen from the eating area. Waiting there too were bowls of potato salad and coleslaw, a basket of puffy brioche buns, and a tray holding mayonnaise, catsup, and a plate of sliced pickles.

In a matter of minutes, and with three pairs of willing hands, the table on the patio was set. Bettina's sage-green pottery plates contrasted with the bright cloth, and the coral napkins picked up one of the tones in the cloth's flowery print.

Across the lawn, Wilfred and Aaron were having a jovial time, trading off between tending the burgers and chatting. They could have been father and son, except that Aaron, with his dark hair and striking good looks, bore no resemblance at all to the Frasers' actual offspring. Wilfred Jr. and Warren had inherited their father's pleasant but unremarkable features and the sandy hair of his youth.

The aroma of grilling hamburgers had begun to waft toward the patio, a combination of sizzling fat and a hint of char.

"They're almost done!" Wilfred called after a few

minutes, but Pamela was already on her way to the kitchen to fetch the side dishes that would accompany the burgers.

Bettina came hurrying after her. "I forgot about the tomatoes!" she exclaimed as she opened a cupboard and took out a small platter that matched her pottery set.

A bowl on the counter near the refrigerator held several tomatoes, their ruddy skins fairly glowing with ripeness. Bettina was soon hard at work slicing and arranging the slices on the platter. Meanwhile, Pamela seized the bowl with the potato salad in one hand and the bowl with the coleslaw in the other and carried them to the table.

Penny, left behind on the patio, was watching the grilling process intensely, with special focus on Aaron, Pamela suspected, and she nearly jumped when Pamela said, "Why don't you bring the buns out."

No sooner had Penny left than Aaron set off toward the patio with a platter that held five of the cooked burgers. The sixth had been cooked with a non-human diner in mind. In a ritual that Pamela had become familiar with in the many years that she had enjoyed the Frasers' barbecues, Wilfred remained behind at the grill. Woofus had been growing more and more interested in the proceedings as Wilfred began to transfer the burgers to the serving platter. As if he knew that one had been held in reserve, he watched serenely as Aaron made his way across the lawn.

Wilfred had begun to tease the reserved burger patty into bite-sized pieces. Sensing that the most interesting part of the process was about to commence, Woofus transferred his attention to his master. Wilfred picked up one of the burger morsels between thumb and forefinger and held it a few inches above Woofus's shaggy head. Woofus raised his muzzle, opened his mouth, and delicately nibbled the morsel from Wilfred's fingers.

On the patio, meanwhile, the table awaited, spread with all that would make the barbecue menu complete. The platter of burgers, seared by the grilling and glistening with fat, formed the centerpiece. Surrounding it were the potato salad, the coleslaw, and the sliced tomatoes, as well as the basket of buns and the tray with the condiments and pickles.

"Beer!" Wilfred exclaimed before sitting down, and he veered toward the kitchen. With Aaron helping, glasses were quickly refilled. Wilfred took his seat and his hearty "*Bon appétit!*" invited his guests to partake.

"You'll be out of the country for a month," he added, addressing Penny and Aaron, "so I planned the most classic USA-style barbecue I could think of."

"I certainly have no argument with that," Aaron said. "Nothing beats a good burger."

"Here you go, then"—Bettina nudged the platter in his direction—"and take a bun." She handed him the basket. "The Co-Op bakery makes these brioche buns, and Wilfred discovered they're perfect for burgers."

No one spoke for a bit, as hamburgers were assembled. Mayonnaise and catsup were applied liberally to the buns, which Wilfred had conveniently split before piling them in the basket. The burger patties were nestled onto the bottom bun, the tomato slices and pickles balanced on top, and the remaining half of the bun lowered onto the completed creation.

Bettina picked up the bowl of potato salad and passed it to Aaron, and Wilfred launched the coleslaw on its way around the table by handing it to Pamela.

Soon everyone's plate had been garnished with a serving of each.

"*Bon appétit!*" Wilfred urged again, and Bettina took the lead, grasping her burger with both hands and lifting it from the plate as tomato juice, mingled with mayonnaise and catsup, dribbled over her fingers.

Pamela followed, tasting the burger first and admiring the way the yeasty texture of the brioche bun stood up to the task of enclosing the plump burger patty, the tomato slice, and the pickle without disintegrating.

"Really, really good," came the verdict from the side of the table occupied by Penny and Aaron, as Aaron echoed Penny's words.

Eating hamburgers inevitably led to fingers in need of wiping, and soon the napkin in Pamela's lap was streaked with mayonnaise, catsup, and grease. Bettina had explained in the past that finger-wiping was, after all, what napkins were for, and somehow when her table linens reappeared, they always looked as pristine as if they were new.

Though the burgers were the meal's main attraction, the potato salad and the coleslaw held their own in their supporting roles. Wilfred's potato salad was simple. He started with steamed potatoes, the Yukon Golds that sliced neatly without disintegrating, and he added chopped hard-boiled eggs, minced onion, and diced celery. The dressing was a mixture of mayonnaise and cider vinegar, with salt, pepper, and celery seed stirred in. As he tossed the potatoes and other ingredients with the dressing, the cooked egg yolks crumbled, scattering flecks of gold through the entire salad.

The coleslaw, too, was Wilfred's own simple creation, a crisp mound of cabbage that intermingled slivers of the dark outer leaves with slivers of the pale inner leaves, and glossy with a judicious amount of mayonnaise.

For a time, conversation was limited to comments about the food, but gradually the pace of eating slowed. The burgers dwindled into mere nubbins of meat enclosed by the crusts of buns, and only a few potato slices or cabbage slivers remained of the salads. The tall glasses were empty but for a trace of foam lingering in their depths.

"So," Bettina said, turning to Aaron, "what will you do for the rest of the summer when you get back from your adventure?"

He lowered his fork to his plate. "Oh!" He looked vaguely confused. "I'm actually not coming back . . . at least not right away."

Penny set her own fork down and addressed Pamela, who was sitting across the table from her. "I thought I told you that, Mom."

"You did." Pamela nodded. "But I didn't tell Bettina. Everyone doesn't have to tell everyone everything all the time."

"But—" Bettina leaned forward to make eye contact with Penny, who was sitting on the other side of Aaron. "But *you're* coming back after a month, aren't you?"

"Of course, of course." Penny waved a hand as if to shoo away any notion that she might be planning a longer absence. "But Aaron . . ." Her pretty lips curved into a fond smile. "Aaron wants to stay in Guatemala and work there for a while, maybe teaching English." The smile grew fonder, and she turned toward him. "He speaks Spanish really well."

She's really smitten, Pamela reflected, *though she said she doesn't want to give up her own plans to follow him*. Penny's dark curls framed cheeks fairly glowing with a blushing intensity. Pamela glanced away, suddenly feeling as if she'd intruded on a lovers' tête-à-tête.

"Well!" Bettina straightened up and leaned back in her chair. "That's a relief . . . that you're coming back, I mean. And it sounds like Aaron has some very interesting plans."

But Bettina, too, had perhaps been startled by the very obvious evidence of Penny's attachment to this handsome young man. She fell silent, as did everyone else. For a few long minutes, diners filled the awkward silence by nibbling up the last fragments of the meal, shredded though the bits of bun might be or forlorn the slivers of cabbage.

When the plates were truly, definitively, empty, Wilfred rose from his chair. He surveyed his tablemates with a chuckling smile and said, "I hope you all have room for homemade strawberry ice cream."

The response was a chorus of "Yes, yes!" and as if a spell had been broken, everyone else rose too, plate in hand.

"Many hands make light work," he observed, and indeed after a few trips between patio and kitchen, the table was bare, save for the flowery cloth.

Wilfred served the ice cream in Bettina's sage-green bowls, mounds of it, pale pink streaked with the bright red of ripe strawberries.

"Homemade," he repeated as he took his seat.

"Delicious," was the verdict as Aaron took his first bite.

"You don't even need one of those ice-cream makers," Bettina chimed in after sampling her own portion. "You stew fresh berries and put them in a kind of custard, and then you freeze it."

Wilfred took up the explanation. "But you have to take it out of the freezer every once in a while and stir and stir. That's what gives it the ice-cream texture."

"Otherwise, it's just a solid block." Bettina set down her spoon and made a gesture that suggested holding a block of ice. "It turned out like that the first time we tried it."

"Well, *this* batch turned out great!" Penny lifted a heaping spoonful as if in a toast to its creator. "Not a solid block at all."

Indeed, the ice cream brought to mind a bowl of just-picked strawberries and cream, but delightfully chilly. The strawberries had retained nearly all their freshness, even to the slight acidic effect of a strawberry plucked right off the vine.

With compliments to the chef out of the way, the conversation turned to other topics. Aaron was familiar with the *Advocate* because, while a student at Wendelstaff College, he had shared a house with friends in Arborville. He asked Bettina how long she'd been reporting for the newspaper and even, flatteringly, recalled an article she'd written after interviewing a local Wiccan about the Wiccan observance of the spring equinox.

"They're very respectful of nature," he observed, "and you brought that out so well."

"Thank you!" Bettina offered a coquettish smile. "Not everyone appreciates the *Advocate*. Some people just leave it in their driveway."

"Dear wife!" Wilfred sounded so shocked that Pamela, Penny, and Aaron all swiveled to face him. "I'm sure they're just on vacation or something. I hear people talk all the time about how much they look forward to the *Advocate* every Friday. Where else will they learn about what's really going on in Arborville?"

"Like Voorhees House?" Aaron's expression contained a hint of mischief, as if he knew he was introducing a topic about which Bettina would have plenty to say.

Pamela smiled to herself as Bettina happily obliged with an overview. Penny and Wilfred meanwhile were discussing his dollhouse project, specifically his plans for applying special dollhouse-scale wallpaper to some of the walls.

"And there will be tiny furniture, of course," he added, "and even dishes."

Listening, Pamela reflected that Wilfred seemed nearly as transported as Bettina at the prospect of having a granddaughter to dote on—and so close at hand. She was about to ask if there had been any word from Maxie about when she—and they—would know whether the expected baby was to be another boy or a little girl. But then she decided against it. Why remind Wilfred that the little girl he imagined as the beneficiary of his handiwork was so far only hypothetical?

Instead, she shifted her chair into a position that gave her a better view of the yard. Twilight had begun its gradual creep, and the sky was darkening in the east. To the west, the sun was slipping behind a band of clouds at the horizon, staining the clouds with streaks of ruby and amber. The lawn glowed deep Technicolor green and released a damp, earthy smell into the evening air.

"Yes, I guess so . . ." Bettina's voice, sounding regretful, summoned Pamela from her reverie. "You've both got a lot to do before you set off on Monday morning . . ." She was addressing Aaron, and Penny beyond him. "You're sure you don't want to stay a bit longer for coffee?"

"This was a wonderful barbecue," Aaron said, glancing back and forth from Bettina to Wilfred, "but I've got a full day tomorrow. My parents and I are driving down to Ocean Grove to visit my grandparents."

"Because he's going to be away a long while," Penny explained. She rested a hand on Aaron's shoulder, and both started to rise.

Things were winding down. Bettina stood up too and led the way toward the sliding glass doors. She opened the nearest one and waved Penny and Aaron, followed by Pamela, inside. Wilfred brought up the rear, slipping an arm around his wife as they followed their guests through the kitchen and dining room and onward till they were all standing on the front porch.

After hugs and a confused chorus of thanks and good wishes, Penny and Aaron set off across the street. Pamela lingered to let them get a little bit ahead, then lingered more as Bettina spoke.

CHAPTER 11

"I'm glad we got to meet Aaron at last," she said, tilting her head to make eye contact with Pamela. That, and her serious expression, suggested she had more in mind than sociable chitchat. That impression was confirmed as she went on. "What do you think will happen? She's obviously head over heels in love."

Pamela suppressed a teasing smile as she replied, "Really? What makes you think so?"

"Pamela!" Bettina's eyes widened, and a furrow appeared between her brows. "You couldn't tell? *I* could tell."

"I asked her about him," Pamela said. "I told you that. She wants to make her own plans about her own life. I suppose she hopes it will include him, but she doesn't want to commit . . . yet."

Bettina nodded. "She's still so young, whereas you're . . ." Bettina's voice trailed off, as if she was aware, even in the gathering twilight, that Pamela was staring at her. When she spoke again, it was to add, "Never mind."

After breakfast the next morning, Penny retreated back upstairs to start packing for her trip. Pamela lingered over the *Register*, happy for the distraction of the Lifestyle section, with its photos of gardens and pretty interiors. She'd sent Penny—a much younger Penny—off to college, after all. How much different was this adventure?

A walk to the Co-Op would be a pleasant distraction too, but not quite yet. There was still a bit of coffee left in the carafe, and she'd only made her way through the first few pages of Lifestyle. But as she was heading for the stove to warm the coffee, the doorbell's chime interrupted her.

Stepping to the entry doorway, she glanced toward the porch. Veiled by the lace that curtained the oval window in the front door was a caller that could only be Bettina, resplendent in a shade of orange that fairly vibrated against the bright summer greenery.

"Good morning, Catrina!" Bettina greeted the cat, who was napping in the sunny spot on the entry's thrift-shop carpet. "And good morning, Pamela!"

The colorful outfit was revealed as a sleeveless linen dress, bright orange and nearly ankle-length, accessorized with a bold turquoise and silver necklace and matching earrings. Bettina was carrying a small shopping bag that bore the logo of the fanciest store at the mall.

"A little something for Miss Penny," she said, extending her arm to display the bag. "I hope she's not finished packing yet."

"She's in her room." Pamela gestured toward the stairway. "We can go up. Or I can make more coffee, and she can come down."

"I can't stay." Bettina waved her free hand to dispel the coffee idea. "We're taking the grandchildren to the Wildlife Center in Timberley."

"Hi, Bettina!" Penny's voice reached them from the landing. "I heard the doorbell, and then I heard your voice." Penny continued the rest of the way down the stairs, and Bettina met her at the bottom with a hug.

"Let's go in the kitchen." Bettina's arm remained around Penny's shoulders, and she took a few steps. "Come and see what I've brought you."

Pamela followed, and in a few moments, they were gathered around the kitchen table and Penny was extracting a tissue-wrapped bundle from the fancy bag.

"You said you were only taking T-shirts," Bettina said, "so I got you a T-shirt."

The garment that was revealed as Penny folded back the tissue was indeed a T-shirt, but quite a splendid one.

A lush design that resembled tie-dye, in shades of rose, violet, and indigo, swirled over the shirt's surface. As if that wasn't decoration enough, the swirls were overlaid with flower shapes outlined in sequins.

"Oh!" Penny lifted it from its tissue nest. "It's really quite . . . remarkable." She held it up to her chest as if to gauge the size. "And beautiful," she added hastily after a glance in Bettina's direction. "I'm *sure* I'll get a lot of use out of it on my trip."

Pamela wasn't convinced her daughter meant that, but she admired her diplomacy.

"Your suitcase is probably already quite full," Bettina said. "So, I didn't want to get something that would take up too much room."

"Well, it's beautiful," Penny repeated. "And I will definitely think of you every time I wear it."

Penny retreated back upstairs with the T-shirt soon after. Pamela offered once again to make coffee, but Bettina insisted that she had to be off, and Pamela accompanied her to the front door. They stepped out onto the porch to see Libby Kimble scurrying toward them, already halfway up Pamela's walk and waving enthusiastically.

She moved quite fast for someone so elderly.

"Your sweet husband said I'd find you here," she said when she reached the bottom of the steps. "You see, I really need your advice, about what the next step for ANGWY should be, because someone else is moving into Voorhees House now and—"

As if the exertion of her sprint across the street had caught up with her, she paused and bent over till all that was visible of her was her back, clothed in a nondescript cotton shirt, and the tidy bun into which her colorless hair was gathered. When she raised her head again, her thin face was flushed, and she was gasping for breath.

"For heaven's sake, come up on the porch and have a seat." Bettina advanced toward the top of the steps, beckoning. "Or here"—she started down—"let me give you a hand."

Pamela realized at that moment that she was still in her robe and slippers. She'd been enjoying a relaxing dawdle over the Sunday paper when Bettina arrived, just about to have a last bit of coffee before dressing and starting her day.

"Let's go inside," she suggested as Bettina made her way back up the steps, guiding Libby with an arm around her waist.

Instead of leading Libby to the kitchen once they were all inside, Bettina steered her into the living room. "Sit here," she said, settling Libby onto the sofa and moving a few pillows aside to make a space for herself.

Precious had been lounging on the top platform of the cat climber, sprawled out to display her Siamese elegance to full advantage. She twisted her head lazily in the direction of the new arrivals and then went back to lounging.

Bettina had already turned down offers of fresh coffee twice. Water seemed a better option for Libby, who was still looking quite flushed, so Pamela headed to the kitchen. When she returned, she slipped the glass of water into Libby's hand, pulled the hassock closer to the coffee table, and lowered herself onto it.

Bettina watched and waited, quite solicitously, as Libby sipped the water. Her friend had a nose for news, Pamela knew, but Bettina was a considerate person. Libby's last words before she paused to recover from her sprint had been "someone else is moving into Voorhees House now." Though Pamela was not a nosy person, with regard to news or anything else, even she had found the statement titillating. Could this be the Chad Donahue, Tassie's "paramour," that the photographer Edmund McClintock had referred to?

No sooner had Libby leaned forward to set the glass on the coffee table, than Bettina spoke.

"You said someone else is moving into Voorhees House now?"

Libby nodded. "Tassie's boyfriend, Chad Donahue. And what I need to know is, do you think ANGWY should pay a welcome call? Do you know any more about him—from your connection with the *Advocate* or Detective Clayborn? Because we don't want to do the wrong thing and make a bad impression by intruding on his grief."

Pamela's gaze strayed from Libby's face to Bettina's. It was hard to judge from Bettina's expression what was going on in her mind. The squint implied puzzlement, but the slight smile hinted that she was amused. Then Pamela realized that she herself was both puzzled and amused by the idea that ANGWY thought it needed Bettina's approval before paying a call on the new occupant of Voorhees House.

Then she blinked, as if her brain was commanding her to take a fresh look at things. Maybe Libby, for some reason, was fishing for information about Chad Donahue.

Still looking a bit puzzled, Bettina asked Libby how she had learned about Chad Donahue and his plans.

"Just neighborhood chatter," Libby said. "I live right around the block from Voorhees House, after all." The flush had subsided, and her skin was pale again, nearly the same tone as the wisps of hair that had escaped from her bun. "It seems odd that he's moving in so soon—or even at all. I wouldn't want to move into a house where a loved one had died."

"Who even owns the house now?" Bettina's sudden lurch as she leaned forward to address Pamela suggested this question had just occurred to her. "I don't think Tassie was officially divorced from her husband yet. Clayborn told me that the husband plans to claim the body and handle funeral arrangements when the medical examiner is finished."

"And why would he do that unless there was still a legal connection?" Libby addressed Pamela, then shifted her gaze to where Bettina sat at the other end of the sofa. "*She* left *him*, so he can't have fond feelings."

"I wouldn't think so," Pamela agreed. "And if there's no will, wouldn't Tassie's husband, even though estranged, inherit the house—setting up a potential conflict with Chad?"

"Maybe there *is* a will," Bettina said. "Maybe there's a will leaving the house to Chad. Maybe the will was even *his* idea."

"Oh, my!" Libby raised a bony finger to her mouth. "That opens a can of worms."

"Worms," Bettina murmured, lifting her wrist to consult her pretty watch. "That reminds me—I have got to get going." She stood up. Circling around behind Pamela as she headed for the door, she paused to glance at Libby and said, "My sweet husband and I are taking our grandsons to the Wildlife Center in Timberley."

"I've got to get going too." Libby stood up and followed Bettina into the entry. "But just one more thing . . ." She reached out a petitioning hand. "You said you'd like to interview my grandson for the *Advocate*, about his wrestling scholarship. Can you come Tuesday morning? At eleven?"

Bettina agreed, and Libby was off, scurrying on her way.

"I really do have to go," Bettina said, consulting her watch again, "but I guess it's true, about Chad moving in—and soon, just like Edmund said."

Then Bettina was off too. Pamela returned to the kitchen, where the *Register* was still spread out on the table and the carafe still held an inch of cold coffee. It seemed too late to return to her morning dawdle, even with reheated coffee, so Pamela tidied up the breakfast dishes, transferred the newspaper to the recycling basket, and climbed the stairs.

"Who was that down there?" Penny's voice emerged from her room as Pamela stepped into the upstairs hall.

"Just someone," Pamela responded. "Someone from the ANGWY committee. She wanted Bettina's advice about something, and Wilfred sent her over here."

"Something about Voorhees House?" Penny appeared at the door of her room. Behind her, the carry-on she was taking to Guatemala lay open on her bed. The colorful T-shirt from Bettina had been added to its contents. Next to the carry-on, Ginger crouched, quite self-contained, with forepaws tucked beneath her breast and tail neatly furled.

"In a sense," Pamela said. "But nothing to do with me—or even Bettina, really."

"I hope not!" Penny turned to step back into her room. "I don't want to have to worry about you while I'm in Guatemala."

Pamela continued on to her own room then and dressed quickly. Downstairs again, she retrieved her shopping list from beneath the mitten-shaped magnet on the refrigerator, collected a few of her canvas grocery bags from the closet, and set off for the Co-Op.

An hour later, she was back at home. Groceries, including a can of fresh crab meat, had been stowed away, and she had shared a lunch of grilled-cheese sandwiches with her daughter. Penny had returned to her room, and with nothing planned for the afternoon, Pamela settled down at her accustomed end of the sofa and opened her knitting bag.

One side of the marigold-yellow donkey was complete, and the other side, a mirror image of the first, was in progress. That effect was accomplished by purling the rows that had been knit the first time around and knitting the rows that had been purled the first time around. After studying her work for a few moments to recall what came next, she sank happily into the trancelike state induced by the rhythmic crisscross of needles and the soft caress of yarn against her fingers.

She knit alone, however. Both Catrina and Ginger had followed Penny to her room after lunch, seemingly aware that she was preparing for a journey and would soon be bidding them farewell. Precious, aloof as usual, napped on the top platform of the cat climber.

Monday morning, Pamela waved one last time as the car, driven by a friend of Aaron's, pulled away from the curb. Penny and Aaron were en route to Newark Airport and the first stage of their adventure. She stepped back into a house that felt newly, curiously, empty. Penny had only been in residence for a month between her graduation from college and now, but mother and daughter had reestablished the comfortable patterns of their earlier life together.

Back inside, she climbed the stairs to her office. Even before having her morning coffee and toast, she had returned to her boss at *Fiber Craft* the three copyedited articles that were due. As she had suspected, her boss had not been idle. A message from Celine Bramley, marked by the stylized paperclip that denoted at least one attachment, waited in her inbox.

The message was characteristically terse: "Here are three articles to evaluate and a book review to copy-edit. I need it all back by next Monday." The attachments were identified as "Weaving Wealth," "Zero Waste," "Fool's Motley," and "Modest Proposal."

The abbreviated titles were all so tantalizing that Pamela couldn't decide which file to open first. But while the cursor was still vacillating between "Fool's Motley" and "Modest Proposal," she was distracted by the phone's demanding ring. She released the mouse and swiveled her chair to pick up the handset.

The voice that responded to her "Hello" was the voice of Pete Paterson, deep and pleasant. The cursor had retreated to a lower corner of the screen, and Pamela allowed it to stay there.

"I hope I'm not disturbing you," Pete said, "but I'm over here at Voorhees House, and I've come upon something sort of interesting. I thought there might be a story in it for your friend Bettina."

Pete's message was tantalizing too. "Don't keep me in suspense," Pamela responded with a laugh, strangely glad that Penny was now en route to Guatemala. "'Sort of interesting' sounds . . . interesting."

"It's a secret room, like in mysteries. There's a huge armoire in one of the bedrooms and when you open its door there's another door inside. That door leads to a whole other . . . room. And the room is full of . . . stuff."

"What kind of . . . stuff?" Pamela had often dozed with her knitting in her lap while British mysteries featuring secret rooms unfolded on the screen before her. But she couldn't bring to mind what they contained.

"A bassinette, like for a baby, with a doll in it. And clothes, I think," Pete said. "Old clothes, lots of them. Even just the idea of a secret room is fascinating. Do you think Bettina would like to see it?"

"I'll ask her. Am I invited too?"

"Sure! I'll be here for several more hours. Just come on over."

CHAPTER 12

"Why would clothes—or anything—be hidden in a secret room if there wasn't something secret about them?" Bettina asked as Pamela nosed into the curb behind Pete's gleaming silver pickup truck.

They had been discussing the errand as Pamela navigated the short drive from Orchard Street to Voorhees House. Bettina had indeed been interested in seeing what Pete had discovered and had hurried over to Pamela's as soon as she hung up the phone.

The porch floor creaked as they made their way, gingerly, to the front door, with the oval window and carved details that Pamela recalled from her earlier visit. The door was ajar, suggesting that Pete didn't expect his visitors to stand on ceremony. Pamela gave it a gentle push, and it groaned as it swung back.

"Hello!" she called. Bettina echoed the greeting as they stepped into the dim entry. The staircase to the second floor rose before them, with the wood-paneled wall on the left and a sweeping but worn banister on the right. The stained-glass window provided the only illumination, streaks of red, blue, and gold on stairs and floor. A glance to the side revealed that the living room was just as it had been the day the ANGWY group paid its call: the stiff-looking sofa against the deep-green walls, with the burgundy draperies hiding the windows.

Pete's arrival offered a welcome contrast then. His cheerful greeting and his confident energy dispelled the gloom that had seemed endemic to the house. He appeared at the top of the stairs and made his way jauntily down, repeating "Good to see you" when he reached the bottom step.

Bettina was the first to speak. "Hello, neighbor!" she cooed with a flirtatious toss of her head that set her earrings to bobbing. Bettina had placed Richard Larkin on "Hello, neighbor" terms quite soon after she noticed his interest in Pamela, and Pamela wondered fleetingly whether she still greeted him the same way.

"I'm sorry you couldn't join us on Saturday night," she went on, "but this . . ." She tilted her head to gaze upward as if intuiting that the secret room lay at the top of the stairs. "I can hardly wait to see what you have to show us. And I do have a nose for news."

"Come on, then," Pete said with a sweeping gesture, and he spun around to lead the way.

"I didn't ask you on the phone"—Pamela addressed Pete's back as they all ascended the stairs—"but I guess you're here for a reason?"

"Chad Donahue," Pete responded without turning. "Tassie's boyfriend—or something. He said he's named in her will as inheriting Voorhees House. He wants to move in, and there's still a lot of clean-out work to do. I guess Tassie didn't mind just closing the doors on rooms full of stuff, at least until she could figure out what to do to the place. But he wants it all gone. Actually he wants a lot more, but I told him I'm not the guy for a major remodel."

At the top of the stairs, a long hall stretched to the right, with doors opening off each side and a door at the end. All the doors but two were closed. Pete paused at the first open door.

"This is the room where she was sleeping," he said and stood aside so they could get a good view. The windows were curtained with lace, considerably the worse for wear, but clean. Faded wallpaper in a flowery print covered the walls, set off by elegant moldings, and an exotic carpet in tones of carmine and indigo hid most of the parquet floor. A wide bed with an ornate carved headboard dominated the room. "The others had been used for storage—hoarding, almost—for decades."

They continued on to the next open door.

"I've made some progress here," Pete said as they entered.

This room had no curtains, and dust motes danced in the sunlight that streamed through the bare windows. Sturdy black garbage bags were heaped along one wall, their lumpy shapes suggesting the miscellaneous nature of their contents. A broom and a dustpan rested in a far corner. The center of the room was occupied by a rolled-up rug, piles of books with old-fashioned buckram binding, a set of china, a box of gloves, and a number of hats decorated with grand displays of feathers and flowers.

"I try to set aside things that might be valuable . . . to somebody." Pete waved toward the hats. "If Chad owns the house now, he must own all this stuff."

Pete's thoughtful concern about something as re-
mote from the male experience as elaborate hats struck
Pamela as quite endearing, particularly in his current
state—sweaty, grimy, and with hair and shirt rumpled
from exertion. She was staring, she noticed with a
start, because she had never quite realized that he was
so . . . sexy.

"But here's the surprise . . ." He edged toward the
wall opposite where the bags were, a wall that featured
an impressive armoire, oak, with carved ornamenta-
tion on its double doors. "I already thought something
odd was going on," Pete said, "because the room next
to this room isn't as large as it should be. So I figured
there had to be something between them, and when I
opened these doors—"

With a theatrical gesture, Pete flung the armoire's
doors open to reveal another door in its back wall. He
stepped inside the armoire and Pamela and Bettina
drew closer. He then opened the second door to reveal
the dim interior of another, smaller, room. Even though
he had invited them to Voorhees House for the specific
purpose of seeing a secret room, Pamela and Bettina
gasped in unison.

"Shall we?" he said, with a grin that suggested he
was pleased with the effect of his dramatic surprise.

He stepped through the second door, and a moment
later a light came on within the secret room, illuminat-
ing an altarlike table in the center of the floor.

"Come on in," Pete urged. "There's lots to see—and
it's handy that somebody added electrical wiring to the
house at some point."

Pamela ventured first, followed by Bettina. There
was lots to see, so much that, though the room was
nearly the size of Pamela's office at home, the avail-

able floor space was barely enough for the three of them.

The surface of the table was littered with candles burned down to nubbins in wax-encrusted candleholders, and vases that held flowers so long-dead that they were crumbling. The room's other main furniture consisted of several massive wooden trunks, with domed tops and iron fittings, as well as a few ancient suitcases. Most eye-catching, however, was an ancient bassinette made of white-painted wicker. Within it lay a baby doll, so realistic that the first reaction on seeing it was shock, given the context. The doll was wearing a christening gown, white, and knitted in a lacy stitch with exquisite attention to detail.

"Oh, my goodness." Bettina leaned over the bassinette, her voice a faint whisper. Somehow whispering seemed appropriate. "What could this mean?" She looked around. "And what's in all these trunks and suitcases?"

"Clothes," Pete said. He stepped toward the nearest trunk and lifted the domed lid.

The clothes were knitted clothes, neatly folded and stacked. Pamela picked up a garment from the top layer, something knitted from soft pink yarn, and held it up. Unfolded, it was revealed to be a pullover sweater, of a size that might fit a child of ten perhaps. Its creator had used yarn in a darker shade of pink to embroider the name Elizabeth just below the crewneck. The ribbing at the bottom was shredded in spots, evidence that moths had discovered the contents of the trunk.

Pamela opened another trunk and began to burrow, but delicately, while Bettina pulled more garments from the layers beneath where the pink sweater had rested. Pete opened a boxy brown suitcase and did likewise. After several minutes of investigation, they paused and looked at each other. Pamela saw in her companions' faces the same wonderment that she imagined they saw in her own.

"It's like a whole wardrobe, many wardrobes," Bettina said. "A wardrobe for every year of some girl's . . . woman's . . . life."

Indeed, in the trunk that she was exploring, Pamela had come upon garments—sweaters mostly, but also a whole knitted dress, in olive green—that she imagined would fit her quite well. Many had been personalized, with the name embroidered or even worked into the knitted pattern in a contrasting color of yarn. Sadly, more than half of the garments had suffered from the ravages of moths, even to the point of gaping holes with ragged edges and trailing yarn shreds.

Bettina was meanwhile lamenting that some baby-sized garments she had come upon, presumably the oldest in the collection, were not only riddled with moth holes but woefully faded, despite, apparently, being consigned to their storage trunk soon after completion.

"I guess this all belongs to Chad too," Pamela commented as she refolded the dress, which was reminiscent of designs she had seen once in a vintage knitting magazine: a simple sheath with three-quarter-length sleeves and a V-neck.

"I haven't showed it to him yet," Pete said. He was tucking a child-sized cardigan back into the boxy suitcase. "I don't imagine he knows about this room, or even that Tassie did either."

"Was this always here, do you think?" Bettina asked.

"I'm not sure." Pete shrugged. "There's no door to the hall from the secret room, but the armoire could have been placed in front of a door that already existed between it and the outer room."

He took a few steps and knocked on the wall that featured the armoire. "Solid," he said. "Real plaster. An extra wall added these days or even within the last several decades would just be Sheetrock."

"Assuming it was like this from the start, why would a house be designed with a secret room?" Bettina had repacked her trunk, and she asked her question with an attentive gaze that implied great confidence in Pete's command of the topic.

"The Victorians could be rather fanciful in their domestic architecture," he said. "The elaborate wood trim on the exteriors, the turrets, the color schemes. Maybe the long-ago Voorhees who had this house built just thought a secret room would be fun—or he wanted a secure place to store important papers and household valuables. I'd say its use as . . ." He paused and glanced around the small, crowded space and then continued. "Its use as . . . this . . . came about more recently."

"It's like a shrine." Bettina nodded toward the makeshift altar. "A combination shrine and . . . museum, but almost everything is packed away."

"I found something else interesting." Pete stepped toward the opening in the wall and extended a hand to suggest they should go through the armoire ahead of him. Once they were back in the larger room, he closed the inner door and the armoire's more elaborate doors.

"Something else interesting?" Eyes wide and lips parted, Bettina tilted her head to focus on Pete, who seemed quite happy to enjoy her obvious admiration. "More interesting than the secret room?"

"Maybe not." Pete waved them toward the doorway.

"I came upon it after I talked to Pamela. You'll . . . both . . . have to tell me if it's more interesting."

He led them back down the hall to the head of the stairs. But they didn't go down the stairs. Instead, he opened a door, revealing more stairs, a narrower flight of stairs, heading up.

"I'll go first," he said, then stepped through the doorway.

The stairs were uncarpeted and creaky, and the stairway smelled of musty wood. At the top, they found themselves in an unfinished attic with a sharply angled ceiling. The walls were gridded with exposed studs, and roughly hewn rafters supported the roof. Sunlight struggled through small, grimy windows near the floor.

A brick chimney rose at one end of the space, with a similar one at the other end. Pete led them to a niche between one of the chimneys and a wall.

"Someone's been living up here," he announced.

But the words were scarcely needed. A sleeping bag lay unfurled on the bare floor, with a few extra blankets nearby in a careless heap, and a pillow in a rumpled case. A plastic container with its lid ajar held food residue: shreds of what looked like carrots, grains of rice, perhaps bits of scallion. A metal spoon completed the tableau.

"Lots to think about," Bettina commented. "It probably wouldn't be Chad. He could sleep in that comfortable-looking bedroom downstairs."

They backed away from the curious sight and retraced their route, first to the second floor and then down the grand staircase.

"What's Chad Donahue like?" Bettina asked when they reached the entry.

Pete shrugged, and his attractive features assumed an almost-comic expression of puzzlement, with one eyebrow raised and lips in a zigzag.

"A normal kind of guy," he said after thinking for a moment. "About my age, I'd say. Unhappy, of course, about Tassie." He paused for another spell of thinking and then went on. "I almost think he wants to do right by the house, or at least what he thinks is right, as a memento of her."

"Why don't you come to Hyler's with us, for a late lunch?" Bettina touched Pete's arm. "My treat, as a thank-you for the tour."

Pete made a sound like a cross between a growl and a sigh. "I'd love to," he said, "but I've got to finish up here within the next few days because I've got some other jobs lined up at the end of the week."

"But what will you eat?" Bettina seemed genuinely alarmed. "It's lunchtime. Even past lunchtime."

"I packed a lunch. I knew I'd be busy today."

"Rain check on Hyler's, then?" Bettina offered one of her most engaging smiles.

"Rain check." Pete nodded.

"My goodness," Bettina commented after they had traversed the creaky porch and descended the steps, "he is certainly conscientious, especially given that he doesn't need money." As they approached the curb where Pamela's car waited, she added, "He's also very handsome."

"Handsome?" Pamela turned away so Bettina couldn't see her mouth twitch. "Do you think so? I hadn't noticed."

"Hadn't noticed?!" Bettina stopped in the middle of the sidewalk. "Why, if I wasn't . . ." She took a deep breath.

"Married?" Pamela suggested.

"Never mind." Bettina strode ahead and stationed herself by the passenger-side door of Pamela's car.

Pamela couldn't hide her smile as she slipped behind the steering wheel.

"You were teasing me, weren't you?" Bettina said. "You *have* noticed that he's handsome."

CHAPTER 13

Pamela and Bettina had their pick of seats at Hyler's. The lunchtime rush that brought Arborvillians from the offices and shops that lined Arborville Avenue was well over, and only a few people still dawdled over coffee at the worn, wooden tables that crowded Hyler's floor, or the booths, with their burgundy Naugahyde upholstery.

Settled in a booth and provided with the oversize menus that were a distinctive feature of Hyler's, they were silent until Bettina looked over the top of hers to say, "Today's Monday, right? The chef recommends avocado, hummus, and tomato on toasted whole-wheat sourdough."

With a new cook had come an addition to the traditional diner fare Hyler's had long offered. A printed card clipped to the menus and headed "The chef recommends" now listed a special sandwich for each day of the week.

"Sounds good," Pamela said. "I think I'd like that."

"I think I'd like a patty melt," Bettina declared and lowered her menu.

The server had been hovering nearby. Seemingly eager for something to do during the slow stretch between the lunch crowd and the afternoon coffee-break crowd, she stepped up to the end of the table as soon as Pamela set her menu down. After noting their orders for a Chef's Special and a patty melt, she waited as Bettina vacillated between a strawberry milkshake and a vanilla one.

"Good choice," she observed when Bettina settled on vanilla, and Pamela requested the same.

"I'm not going to write about the secret room and its contents," Bettina announced as the server went on her way. "Marcy Brewer would do it, but I won't. The *Advocate* doesn't need to pander to sensation-seekers." She paused to adjust the paper placemat with its scalloped edges. "That poor, reclusive woman deserves her privacy, even in death."

"Do you think the nosy neighbor, Win, knows about the secret room?" Pamela asked. "She certainly knows about Edith's marathon knitting—remember, she showed us that she had a perfect view of Edith's porch from her armchair, and she said that Edith was knitting, knitting, knitting, all the time."

"I wonder if Win ever talked to Edith," Bettina said. "She didn't seem shy about tending to her neighbors' business."

"What would she say? 'What do you do with all that stuff you knit? Nobody ever comes to see you, and you don't seem to have anybody in your life.'"

"Oh, Pamela!" Bettina reared back, and her brows contracted in a scowl. "No one would say that. It's terribly cruel."

"I didn't mean she'd really say it." Pamela smiled and reached out to pat one of Bettina's hands. "I just meant that it would be hard not to sound . . . nosy. Most people aren't as skilled as you are when it comes to finding things out. And"—she looked up—"I think our food is coming."

The server approached with two large oval platters, which she set down, almost simultaneously, between the silverware already waiting on the paper placemats.

"Back in a jiffy with your milkshakes," she said and added, with a teasing glance at Bettina, "vanilla, not strawberry."

"Strawberry would have been okay," Bettina murmured as she departed. "I like strawberry too."

Pamela's sandwich was oval, centered on its oval platter, but cut in half and angled to expose the cut surfaces to better effect. The bread was a light toasty brown, and visible between the top and bottom slices were layers: thick and creamy hummus the color of chickpeas, dark green avocado shading to pale gold, and the vivid pop of bright red tomato. Tucked alongside the sandwich were a few black olives and a curly twist of lettuce.

Bettina's patty melt brought with it more traditional accompaniments, a scoop of coleslaw in a pleated paper cup and a long, glistening pickle spear. The patty melt itself was a plump creation, likewise cut in half and angled to reveal the cross section of a burger patty seared on the outside but pink and juicy inside. The bread was rye, rendered golden brown on the grill, a process that had also melted the Swiss cheese layered above and below the burger patty. Shreds of sautéed onion topped the patty to complete the creation.

"This certainly looks good," Bettina commented as she reached for her knife and fork. But the milkshakes were en route, in tall frosted glasses. When they arrived, she paused to sample hers, leaving a bright print of lipstick on the straw.

The patty melt was clearly meant to be eaten with knife and fork, but Pamela's sandwich seemed manageable as finger food. She picked up one of the halves, took a big bite, and savored the combination of the lemony hummus, the buttery avocado, and the tomato with its acidic tang.

Bettina had soon tackled her sandwich as well, and pronounced it to be just as good as she had expected, prefacing the comment with an extended purr of satisfaction.

"And the Chef's Special?" She set her fork down and leaned across the table. "Is it really special?"

"Very good," Pamela assured her. "Very good."

No more was said for a time, as bites of sandwich alternated with sips of milkshake. Hyler's milkshakes were legendary, cool and sweet, and flavored subtly so as not to overwhelm the rich dairy taste of the milk and ice cream that formed their basis.

Bettina looked up at length, midway through the second half of her patty melt and having just taken a bite of pickle.

"Do you think Win knows about the person who's been sleeping in the attic?" she inquired after she had swallowed.

Pamela's response was delayed by the fact that she had just started on the second half of her sandwich. "I doubt it," she said when she could speak again. "If she did, I imagine she'd have figured out that a flesh-and-blood person and not a ghost was responsible for the lights and sounds she was keeping track of in her notebook."

Bettina frowned slightly, as if pondering that idea, then she took another bite of pickle.

"I'm interviewing Libby's grandson for the *Advocate* tomorrow morning," she said after a bit. "Libby's house is just around the corner from Win's. Why don't we stop by Win's for a chat?"

"*Is it a ghost?*" Pamela opened her eyes and mouth wide in a comic expression of suspense. "*Or is it a squatter? Read all about it in this week's Advocate.*"

"It's not for the *Advocate*!" Bettina slapped the table. Her knife and fork, which were resting on the platter before her, jingled. "The *Advocate* does not pander!"

"I wonder if Edmund McClintock knows that someone's been sleeping in the Voorhees House attic," Pamela said mildly.

Bettina tried to look stern, but her mobile features, accustomed to cheer, were uncooperative. "The *Advocate* does not pander!" she repeated.

"I know." Pamela smiled. "But I really do wonder if Edmund McClintock knows that someone's been sleeping in the Voorhees House attic, and also if he knows that Voorhees House has a secret room."

Bettina wiped her fingers on her napkin and began to rummage in her handbag. Soon she produced the visiting card Edmund had given her. She glanced at it and then said, "He doesn't have a phone number."

"I didn't think he would. But the card gives his address, doesn't it?"

Bettina nodded. "He's right in Arborville, off Arborville Avenue on one of those cross streets between Orchard and the Co-Op."

"Let's go there." Pamela picked up her sandwich and recommenced eating, as if the matter had been settled.

"We'll talk to Win first though." Bettina seized her knife and fork and teased a bite from what remained of the patty melt. "Because we'll be in the neighborhood tomorrow morning anyway—that is, assuming you want to come along when I interview Libby's grandson. Then we'll figure out when to visit Edmund."

"I am curious to see what Win will say." Pamela put the sandwich down and drew a long swallow of milkshake through the straw that emerged from its crest of foamy bubbles. "Though I certainly wouldn't conclude that lights and sounds meant a house was haunted if I knew perfectly well that a flesh-and-blood person was in residence."

"Well . . ." Bettina shrugged. "We'll see what she says."

Pamela sampled an olive and returned to her sandwich, alternating olives and bites of sandwich until all that remained on the platter was the curly twist of lettuce. The olives were Kalamatas, salty and infused with deeply flavored olive oil, and they provided a lively accent to the mellower flavors of hummus and avocado.

Bettina too had finished her sandwich and was scooping delicate forkfuls of slaw from the pleated paper cup. Soon all that remained of the meal were the dregs of the milkshakes. Those were soon dispatched with contented slurping.

As the server cleared, Pamela extracted a few bills from her wallet. "My turn to pay, I think," she said.

Soon the table was bare, but for the salt and pepper shakers, little bowls offering sugar and less caloric sweeteners, and a bottle of catsup. The check lay in the center of the table with bills tucked underneath.

"Tomorrow morning, then?" Bettina slid to the end of the bench on her side of the booth and leaned on the table to propel herself to her feet. "I'll ring your doorbell at a quarter to eleven."

Pamela agreed, slid to the end of the bench on her side, and rose. They threaded their way among the tables between their booth and the exit and went on their way back.

Back at home, Pamela brought in her mail, greeted the cats, and climbed the stairs to her office. Penny and Aaron were still en route to their destination, so it was too early to expect an email from Penny, but she checked her inbox and deleted messages offering coupons to the hobby shop and suggesting she pay her water bill online.

She had been about to start work on the new assignments from *Fiber Craft* when Pete called. Now she pondered the abbreviated titles strung across the top of Celine Bramley's message and clicked to open the one labeled "Fool's Motley."

The article was to be evaluated, not copyedited, so it required only to be read, keeping in mind the mission of *Fiber Craft* and the interests of the magazine's subscribers. And, of course, she had to take into account the author's credentials, as well as determining whether the article was backed up by sensible research and appropriate references.

The full title of "Fool's Motley" proved to be "Clothes

Make the Man: Fool's Motley and Speaking Truth to Power in Renaissance England." Soon Pamela was immersed in the world reflected in Shakespeare's plays, a world in which a court fool could say things that would send a courtier to prison. The author's focus, given that she was writing for *Fiber Craft*, was on the fool's *motley*, the distinctive variegated clothing that marked him as outside the social hierarchy and allowed him to ignore its customary constraints.

The illustrations, reproductions of woodcuts from the era, demonstrated how the English Renaissance fool's garb derived from the costume worn by the Harlequin character in Italian comedy. Given the nature of the medium, the woodcuts were unfortunately not in color. Thus the vivid reds, blues, and greens of the diamond-patterned Harlequin outfits described in the text had to be imagined.

Nonetheless, Pamela wrote an enthusiastic recommendation that the article be published. Leaving the other two articles for another day, she opened the file labeled "Modest Proposal" and set to work copyediting the review of *A Modest Proposal: Fashion in the Islamic World*.

Dinner had been chili, from a huge pot made with the intention of eating chili for several more days, and the cats had eaten their dinner as well. The sky was still bright on this near-midsummer evening, however, and a retreat to the sofa with knitting and a British mystery seemed a waste. Pamela accordingly took her knitting to the porch. There she enjoyed the mild air and the vista of lawns and gardens as the second side of the marigold-yellow donkey neared completion.

* * *

On Tuesday morning, Pamela opened her eyes to find two pairs of eyes staring back, one pair amber, the other the color of jade. The sun had set the white eyelet curtains aglow, and the room was bright. Quite aware that Penny was no longer in residence, Ginger had followed Pamela and Catrina up the stairs the previous night. She had slithered under Pamela's covers, knowing that for the foreseeable future, only this bed would be occupied by a human.

Pamela tossed the covers back, and the cats hopped to the floor. They led the way to the doorway and darted into the hall, barely allowing Pamela time to slip her feet into her slippers and slide her arms into her robe.

A few minutes later, the morning ritual had commenced. A can of liver-chicken medley provided several generous scoops of breakfast for Catrina and Ginger in their communal bowl, and Pamela spooned Feline Gourmet salmon into a smaller bowl for Precious. She filled the kettle, set it to boil on the stove, and dashed down the front walk to retrieve the *Register*.

Back inside, she nestled a paper filter into the carafe's plastic filter cone and ground fresh beans for coffee, by which time the kettle was hooting its signal that the water was ready to be poured. As the welcome aroma of brewing coffee began to fill the little kitchen, she lowered a slice of whole-grain bread into the toaster. Soon she was sitting at her kitchen table with coffee at hand in a wedding-china cup and buttered toast before her on a wedding-china plate, as contented with her breakfast as the cats had been with theirs. The fact that the *Register* had no startling news to report added to her pleasure.

Bettina rang Pamela's doorbell at precisely a quarter to eleven. The scheduled visit to Libby Kimble's house was, technically, work—since Bettina would be interviewing Libby's grandson for the *Advocate*. She had, therefore, dressed for the occasion in a stylish summer dress accessorized with coordinating pumps, matching handbag, and carefully chosen jewelry. The dress was a fit and flare style, sewn from lustrous cotton fabric featuring giant white camellias with deep green leaves on a pink background. Shoes and bag were pink, and a necklace and earrings crafted from silver and green jade completed the ensemble.

Their route took them along Arborville Avenue past the commercial district and then partway up the hill that formed the backside of the cliffs overlooking the Hudson. Soon they had reached Libby's house, with its charming storybook half-timbering, and Bettina nosed the faithful Toyota into a spot along the curb.

Libby's yard was as lush with summer blooms as those of her neighbors. A row of pink hydrangeas accented the house's foundation, while clumps of blue-flowered salvia intermingled with yellow daylilies in the foreground, and the air was fragrant as Pamela and Bettina made their way up the walk toward the front door.

Libby's grandson responded to the bell. They had only gotten a glimpse of him the previous week, when he came home while they were having coffee at Libby's after the shock of finding Tassie's body. Pamela had noted then that he was tall and handsome in a young man sort of way, athletic-looking as befitting a wrestler, but not bulky.

"Ms. Fraser, Ms. Paterson," he said, dipping his head in a slight bow after he had gestured for them to enter. "I'm Zach. Thank you for coming." He glanced toward the hall, which, judging from the sound of dishes clanking beyond, led to the kitchen. "The interview was Grandma's idea," he added in a whisper. "The scholarship isn't really that big of a deal."

"Don't be silly!" Bettina's voice and expression reflected coquettish shock. "A scholarship is a very big deal, and wrestling . . ." She allowed her gaze to suggest a tasteful appreciation of his physique. "I can see that you must be very good."

"Well, I . . ." Zach dipped his head again, perhaps in an unsuccessful attempt to hide the fact that he had turned quite pink.

At that moment he was rescued by the entrance of Libby. She was bearing a wide silver tray that held napkins, cream and sugar, silverware, cups and saucers, and little plates, obviously good china, in a pattern that involved deep blues, vivid reds, and gold filigree. Her slenderness did verge on frailty, as Pamela had noticed before—a frailty underscored by her colorless hair and skin. But the tray, with its elegant cargo, lent her a kind of presence—especially here, in her own pretty living room, and more relaxed than she'd been the first time Pamela and Bettina paid a call. It struck Pamela that she must have been quite lovely once, with light hair and a fair complexion.

"Please sit down," Libby said as she bent to set the tray on the coffee table.

Pamela took a step toward the dusty-pink sofa, but Bettina did not move. "Let us help!" she exclaimed. "Is there more to carry?"

"A few things." Libby nodded. "I remembered that you're both coffee drinkers, and then there's the teapot, and something to nibble."

She led the way, with Bettina following and Pamela bringing up the rear, across the hall and into the kitchen, very cozy with its frilly curtains, pie cooling on the stovetop, and cat curled up on one of the chairs at a small table.

"Baking day," Libby commented. "Taking advantage of blueberry season. Wrestlers have big appetites. And I made some tea cake for your visit."

A squat china teapot waited on another tray, flanked by an elegant silver coffeepot and a plate holding slices of something involving currants.

Back in the living room, Libby performed hostess duties, tipping the elegant coffeepot over cups assigned to Pamela and Bettina, pouring herself tea, serving tea cake on the little plates, and making sure cream and sugar were within reach.

Pamela and Bettina had settled onto the sofa, with Libby in the matching chair that faced it across the coffee table. Zach was perched on a straight-backed chair that he had pulled up alongside his grandmother. He too had been served coffee, and the delicate china cup looked incongruous in his large hand—not to mention the very fact of his athletic presence at a table laid out as if for a classic British tea.

"Well"—Bettina surveyed the pretty room and took a sip of the coffee that she had transformed into the sweet mocha concoction that she favored—"this is certainly a treat." When her gaze landed on Zach, she added, "And I so look forward to hearing all about your high-school wrestling career and the sports program at . . . what was it? Millford University?"

Zach had just conveyed a large chunk of tea cake to his mouth, so he had to be content with a nod. Pamela too had sampled the tea cake, which was rich and buttery, with a moist crumb, and studded with currants.

Fortified by the refreshments, Bettina soon got down to business. She asked if she could record the interview, and upon being told yes, retrieved her phone from her handbag and used a pink-tipped finger to launch its recording function.

Soon Zach was happily chatting away, encouraged by Bettina's attentive head-tilts and appreciative murmurs. He hadn't gone to Arborville High, but to a larger high school in a larger town, and its wrestling team had competed all over the state. When they made it to the state finals, college recruiters had shown up at the matches, and he had been approached by several.

Zach's evident surprise as he related this was appealing—evidently it hadn't occurred to him before then that mastery of his chosen sport could result in anything other than the respect of his teammates and the satisfaction of a good match.

His academic accomplishments didn't hurt either, he added, not quite as humbly. He received offers from four schools but chose Millford because it was close enough to New Jersey to make visits home easy but far enough away to feel independent.

The coffeepot was empty by the time Bettina picked up her phone and clicked it off with a satisfied smile. The plate that had held the tea cake was empty too, but for a few crumbs scattered over its pale center and the swirling reds and blues of its gold-filigreed border.

Zach had to hurry off to his job at the mall and excused himself as soon as Bettina had taken a few photos.

"The *Advocate* publishes all the news that fits," she reminded him—though perhaps not being a native Arborvillian, he hadn't been aware of the weekly's reputation in town. "So I can't promise you'll see yourself in the *Advocate* as soon as this week's issue."

Pamela and Bettina lingered to help Libby tidy up and then went on their way as well.

CHAPTER 14

Win Colley wasn't expecting them, but she stepped out onto her porch just as Bettina switched off her ignition.

"Hello!" she called eagerly, waving and running toward the car. "I happened to be at the window," she added once Pamela and Bettina had joined her on the sidewalk, "and I saw you pull up. There have been comings and goings next door. I was wondering if you knew."

"Actually"—Bettina laughed—"one of those comings and goings was us."

"Oh!" Win's bright eyes and sudden head-twitch brought to mind a startled bird. "I must have been busy inside. I only noticed . . . in fact, I met—" She paused, then seized Bettina's arm with one hand and Pamela's with the other. "Come inside! Come inside! No reason to stand around talking on the sidewalk.

"Anyway," she said once she'd settled them amidst

the needlepoint pillows on the sofa in her pleasant living room and they had refused her offer of coffee, "I did meet your husband, Pamela. So handsome!"

Pamela felt her mouth open, but the sudden confused whirl in her brain refused to coalesce into words, so she closed it again. What on earth was the woman talking about? Perhaps, a voice in her brain suggested once the whirling had stopped, since Win believes there are ghosts haunting the Voorhees House, she also believes that Michael Paterson has for some reason reached out to her from beyond the grave.

When Win spoke again, it was to say, "You hadn't mentioned that he was doing work next door. Pete Paterson, Pamela Paterson. I made the connection right away."

Bettina responded first, with a delighted, protracted giggle. "Pete Paterson isn't Pamela's husband," she explained once she had calmed down. "He just has the same last name. Lots of people are named 'Paterson.'"

"It's just a coincidence," Pamela felt compelled to add. "I'm actually a . . ." Her voice trailed off, and she started over. "I lost my husband several years ago."

"I'm so sorry!" Win had been perched on the edge of the comfortable armchair that faced the window, as if ready to take flight at any moment. And take flight she did, hopping up, perching next to Pamela on the sofa, and grabbing her hand. "But you know him, this other Paterson," she chirped, focusing attentively on Pamela's face. "I mean, it sounds like you know him. So perhaps the two of you will end up together, like fate, since you both already have the same last name."

The confused whirling had returned, and Pamela was once again speechless—and probably blushing too, she thought, though with her olive skin a blush seldom showed. She raised her free hand to her cheek and soothed it with the coolness of her palm.

Bettina seemed to sense her friend's discomfort. "A squatter has been living in the attic next door," she announced, causing Win to drop Pamela's hand and stare at Bettina instead.

"Yes." Bettina nodded, setting her silver and jade earrings atremble. "Pete Paterson—the other Paterson—showed us when we were here yesterday. There's a sleeping bag up there, and a pillow, the remains of meals . . ."

"A squatter?" Win frowned, a startled frown, as if confronted with an idea that had never occurred to her.

"I guess you haven't noticed anyone sneaking around, probably at night?" Bettina's tone implied that she expected the answer to be no.

"Sneaking?" Win squinted. "Not sneaking. Pete Paterson, and you two—you said that was you, yesterday—and that boyfriend of Tassie's. But nobody with a reason to sneak."

"This attic person . . ." Bettina studied Win's face. She hesitated, the way a person about to impart bad news might hesitate. "This attic person," she said at last, "is probably responsible for the lights and the weird noises."

"Ohhh . . ." Win raised both hands to her cheeks. Only her tragic eyes were visible above her fingertips as she uttered the words "my notebook" in a muffled voice.

"Voorhees House probably isn't haunted," Bettina said matter-of-factly.

Win sagged. Her gaze strayed toward the doorway leading to the dining room. The notebook she had consulted as she described the curious phenomena next door still lay on the dining room table.

"But there's still a mystery." Bettina smiled. *Every cloud has a silver lining*, Wilfred might have said had he been there. In an attempt to cheer Win up, Bettina had seized on the fact that, indeed, the idea of a Voorhees House squatter—if not quite a ghost—was compelling in its own right.

"Who is this person?" Bettina went on. "And why is this person hiding out in the attic next door?"

"Ohhh!" Win shivered—with delight? Pamela wasn't sure. "I don't know. Why *would* someone want to sneak in to live in that spooky place? And it *is* spooky, even if it's not really haunted . . . although . . ." Win's voice trailed off, and her eyes widened. "Why couldn't it be haunted too? Those sounds were awfully weird. I can't imagine how a human person could make them . . . or why a human person would want to."

Her gaze strayed toward the dining room again. "I'll keep track!" she announced. "I'll keep track of when I hear the especially weird sounds."

"Do!" Bettina clapped her hands in confirmation. "And the lights too. And call me as soon as you see or hear anything."

"Oh, yes, definitely!" Win was sitting up straight now, her face alight with new purpose. "I *will* call you. And I'll watch for sneaking."

Sensing the visit was drawing to a close, Win sprang up from the sofa. She turned to extend a hand when she realized that Bettina, though considerably younger, wasn't as spry as her hostess. Soon they were all on their feet and moving toward the door, but as Win reached for the door latch, Bettina spoke.

"I have a question," she said. "Something that just occurred to me."

"Ummm?" Win signaled her attention by opening her eyes wide.

"Did you ever ask Edith what all her knitting was for?"

Win shook her head. "As I said, she was a complete recluse. It was sad too. *She* was sad. We wondered what had happened, aside from losing her husband." She glanced at Pamela and added, "I mean, that's sad, of course. I lost my husband, but people get over it . . . I hope." She went on, in a rush of words, perhaps trying to distract from the possible faux pas of mentioning lost husbands in conversation with a woman who had just revealed that she was a widow.

"Yes, Edith just sat on her porch and knitted all the time. She must have already been in her fifties when we bought our house, but she was still quite beautiful—though she didn't dress like a person who knew she was beautiful, or who even cared to be beautiful. And she never wore knitted things, so I did wonder who all the knitted things were for—but I never asked her. They couldn't have been gifts because no one ever came around.

"She just sat there," Win repeated, "knitting all the time."

"Knit and Nibble tonight," Bettina observed as she steered the Toyota toward the corner where Beech Street crossed the road that would take them to Arborville Avenue.

Pamela nodded. "At Karen's. It's been a while since we met there."

"I know you'll want to walk," Bettina said. "You'll say it's going to get hot soon but it's not hot now and it's a shame to drive a short distance like that on a cool summer evening. But I'm not walking up that hill, so I'll pick you up at a quarter to seven."

A pleasant surprise awaited Pamela when she sat down at her computer upon returning home. An email from Penny had arrived, with photos attached. The photos showed a landscape of lush green fields, verdant hills, and palm trees. The village itself was a cluster of stucco bungalows roofed with thatch.

"It looks beautiful and peaceful and quite other-worldly," Penny had written, "and it is—but incredibly there's cell phone reception. A lot of the villagers have cell phones, and they use them to communicate with relatives working in the US, even New Jersey."

Penny went on to say that she and Aaron were fine, as were the other members of the group building the school, and the trip had been tiring but okay, and Guatemalan food was really good.

Smiling to herself, Pamela checked the other messages that had arrived while she was out with Bettina: a note from her mother, a reminder from the town that road resurfacing in the Palisades neighborhood would begin after the Fourth of July holiday, and a schedule of upcoming events from the library.

After a quick grilled-cheese sandwich for lunch, she returned to her office and opened "Weaving Wealth," whose full title proved to be "Weaving Wealth: Cloth as Currency in Medieval Iceland" and whose author, Ingrid Thorsdottir, was a professor at the University of Iceland. Pamela was fascinated to learn that in medieval Iceland, the cloth that woman weavers produced was not only used as cloth but also as a form of currency. To this end, the number of warp and weft strands per inch had to be standardized in order to assign a particular value to a piece of cloth of a certain length and width. The author had researched medieval legal texts to learn the specific numbers required per inch and had then examined actual fragments of cloth preserved from archeological digs to discover that, yes, she was holding in her hands examples of centuries-old legal tender.

So interesting, Pamela murmured as she reread the article's last few sentences. It hadn't occurred to many male scholars, it seemed to her, that the work of women's hands could have an importance beyond creating domestic comfort for their families.

"*Fiber Craft* should definitely publish this," she wrote in her evaluation, and added a paragraph citing Ingrid Thorsdottir's qualifications and summarizing her argument.

"I wrote that article about the haunting," Bettina announced as Pamela stepped across the threshold to join her on the porch that evening. They were on their way to Karen Dowling's house for the Knit and Nibble meeting. Bettina was still dressed as she had been that morning, in the dress whose print involved white camellias with green leaves on a pink background, but she had added a light cardigan in mint green.

"My editor insisted," she went on, "but I refused to play up the spooky angle. Now I'm wondering, though, is there even any point in the article if the squatter in the attic accounts for what Win saw and heard?"

Bettina led the way down the steps, and Pamela followed, speaking to Bettina's back. "There *is* a new mystery now though. Who is the squatter?"

"I don't know about putting that in the article though." Bettina glanced over her shoulder to respond. "I probably shouldn't. That's Chad Donahue's business, really. I imagine Pete will tell him what all he's discovered. And there's no point in telling Clayborn, is there? He'd probably just think I was being a busybody."

They had reached the curb, where Bettina's faithful Toyota waited. A sudden thought had occurred to Pamela as she walked. Reading about the Icelandic woman weavers had been so engrossing that it had been hours since anything connected with Voorhees House had occupied her mind.

But now, just as a vacation can bring a new perspective to a much-pondered issue, Pamela realized that a few hours of *Fiber Craft* work, with no thought of Voorhees House intruding, had given her a new perspective on the topic of the squatter. She waited until she was settled in the passenger seat of the Toyota, however, before saying anything.

"Maybe Tassie really did die of fright," she commented as Bettina inserted her key into the ignition.

Bettina's explosive "What?" overlapped with the engine's throaty rumble.

She eased up on the gas pedal and turned to Pamela. "Don't tell me you're having second thoughts about the haunting issue?"

"We've decided that the ghost was the squatter, right?" Pamela waited until Bettina's smile and slight head-tilt signaled her agreement, then she went on. "The lights, the weird sounds . . . ? They were all produced by whoever's been living—or at least sleeping—up there in that attic."

"Yes," Bettina said. "That seems the sensible explanation. But you think Tassie could have died of fright anyway?"

"From an encounter with the squatter." Pamela resisted the urge to add *duh*. "I assume she had no idea there was a person in the attic. I'd be terrified if I was home alone in a big, spooky house, and I heard feet on the stairs and then a strange person appeared. Harold Bascomb did say that an adrenaline spike caused by fright can kill somebody by interrupting the normal rhythm of the heart."

"Oh, my goodness!" In her excitement, Bettina stomped on the gas pedal, and the Toyota sprang forward.

Pamela laid a calming hand on Bettina's arm. "Let's drive or talk," she suggested.

"Talk!" Bettina exclaimed and switched off the ignition. She turned to face Pamela. "What if the squatter was purposely trying to scare Tassie away? What if the squatter had some reason of his own . . . *her* own . . . whatever? Some connection with the house, some resentment of Tassie for inheriting it?"

"Or some connection with Edmund McClintock," Pamela added. "Part of a crusade to keep Voorhees House from being *remuddled*, as he put it."

"We can ask him tomorrow." Bettina twisted her key in the ignition, revved the Toyota's engine, and slowly pulled away from the curb.

"Would he tell us the truth?" Pamela asked. "If the squatter scared Tassie to death, there might be some liability there, not to mention that it has to be illegal even to sneak into a house that's not yours—let alone move in."

"The medical examiner is taking his time," Bettina observed as they approached Arborville Avenue. "But I suppose even if there's evidence of, let's say, a heart attack, what caused it could never be proved."

The welcoming wreath on the Dowlings' front door was shaped from silk flowers in shades of indigo and violet, harmonizing with the soft gray-blue of the clapboard siding. The house was the same vintage as Pamela's house, and the same style, and it had been a fixer-upper. That was several years ago. Now the once-sagging porch was stout and trim, the faded paint had been refreshed, and the front door opened to a lovingly decorated living room.

The first Dowling to greet them once Karen had beckoned them inside was not, however, either Karen or Dave. It was a much smaller Dowling.

"Tina! Tina!" crowed a child with wisps of blond hair framing a wide-eyed face. "Tina's here, Tina's here," she elaborated, hopping up and down.

Bettina, for that was the "Tina" Lily Dowling was referring to, bent down until her head was on the same level as Lily's.

"How is my girl?" she cooed. "How is my Lily?"

"She's fi-i-ne." Lily grasped one hand with the other and shivered with glee, smiling a smile that displayed a few tiny, perfect teeth. "Daddy's going to read to Lily."

A voice came from behind Pamela, who had remained standing near the open door as Bettina rushed forward and stooped.

"Not late, I don't think," said the voice, which was Roland's.

Karen had been watching delightedly as Lily and Bettina conversed. Now she turned to greet this latest arrival.

"I had to backtrack to check the alternate-side parking signs," Roland said as he edged around Bettina, holding his briefcase aloft. "I lost about five minutes, but I don't believe it's seven yet." He glanced around the room and added, "I see everyone else is here though."

Nell appeared quite at home in the antique rocking chair that Dave Dowling had refinished, and Holly was perched at one end of the sofa, which was a pretty shade of blue and simple in style.

"Plenty of room," she called, patting the sofa. "Pamela? Bettina? Roland?"

"Thank you, thank you," Roland murmured, "but I'll just . . ."

He'd reached one of the twin armchairs, upholstered in blue and cream stripes, that faced the sofa across the coffee table. But before he could sit down, he was intercepted by Dave Dowling, who had just descended the stairs. Dave was a slender, pleasant-looking man, blond like his wife.

"Roland, my man!" Dave exclaimed, seizing Roland's hand and giving it a hearty shake. "Pamela! Bettina!" he added. "Welcome! And"—he nodded toward the sofa—"Holly knows we're always glad to see her."

"Daddy's here! Daddy's here!" came Lily's voice, as she abandoned Bettina for this new object of interest. "Reading, reading. Daddy's going to read to Lily."

"And here we go," Dave sang out as he swept Lily up and headed for the stairs.

CHAPTER 15

"So cute!" Bettina was beaming, and Pamela suspected she had been imagining similar interactions to come with her own Arborville granddaughter if Maxie's baby turned out to be a girl.

Roland lowered himself into the armchair, hoisted his briefcase onto his lap, and nudged the button that clicked the latch open. Pamela and Bettina joined Holly on the sofa, and Karen took a seat in the other armchair.

Pamela had finished both halves of her marigold-yellow donkey, and it was time to start the gusset that would form the stomach and the inner sides of the legs. A contrasting color had seemed like a fun idea, though Nell had said it wasn't mandatory, but since some donkeys were lighter on their undersides than on their backs, she had explored her bins of leftover yarn and found a pale yellow. Now she consulted the directions Nell had provided and cast on four stitches.

Next to her, Bettina was already hard at work. A

skein of royal-blue wool shared her sofa cushion, linked to the swath of knitting hanging from her needles by a long strand that she looped and twisted as, stitch by stitch, her project grew.

"I guess there's nothing going on anymore with the Voorhees House story?" Holly spoke up from her end of the sofa, turning toward Bettina, who sat in the middle.

Bettina caught Pamela's eye, and her lips twitched with a tiny smile, then she swiveled to face Holly. "There might be a story in the *Advocate* this week," she said. "But not about Tassie. The house seems to have secrets of its own."

"Spooky?" Roland inquired from the other side of the coffee table.

"You'll have to wait for your *Advocate*." Bettina's voice had a teasing lilt. "Maybe even *more* than a week. All the news that fits, you know."

"I'm not personally interested in spooky," Roland said, summoning an extra-serious expression, as if embarrassed that anyone might have assumed he was looking forward to a titillating read. "But I know there are those in Arborville who don't find enough stimulation in their everyday lives."

"Well!" Bettina lowered her knitting to her lap and scooted forward, causing the sofa to wiggle. She leaned across the coffee table and met Roland's gaze. "The *Advocate* does *not* stimulate," she said firmly.

"But wouldn't a newspaper want . . . ?" Holly's voice trailed off, perhaps because, as an ally of Bettina's and an ardent supporter of the *Advocate*, she sensed this wasn't the time to argue in favor of stimulation as a journalistic objective.

Nell had started speaking at almost the same time, and her voice didn't trail off. "Many people lead challenging lives," she observed, "and if they want to escape into another world by reading about ghosts for a bit, I don't think we should begrudge them. I myself enjoy Halloween—and who knows for sure, really, that there isn't more . . . more . . ." She tilted her head and scanned the room, paying extra attention to its upper reaches, and extended her open palms in a welcoming gesture, looking for all the world like an ancient priestess.

Then she shook herself, blinked a few times, and said, "Not that *I* believe in ghosts."

"Neither do I"—Bettina sat up straight—"and the *Advocate* doesn't pander."

"No, of course not." Nell picked up her knitting again. A curious, seemingly free-form, shape dangled from her needles, but Pamela recognized it as yet another in-progress donkey. This one was blue, and Nell was partway through one of the mirror-image donkey halves. The head and one leg had been completed, and the midriff section was underway.

Pamela herself had let her knitting lapse during the brief discussion that had just ended. Now she took her work up again and embarked on one of the long rows that would form the insides of her donkey's front legs. When the gusset was complete, it would resemble the letter *H*, with a wide crossbar that would become the donkey's stomach.

The pleasant whisper of yarn against her fingers was so soothing and the rhythmic dance of the criss-crossing needles was so mesmerizing that she was scarcely aware of the quiet conversations underway around her: Bettina and Holly to her left on the sofa and Karen and Nell to her right, with Karen in her armchair and Nell in the wooden rocker.

It wasn't until Holly raised her voice to address Roland that Pamela looked up from her project. "Do you and Melanie have plans for the long weekend?" Holly inquired.

"Long weekend?" Roland's bewildered expression became defensive as, momentarily at a loss, he pondered Holly's meaning.

"The Fourth of July," Bettina chimed in. "It's only a few weeks away."

"I expect to be working," Roland said as he completed the stitch Holly had interrupted. "And it's not really a long weekend this year, because the Fourth of July is on a Thursday."

"But lots of people will take the Friday too. It's a chance for a getaway, right in the middle of summer." As if moved to sympathy by the image of Roland forgoing pleasure for work, Holly stared, and her pretty brow puckered.

"I will not be *getting away*." Roland's tone suggested he found the term distasteful. "And I certainly won't be skipping work on Friday so I can *get away*."

Holly summoned a meek version of her usual smile, too meek to bring her dimple into play. "Well," she ventured, "even if you don't leave town, there will be plenty of fun events right here in Arborville." She shifted her gaze from Roland and tilted her head toward Bettina, who was beside her on the sofa. "And I imagine that the *Advocate* . . ."

"Yes!" Bettina recognized her cue. "The *Advocate* will print a full schedule of the town events in the paper that's delivered the Friday before: the parade, the speeches, the fireworks, of course."

"*Of course*," Roland said sarcastically. "As if the town didn't waste enough of my tax money on wasteful expenditures, it's necessary once a year to invest it in *fireworks*, so my money can be shot into the air and incinerated in an explosion." He'd been working steadily since he started up again after Holly's interruption, with his swath of turquoise knitting lying smoothly over his pinstripe-garbed thigh. But now he lowered his needles. "Not to mention that fireworks are dangerous, and they terrify the dogs."

"It's once a year," Nell observed. "And it's patriotic—'the rockets' red glare, the bombs bursting in air' and all of that. I'm a pacifist, but even I have to admit that the marching and the music and the fireworks are very stirring."

Roland seemed disinclined to respond, and Nell continued the maneuvers of fingers and needles that would eventually transform the ball of blue yarn on the floor at her feet into a complete blue donkey.

Karen's armchair was empty, Pamela noticed. Their hostess had slipped out of the room unobserved while Roland let his views on the upcoming holiday be known. The room was silent now, but a seductive aroma from the kitchen had begun to engage another of the senses: coffee. Though Karen herself was a tea drinker, she'd mastered the subtleties of the coffee grinder and filter cone, and she served the coffee-drinking knit and nibblers as good a cup of coffee as they'd find in their own homes.

Holly had seemingly been privy to Karen's plans for the evening's refreshments. She rose from her end of the sofa and announced, "Dessert will be served in the dining room. Please come and take your seats."

Roland looked up with a shocked expression, as if wondering how break time could occur on schedule without his reminder. He pushed back his starched shirt cuff to consult his watch and then set his knitting aside.

The Dowlings' dining room table was made of oak, oval, and supported by a pedestal with feet carved to resemble lions' heads. Six placemats woven of lavender raffia were arranged around it, each with a blue-and-lavender striped napkin, a fork, and a spoon. The chairs were oak too, the classic old T-back style. Chairs with arms had been placed at the table's head and foot, and the chairs along the sides were armless.

"No seat for Dave?" Bettina inquired as they entered the room. Karen was still busy in the kitchen, but Holly knew the answer.

"He's teaching a summer course," she said, "and there's loads to prepare because it's a whole semester's worth in six weeks." She gestured toward the chairs. "Please, everyone, sit wherever you'd like."

They had scarcely arranged themselves in their seats than Karen appeared in the kitchen doorway. She carried a small plate laden with something delicious-looking in each hand. As she stepped into the dining room, Holly scurried past her and disappeared into the kitchen.

"It's a recipe from one of Holly's vintage cookbooks," Karen explained. "Lemon icebox cake, made with vanilla wafers and whipped cream, mostly."

After a few minutes of busyness, with Bettina rising to help, a white china plate containing a generous portion of the icebox cake had been placed in front of each knit and nibbler. Coffee and tea had been provided as well, served in white china cups nestled on matching saucers. With a pleased glance around the table, Karen took her seat at its head.

While the tea drinkers and Bettina availed themselves of the cream and sugar, Pamela studied the icebox cake. Layers, she thought, but the whipped cream had softened the vanilla wafers to the point that they scarcely resembled cookies anymore. Still, layers were apparent—many layers—golden-brown alternating with creamy white. And as a preview of the flavor, the creamy top layer had been garnished with a bright sprinkling of grated lemon rind and a curl of lemon peel.

Karen finished sugaring and creaming her tea and picked up her fork. As if choreographed, then, five other forks were raised in unison. Pamela nudged off a forkful that included a bit of the cookie layer and a bit of the creamy layer, and discovered upon tasting it that the lemon component wasn't confined to the garnish on the top. The creamy layer, which she suspected was composed of cream cheese as well as whipped cream—and sugar, of course—had been infused with an intense lemon flavor. The whole effect, chilly as ice cream and evoking lemonade, made for a perfect summer dessert.

"Very, very good!" Nell was sitting directly to Karen's left and turned toward her, holding a forkful of the cake aloft. And she uttered Pamela's thought aloud: "Just right for a summer evening."

"I didn't follow the recipe exactly though," Karen said, "because that cookbook was written before people had real refrigerators. So I looked online, and all the icebox cakes go in the freezer now."

"My mother grew up in a house with an icebox."

Nell nodded. "It kept things cold, but it didn't freeze them."

Holly spoke up. "The ice would melt."

"Indeed, it would." Nell smiled. "And the iceman would deliver more. My grandparents had a nice house, with a special feature in the kitchen. The icebox backed up against an outside wall with a little door in it. My mom said that her mom would put a card in the front window alerting the iceman when she needed more ice, and he would just open that little door and put in a new block."

"The icebox cake wouldn't be as cold." Roland had apparently been pondering the implications of an icebox cake that was literally an *icebox* cake. "It would be cold," he said, "but not as cold as this." He waved his fork toward the small bit of cake that remained on his plate.

"People didn't have air-conditioning then," Nell explained, "and they didn't like to heat up their big stoves in the summer because the house was hot enough already. But they liked desserts."

"Who doesn't?" Bettina inquired with a giggle.

"So, an icebox cake was a way to make a fancy dessert that didn't need to be baked," Nell concluded.

Only a last few bites remained on the white china plates, and for the next minute or so, the sound of human voices was replaced by the clicking of forks against china. Once the plates were empty, conversation resumed as cups were lifted from saucers and coffee (or tea) provided an aromatic complement to the piquant lemon flavor.

After a chorus of praise for the icebox cake, as well as Karen's pretty table setting, talk remained on the subject of food. Mention of a new restaurant in Timberley that advertised its farm-to-table menu as a selling point prompted Holly to note that the menu at Arborville's own Caleb's Table had always featured produce from its own gardens, so farm to table was hardly unheard of in northern New Jersey.

"And not only that," Bettina pointed out, "but the Timberley restaurant hasn't even bothered to place an advertisement in the *Advocate*—as if they think people in Arborville don't appreciate good food."

"Snobby." Holly observed. "And it's probably not all that great, anyway. So what if it's farm to table. The cooks still have to know what they're doing."

Roland's chair squeaked slightly as he shifted position, and five pairs of eyes focused on his lean face with, at the moment, brow furrowed and lips parted as if eager to contribute to the discussion.

"Have you and Melanie tried the Timberley restaurant?" Holly inquired.

Without answering that question, he made a show of pushing back his immaculate shirt cuff to display his impressive watch. "It's well past time that we returned to our knitting," he intoned. And with that, he rose from his seat and stepped toward the living room.

Everyone else rose, but no one followed him. Many hands make light work, Wilfred would have said, as five people applied themselves to the task of clearing the table. A few minutes later, plates and cups and saucers had been transferred to Karen's kitchen counter, along with silverware and the other accoutrements of coffee and tea service. Holly had perched on a chair at Karen's kitchen table and Nell on another, and they were deep in conversation about the progress of Nell's vegetable garden.

"Plenty of lettuce and spinach," Nell reported, "but

tomatoes are a ways off, and peas and beans even a further ways. No carrots for a while either."

Bettina was studying the portion of icebox cake, something less than half, that remained in the rectangular Pyrex pan where Karen had assembled it.

"You could make it almost any flavor, couldn't you?" she commented. "And layer other things with the cookies and cream, like strawberries—strawberry jam, or even raw strawberries, or strawberry jam *and* raw . . ."

"Yes," Karen said. "There are versions with all kinds of fruit, and versions with chocolate too." She crossed the floor, peeked through the doorway, and then stepped into the dining room. "He's knitting," she whispered, "and I don't think he misses us."

"Knitting and nibbling are the stated purposes of the group, as Roland often reminds us." Nell chuckled. "It goes without saying that chatting is permitted too, but . . ." She rose and moved toward the doorway, adding, "I have a donkey to finish."

"And I have an eggplant to finish," Holly noted.

Pamela and Bettina followed Nell into the dining room and the living room beyond, with Holly bringing up the rear.

Indeed, Holly's project from the previous week was still underway, several inches longer and beginning to take on the curved effect that would mimic an eggplant's shape. She took her place at the end of the sofa, patted the skein of deep-purple yarn at her side, and picked up her work.

Roland, meanwhile, was checking his watch, and not inconspicuously, though he refrained from speaking.

"Are you going to knit a whole garden?" Nell inquired with a fond glance in Holly's direction.

"I'll see how the eggplant turns out." Holly looked up with a dimply smile. "Maybe a tomato. Some things would be harder . . . peas? In a pod?"

"Yes." Roland spoke unexpectedly. His voice was quiet, as if his intended audience was simply himself. "Very imaginative. A person can wear only so many sweaters. Gifts, of course, but even there . . ." His busy fingers remained in motion as he ruminated. "The knitting goes on," he continued after a bit, "and the question becomes, what else to knit? Two hours a week for fifty-two weeks equals one hundred and four hours of knitting. Minus fifteen minutes a week for the break, but still . . ."

"You've knit other things besides sweaters," Nell reminded him.

"Yes. Yes, I have. But not many other things, and not for a while." He was silent then, but a sharp little crease between his brows suggested that his ruminations continued.

The silence was not prolonged. Soon a conversation sprang up between Karen and Nell, with Nell's rocking chair close enough to the armchair occupied by Karen that they could chat easily. From her seat at the end of the sofa, Pamela could make out only enough words to recognize that the topic was the summer activities the library was offering for the preschool set.

Bettina was chatting too, turned toward Holly, who sat at the other end of the sofa. So, Pamela was left to join Roland in solitary rumination. Her mind drifted from picturing the completed state of the donkey now in progress on her needles, to wondering how soon she'd find another message from Penny when she checked her email, to the very mundane question of whether the last few days had been hot enough to add watering the lawn to Wednesday's schedule.

The snap of the latch on Roland's elegant briefcase summoned Pamela back to the present. She watched as he folded his project and laid it inside the briefcase, arranging his empty needle parallel with the one that held the swath of knitting. After tucking the skein of turquoise yarn alongside, he lowered the briefcase lid and clicked the latch back into place.

"Particularly enjoyable tonight," he commented as his eyes sought out his hostess, "though Knit and Nibble meetings are always enjoyable." He double-checked that his briefcase was latched and then added, "I look forward to next week."

Before Pamela and Bettina took leave of each other in Bettina's driveway, they agreed to pay a call on Edmund the next day at one p.m., with Pamela driving—though the distance, as she pointed out, was certainly walkable.

CHAPTER 16

As Edmund welcomed Pamela and Bettina into his living room, Pamela's attention was immediately drawn to the stuffed pheasant. Protected by a bell-shaped glass cover, it peered haughtily back at her, as if glorying in the coppery iridescence of its feathers, shading to green at the neck and then red. And with his handsome features, Edmund was the perfect Victorian gentleman, in a summer suit tailored from crisp white linen.

"To what do I owe the pleasure?" he inquired once they were seated on a tufted velvet loveseat, maroon, with a carved wooden frame. "This is unexpected."

"You don't have a phone," Bettina explained, "or at least there was no phone number on your visiting card."

As if anticipating that Edmund would receive them with the formality of a bygone age, Bettina had dressed to impress, in linen too, but pale yellow. She was wearing a vintage-looking mid-calf-length sheath, with a wide portrait collar that set off the triple strand of pearls at her neck.

Edmund's residence was a cozy guesthouse behind a larger house. The décor of his small living room reflected his taste for all things Victorian, though perhaps sourced from thrift shops rather than antique dealers. The walls were a deep rose, the drapes were indigo, and the furniture was dark and imposing. A large mirror in a scalloped gold frame reflected Pamela's and Bettina's images back at them from the opposite wall.

"I know you're interested in Voorhees House," Bettina said. "In fact, you said you'd be happy to make your views known to readers of the *Advocate*."

"Of course." Edmund was still on his feet. He bowed slightly and then lowered himself into a wooden chair near the small pedestal table that held the pheasant.

"I wonder . . ." Bettina paused, and Pamela hid a smile as the Bettina reflected in the mirror adjusted her mobile features to express both curiosity and admiration—with more admiration to come if her curiosity was satisfied.

"I wonder," she repeated, "whether you know the person who's been living in the Voorhees House attic."

"What?" Edmund twitched, and his chair creaked. "I had no idea a person had been living in the Voorhees House attic, and I don't see why you'd think I would know such a person." His tone was that of an affronted gentleman in a period drama, and he seemed about to rise to his feet.

"Your interest in the house . . . in protecting the house . . ." Bettina's voice was as soothing as if she was comforting Woofus.

Edmund relaxed, though the air of formality remained. "How do you know about this . . . *person*?"

"I saw the evidence," Bettina said. "There's a sleeping bag, and a pillow, and even the remains of food. And since you'll ask anyway, a local handyman has been doing some work there—just cleaning up, no *remuddling*. He's a friend of mine, and Pamela's"—she nodded toward Pamela, on the loveseat beside her—"*mostly* Pamela's, and he found the evidence and invited us there to see it too."

Edmund relaxed more. He even laughed. "I imagine you've found your ghosts, then," he said.

"I wasn't actually looking for them . . ." The Bettina reflected in the mirror looked puzzled. "I didn't really think Tassie died of fright."

"The haunting effect," Edmund explained. "Lights coming on and off, which could have been candles or a flashlight, maybe doing things on purpose to keep the house uninhabited." He paused, his eyes widened, and then he frowned, as if having second thoughts about what he had just said. "Not that I know the person, or even *know of* the person."

Had the affronted-gentleman reaction been an act? Pamela wondered. Was the squatter actually a fellow devotee of Victorian architecture, bent on preserving Voorhees House by whatever means?

"But"—he laughed and went on—"that didn't work, did it? Because she *did* move in. And the boyfriend doesn't seem to have been scared off, either."

"There were sounds too," Bettina said, "according to Win Colley, the neighbor. And not normal sounds. *Spooky* sounds, maybe on-purpose spooky sounds, like . . ." Pamela shrank away as Bettina suddenly

unleashed an amazingly close imitation of the *wheee—
ooo—aaa—wahh wheee—ooo—aaa—wahh* that Win
had demonstrated. "The lights could be a person just
squatting there, using candles and flashlights to find
their way around in that big house. But the sounds, the
nature of the sounds . . ." She paused and fingered her
chin thoughtfully as a frown disturbed the effect of her
careful makeup.

Edmund took up the thought. "Definitely haunted-
house sounds. And the word got out, and people were
spooked, but Tassie moved in anyway."

He jumped up from his chair and whirled around to
face an elaborately carved cabinet, with shelves above
and drawers below. Glancing furtively around, he
opened one of the drawers and took out a small, velvet-
covered case.

"You won't tell anyone I have this," he whispered
ominously.

"No, uh, of course not." Bettina whispered back,
and Pamela nodded and murmured agreement.

Edmund returned to his chair, lifted the lid of the
case, and extracted a smartphone.

"It's a concession to modern life." He was still
whispering. "My mom insists, but I don't put the number on my visiting cards."

He fingered the phone's screen for a minute, nodded
with satisfaction, then held out a hand with the phone
resting on it like an offering. From the phone came a
remarkable sound: high-pitched and delicate at first,
violinlike, but more ethereal, then moaning and swoop-
ing and dipping through octaves.

"Cool, no?" Edmund remarked when the brief con-
cert had ended. "Ooops," he appended, using his free

hand to cover his mouth. "'Cool,' in that sense, was not in the Victorian lexicon."

Bettina had seemed quite transfixed by the music and remained staring at the phone even after it ended. "What was that?" she inquired after a few silent moments had passed.

"Electronic music. It's a thing, very twentieth century. You can find all you want on YouTube. Not really to my taste though—too modern." He pressed a spot on the phone's screen and lowered the phone back into its velvet-covered case. "That was a theremin, invented in nineteen twenty-eight."

"It did sound spooky," Bettina commented. "Maybe the squatter likes electronic music."

"Old houses didn't have central air-conditioning, and attics get hot. A person spending a lot of time in an attic would likely need to open windows." Edmund rose, whirled toward the cabinet again, and tucked the case away in its drawer.

"I guess you've never been inside Voorhees House," Bettina said once Edmund had taken his seat again. "Or at least never really explored—or you'd have come upon the sleeping bag and other things in the attic too."

"Never been inside." Edmund shook his head and smiled a tight-lipped smile. "Not sure if I'd want to. Too sad to see all that beauty—the parquet, the moldings, the graciousness of it all—and think that any day now, *any day now*, it's going to be torn out and *remuddled*. Turned into a white box with no character, and there's nobody alive anymore who can replicate that craftsmanship, and . . . and . . . they all just want to *mod-*

ernize. Why is that good? I ask you. What is one thing about the modern world that's actually good?"

He buried his face in his hands and remained in that position, whimpering slightly. Then he allowed his head to droop further until his fingers were buried in his abundant hair. When at length he raised his head, his hair was so disordered and his eyes so wild that he seemed transformed, like a Dr. Jekyll who had become Mr. Hyde.

Bettina was staring at him with alarmed fascination, but it was Pamela who spoke. Seeking to change the subject, at least slightly, she said, "Our friend—the handyman—also showed us a secret room."

"Armoire." The distraction had worked. Edmund actually smiled. "You open an armoire, and there's another door inside, you step through that door into a secret room—"

Bettina interrupted, sounding more accusing than curious. "How did you know, if you've never gone into Voorhees House?"

"They're almost always like that," Edmund said. "The secret rooms. Or else there's a bookcase that swings back. But I didn't know Voorhees House had a secret room until right now. All the more reason that it should be maintained exactly as it is, because a *remuddling* would just . . . would just . . ." His eyes widened. Inhaling deeply, he probed at the air as if trying to capture the words he was looking for.

"Are the secret rooms always piled with suitcases and trunks filled with hand-knit clothes?" Bettina inquired.

Edmund smiled again. "That's what's in there? You're quite the snoop—a real Sherlock Holmes. But now I have an appointment . . ."

· He pulled out a gold pocket watch on a chain, snapped it open, and rose. They took the hint that they were being dismissed.

"Do you think he was telling the truth?" Pamela asked Bettina after they left the guesthouse. They were walking along a brick path that intersected a backyard thick with native plants in blossom, lush and almost weedy, and alive with bees and butterflies.

Bettina veered out of the way of a bee on its way to a stalky blue flower, stumbling a bit as she negotiated the uneven bricks in the open-toed pumps she had paired with her chic linen dress. Regaining her balance, she said, "He seemed very sincere in his concern for the fate of Voorhees House. But is he *so* concerned that maybe he himself is the squatter?"

Pamela nodded. "That electronic music he played certainly sounded like something you'd hear in a haunted house. He could have been sitting up in the attic on random nights, opening the windows, and maybe hooking his phone up to speakers."

"The windows would have had to be open," Bettina agreed, "for Win to hear the sounds." They'd reached the driveway, also brick, of the main house and were heading toward the street. The streets in this part of Arborville departed from the grid system that prevailed in most of the town. One street curved to intersect the others at unexpected angles, and the lots were curious sizes and shapes.

"So, like Edmund said, the sounds would mostly have been heard in warm weather." Pamela stopped suddenly, and Bettina, who had fallen behind, bumped into her. Pamela turned to face her. "Do you remember if Win gave us specific dates for her notes on the spooky sounds?"

"I don't," Bettina said, "and I'm not going back there to sit through another session with that notebook."

They had reached Pamela's car. A thought had occurred to her the moment she raised the question of the dates for the sounds, but she waited until they were settled in their seats to put it into words.

"The dates might not matter," she said then. "Summer, winter, fall . . ."

"So, we don't have to talk to Win again?"

"If we imagine that the squatter is living in Voorhees House for whatever reason—maybe even just needed a free place to stay—and is up there listening to his, or her, favorite weird music . . . then, of course, the windows would only be open in hot weather."

"True." Bettina nodded. "Attics get very hot in the summer."

"*But*"—Pamela raised her right hand with index finger extended (a schoolmarmish pose, she knew, but sometimes she couldn't help it)—"if the intention was to scare away potential inhabitants of Voorhees House by making it seem haunted, then no matter what season—hot or cold—the squatter could have been broadcasting those sounds out open windows."

Bettina nodded again, so enthusiastically that the scarlet tendrils of her hair vibrated. "Even windows on other floors," she added. "But I'm still not going back to Win Colley's."

When they reached the corner where a right turn onto Arborville Avenue would take them back to Orchard Street, Pamela clicked on her turn signal. Before she could make the turn though, Bettina reached out as if to seize the steering wheel.

"I just thought of something," she said. "It's Wednesday already, and I should check with Clayborn to see if he has anything for this week's *Advocate*."

Pamela clicked off the turn signal, and Bettina added, "Do you mind a detour?"

"Of course not."

She turned the other direction, and five minutes later, the serviceable compact was pulling into a spot in the parking lot that served the library and the police department.

"I'll find a bench to sit on while you're inside," Pamela said after they'd both stepped out onto the parking lot's asphalt. As Bettina headed for the brick building with its heavy glass doors, Pamela meandered toward the kiddie playground.

On this mild June afternoon, the playground was buzzing with activity. Under the watchful eyes of moms, and the not-so-watchful eyes of chatting au pairs, children hurtled down the slides, clambered about on the jungle gym, and shrieked as the merry-go-round spun ever faster. Pamela found a spot on a bench in the welcome shade of a huge tree and let her mind wander.

The first stop it made in its wanderings was a recollection of sitting on perhaps this very bench fifteen or more years ago, watching Penny as she explored the delights of the kiddie playground. Michael Paterson had still been alive then, and now he wasn't, and Penny was all grown up and spending a month in Guatemala with her maybe-boyfriend and . . .

Bettina's voice cut into her musings, calling from somewhere behind her: "*Pamela, Pamela.*" The voice grew louder, and the next thing she knew Bettina had circled the bench and was standing before her. The contrast between the serene cheer implied by Bettina's bright makeup and carefully coordinated ensemble and her present demeanor was striking. She was blinking rapidly, and her breath was coming in short gasps.

"I cannot believe this," she said, whispering because Pamela was sharing the bench with a few other people. "Let's go back to the car." She turned and led the way.

Following her, Pamela felt her heart rearrange itself in her chest as the prelude to an alarmed *thump*. What on earth could have happened in the meeting with Detective Clayborn?

Bettina scarcely waited for Pamela to unlock the passenger-side door before she spoke. And when she did, it was to say, "Tassie Hunt was *murdered!*"

She pronounced each word slowly and carefully, with an almost-questioning tone, as if she herself still needed time to process the information.

"Let's . . . let's . . . get in the car." Pamela laid a soothing hand on Bettina's arm before circling around to open her own door and slip behind the steering wheel.

"The medical examiner's report came through," Bettina explained once she had settled into the passenger seat. "Tassie didn't die of natural causes. She was suffocated. Traces of down from a pillow were found in her nasal passages."

"That complicates things," Pamela said. "The squatter, who we thought might be trying to scare people away from Voorhees House, and who we thought might have accidentally caused Tassie to die of fright—"

Bettina took up the thought. "—could have killed her on purpose." She paused, raised a brightly manicured finger to her lips, and inhaled deeply. "There was a pillow in the attic, along with the sleeping bag."

"What if Edmund is the squatter?" Pamela asked.

"He seemed excitable, and so passionate about the house." Bettina nodded sadly. "I'd hate to think he'd stoop to murder though. What would his mother say? She sounded protective, insisting he have a phone, even if he keeps it hidden."

"Maybe Chad killed Tassie," Pamela said, "so he could inherit the house."

"We don't know if he *would* inherit it," Bettina reminded her. "We have no idea whether Tassie had made a will, or what was in it."

"Umm-umm." Pamela shook her head. "He told Pete he *had* inherited it."

"Maybe he was lying—though Pete seemed to think he was an okay sort of guy, and that he really cared about Tassie."

With the subject seemingly exhausted, Pamela backed out of the parking spot, and soon they were on their way to Orchard Street.

"Wilfred baked cinnamon rolls this morning," Bettina said as Pamela pulled into the Frasers' driveway. "Do you want to come in for a bit? I can make a fresh pot of coffee to go with them."

"It pains me to turn down Wilfred's cinnamon rolls," Pamela replied, "but I have to get home and start cooking because Pete is coming for dinner tonight."

Bettina, still sitting in the passenger seat, whirled to face her. "Why didn't you tell me?"

"I'm telling you now." Pamela laughed.

"Is this a . . . development?" The question was accompanied by a teasing smile and a raised eyebrow.

"I've cooked dinner for him before."

"What are you making?"

"Ribs," Pamela said. "I walked up to the Co-Op this morning before we went to see Edmund."

* * *

The ribs had been a great success, baking long and slow in the oven with homemade barbecue sauce. Pamela had served them with coleslaw from the Co-Op deli and macaroni and cheese of her own devising. Now she and Pete were lingering over strawberry shortcake in a dining room lit by flickering candles, as the sky beyond the windows gradually darkened.

Pamela always took the chair at the back end of the table because it was nearest to the kitchen door for food service. From the vantage point of that chair, she could look through the arch separating the dining room from the living room and see all the way to the windows that looked out onto the front porch.

Now, in a conversational lull after Pete had shared fond reminiscences of the cocker spaniel that had been his childhood companion, Pamela shifted her gaze from his face to the view through the arch. Not expecting to see anything out of the ordinary, she was at first puzzled by the shape moving across the shadowy porch. But when it stopped to look back at her through one of the windows, she felt her chair quiver as she gave a start.

A moment later, though, laughter bubbled up. She realized she was staring at Bettina and Bettina was staring back. A few more moments later, Pamela was standing on the porch. En route, she had flipped the switch for the porch light, and Bettina was blinking at her in the sudden glare.

"You could have rung the doorbell," Pamela commented, aware that the expression on her face was likely not the most welcoming. "What are you doing out here?"

Bettina mustered a smile, but an unhappy one. "I

knew Pete was here, and I didn't want to interrupt if you were . . . you know . . ."

"If I was . . . you know . . . what?" Pamela felt her forehead crinkle into a frown.

"Not *you*." Bettina pointed at Pamela. "But both of you . . . you know . . ."

Pamela sighed, explosively. "If both of us were . . . you know, we wouldn't be doing it in the living room with the curtains open."

Bettina stepped back, eyes open wide. "Does that mean that you and Pete *have* . . . ?" The unhappy smile was replaced by a delighted one.

Pamela was spared answering by the fact that Pete had just stepped over the threshold and joined them on the porch.

"Oh, my goodness!" Bettina's smile morphed again, signaling surprise this time. She tilted her head to focus on Pete. "You're here! I had no idea . . ."

Pamela fought back the urge to point out that her friend had known perfectly well that Pete was there and that that knowledge had been the reason for her covert surveillance. Had she obeyed the urge, she would have had to interrupt—because Bettina was still talking, and quite breathlessly.

Words gushed out. "The lights are back! In Voorhees House—the weird lights in the weird places! That's what I came to tell you, Pamela. Win Colley just phoned, because she remembered I asked her to keep me posted." Bettina paused to take a deep breath. "So I think the only sensible thing is to go there, and—"

Her lips parted in apparent amazement (a bit overdone, to Pamela's mind). She gasped and raised a graceful hand to her mouth. "This is such a coincidence," she exclaimed, aiming a flirtatious glance at Pete. "*Such* a coincidence that you happen to be here, because you have a key to Voorhees House."

Pamela groaned. She stared at Bettina, afraid to even contemplate what Pete must be thinking. Fortunately, he was standing behind her, so she was spared a view of his face. And as if things weren't awkward enough, a snuffling bark from the street called her attention to Woofus, loping into the circle of light cast by the streetlamp. Following him, at a distance marked by the length of a leash, was Wilfred.

They neared the steps leading up to Pamela's porch, and Woofus fell back, allowing Wilfred to take the lead. The next thing she knew, Wilfred and Pete were greeting each other with a hearty handshake.

"Dear wife," Wilfred said after the handshake concluded, "I insist on coming with you and Pamela."

"Uh . . ." Pamela became aware that she had seized one hand with the other and was kneading her fingers quite mercilessly. "Uh," she repeated, "I'm not sure . . ."

Suddenly Pete's voice came from behind her, sounding unexpectedly matter-of-fact. "I do have a key," he said, "and given that Chad has trusted me with a key, it might even be my duty to look into 'weird lights in weird places.' There could be a glitch in the wiring. So"—Pete moved toward the steps—"shall we be off?"

"Let's take my car," Wilfred suggested, turning to follow him. "There's more room in the back seat. After all, there are five of us."

"Five?" Pete had already started down the front walk.

"We'll want to have Woofus along," Bettina said, "in case the weird lights in weird places aren't just a glitch in the wiring."

Pamela hurried back into her house to fetch her purse and her keys. A minute later, the small procession was making its way toward the Frasers' driveway, where Wilfred's ancient but lovingly cared-for Mercedes waited.

Pete detoured to his own car to collect a flashlight. Then he and Wilfred led the way, chatting about the Mercedes, which Pete confessed to having admired since the day he first showed up on Orchard Street when Pamela hired him for her rescreening job.

"You've got a pretty nice set of wheels too," Wilfred observed in response. "Two sets, really. I've always wanted a pickup truck."

Bettina, meanwhile, had taken charge of Woofus's leash, and he pulled her along after him in his attempt to keep up with Wilfred. Pamela brought up the rear, not convinced that the mission they were embarking on was a wise one—or even a necessary one—but somehow impressed by Pete's willingness to join in. She would make sure, though, to let Bettina know that pretending to be surprised when Pete stepped out onto the porch had been a most unconvincing piece of acting.

It seemed only natural for Pete to join Wilfred in the front seat of the Mercedes, given that the two men were still deep in conversation. Pamela and Bettina took seats in the back, with the furry bulk of Woofus between them.

The drive to Voorhees House seemed unfamiliar by night, with most storefronts along Arborville Avenue shuttered and the meandering climb up the hill seeming an adventure in a landscape with familiar landmarks hidden by darkness. Wilfred followed Pete's directions, turning left and then turning again, and soon the Mercedes was coasting to the curb.

Voorhees House loomed inky black against clouds infused with moonlight. Once out of the car, Pamela scanned the side that faced the street, seeing only darkness behind each window. Pete walked to the spot where Win Colley's yard began and turned to get a look at the house's actual front. Wilfred and Bettina stood on the sidewalk near the car with Woofus, who seemed puzzled, sticking close by.

"I don't see any lights, weird or otherwise," Pete announced after a bit. "But since we're here . . ." He circled back to the steps that led up to the rickety porch, clicked on the flashlight, and made his way to the front door.

The three other humans, plus the dog, gathered at the bottom of the steps. The porch floor creaked as Pete approached the door, and the click of the key as he turned the lock seemed unnaturally loud. The door itself moaned ominously as he pushed it open.

It was a surprise, then, when his next words were, "Hello. I didn't mean to startle you."

CHAPTER 17

"Someone's in there!" Bettina exclaimed and darted past Pamela. Grasping the handrail, she hurried up the steps with Wilfred close behind. Pamela was about to follow but had to veer out of the way as Woofus bounded after his master and mistress. Neither Bettina, Wilfred, nor Woofus had ventured across the threshold by the time Pamela joined them, though the discovery Pete had made was far from frightening.

In the beam of Pete's flashlight, a young blond woman, so small and slender as to be almost waifish, was cowering against a wall in the living room, near a window whose heavy drapes were drawn. The only light other than Pete's flashlight came from a flickering stub of a candle in a low candleholder on a nearby table. The scene could have come from a Gothic novel. The young woman was even garbed in white, though the garments were a basic T-shirt and a pair of gauzy drawstring pants.

"I'm a local handyman," Pete said, "doing some

work for Chad. I just came by to check that everything's okay with the house. I guess you're a friend of
his?"

The young woman took a few steps away from the
wall. "Not exactly."

At that point, Bettina stirred, slipping past Wilfred
and tiptoeing to Pete's side. "I'm Bettina Fraser," she
said, "and this is Pete Paterson, and yes, he is doing
some work for Chad. You don't need to be afraid."

Such was the comforting power of Bettina's voice,
even in the gloom, that the young woman advanced
farther.

"There's a light switch somewhere," Pete murmured.

He retreated toward the doorway, and in a moment
six frosted glass globes in an elaborate brass chandelier came alight. Wilfred, Pamela, and Woofus edged
across the threshold.

"I'm Bettina Fraser," Bettina repeated, with a mean-
ingful look at the young woman, "and you would be?"

"Esme Grindale?" The young woman's voice was
tentative.

"Why don't we all sit down," Bettina suggested,
moving toward the stiff-looking sofa, which was posi-
tioned against the right-hand wall.

The sofa was flanked by long windows, and Esme
had been cowering in the corner beyond the farthest of
them when Pete first entered. Now she edged around
the sofa's arm and perched at its end. Bettina settled
right next to her and offered a companionable smile.

"Now then," she said, "something tells me you're
here for an interesting reason."

A few stiff-looking chairs in the same dark hue as
the sofa faced it, with an ornate table, taller than a normal coffee table, between them. Pamela and Pete slipped

unobtrusively into the chairs while Wilfred lowered himself gently onto the sofa beside his wife.

"I've always been fascinated by Voorhees House," Esme explained. "I live in Haversack now, in a commune with friends from college, but I grew up in Arborville."

Esme looked barely old enough to be on her own. Her delicate features still had a childlike softness to them, and her gaze was trusting.

"When I heard that Edith Voorhees had died and the house was empty, I started coming around, at night mostly. I'd visit my parents, and then I'd ride my bike over here, sit on the porch, imagine all the things that had gone on in the house, the things people had lived through."

Pete was nodding, his evident sympathy rendering his handsome features all the more appealing. Pamela remembered that one of their first conversations had been about his fondness for old houses.

"Then one day"—Esme's voice quickened—"I discovered that the back door doesn't actually lock very securely, so I started coming inside, even staying here on and off, hiding my bike in the basement."

She had been addressing no one in particular, focusing, in fact, on the carpet. But now she turned toward Bettina and said, with a pleading note in her voice, "I wasn't hurting anything."

"Of course you weren't." Bettina offered a comforting smile.

"I came to believe," Esme said, "that I was always destined to live here, or maybe that I *had* lived here in a past life. I hoped it would stay empty forever so I could keep coming."

"You weren't frightened"—Bettina leaned closer to

Esme and studied her face—"by the weird noises? One of the neighbors believes Voorhees House is haunted, and she suggested that I write an article for the *Advocate*. I see now that you were responsible for the weird lights, but she also heard weird noises."

"Oh!" Unexpectedly, Esme laughed. "I didn't know I had an audience."

"An audience?" Pamela's voice echoed Bettina's.

Esme tilted her head to stare at the ceiling and then closed her eyes. Her body stiffened, and from her barely open lips there came a sound, high-pitched and ethereal, vibrating from soft to loud and back to soft again. It rose in pitch until it seemed to fade away, though Woofus's attentive pose suggested it remained audible for some time to ears other than human.

"'Voorhees Suite,'" Esme announced in her normal voice once she had returned to herself. "My magnum opus. It's all about the house, the way the old wood vibrates, like a Stradivarius. My voice, plus echoes and ambient noises. It was almost finished, then Tassie moved in and interrupted me."

She had become quite animated, with her large, pale eyes appearing even larger and her gaze shifting rapidly from face to face.

"And now there's this new person, moving in any day, and—"

She flopped forward until her head was nearly between her knees. "Oh, oh, oh!" she moaned, and the sound was not ethereal at all. It was the sound of a young woman in great distress. "All my work will have been for nothing," she concluded.

A plaintive whimper joined Esme's moans to create the effect of a curious duet. Looking around for the source of the whimper, Pamela realized that Woofus had wandered from the post he had taken up at Wilfred's end of the sofa when they all found seats. He was instead standing in the doorway that led to the dining room.

Esme remained bent over, moaning, and Bettina laid a gentle hand on her back, but Wilfred stood up and slipped around the back of the sofa. As he approached Woofus, the shaggy creature dipped his muzzle and directed a beseeching glance upward, revealing the whites of his eyes. He continued whimpering, even more plaintively.

"What is it, boy? What is it?" Wilfred stooped and stroked the dog's head.

Woofus turned and took a few steps into the dining room. He paused and swung back to check whether Wilfred was following him. Wilfred grasped the doorframe to aid in hoisting himself to his feet, and Woofus scampered ahead, disappearing around the corner. Wilfred disappeared around the corner soon after.

Bettina was still occupied with Esme, who was now sitting upright. She was dabbing at her eyes with a tissue that Bettina had produced from her handbag, and Bettina's soothing voice seemed to be having an effect.

Several moments passed. Both Pete and Pamela had been staring toward the empty dining room doorway ever since Woofus and Wilfred disappeared. Now Wilfred reappeared, and then Woofus, huddling close to his master's thigh.

Wilfred focused on Pete, mouthed Pete's name, and tipped his head in a "*come here*" gesture. Pete rose, concern emphasizing the melancholy cast to his eyes, and circled around behind Pamela to join Wilfred in the doorway.

Pamela rose too. Wilfred's chivalry was appreciated. His capable, masculine presence had always been a comfort in troubling situations, and whatever Woofus had led Wilfred to in the dining room perhaps required Pete's presence especially, given that they'd entered under his auspices. But Pamela was curious—and she didn't like to think she had to be spared if the scene was disturbing.

The dining room was brighter than she had expected. The heavy drapes were open, and the main windows looked out on the driveway of the neighboring house—not Win's house, but Spud Birdsall's, on the other side. The driveway was illuminated with a large spotlight, perhaps a burglar deterrent. The light spilled into the Voorhees House dining room, where it created bright, windowpane-shaped patches on the carpet and on the parquet floor where the carpet left off.

Visible in one of those bright patches was the head and upper torso of a man—not young, but not old—fit, and dressed in a summery cotton shirt. He was lying on his back, staring at the ceiling.

"Chad Donahue," Pete said. "What a thing to have happen."

"It never rains but it pours." Wilfred shook his head and pulled his phone out of a side pocket in his overalls. "First Tassie and now this."

Bettina stepped through the doorway then. She stared at the body on the floor, and a tiny squeak emerged from her throat.

"Dear wife!" Wilfred was at her side in an instant, holding out his arms in welcome as she slipped into them. "Someone *really* doesn't want this house to be inhabited again."

Pete had continued studying Chad's body. Pamela wasn't sure what was going through his mind, though she doubted it was anything as mundane as wondering about the future of Voorhees House and his role in that future. When he looked up, his thoughtful expression remained unchanged, but now his attention was on Pamela's face.

"How are you doing?" he inquired softly.

"I'm okay," Pamela responded, grateful for his presence.

Wilfred had spoken briefly on his phone, leaving one arm wrapped around Bettina. "Police are on their way," he announced, "and I guess we can . . ." He headed toward the doorway with Bettina at his side and Woofus at his heel. Pamela and Pete followed them into the living room.

"Esme's gone!" Bettina's tone suggested curiosity rather than certainty. She peered around the room as if perhaps her first glance had missed something. But the candle and candleholder were gone too.

"Probably just retreated to the attic," Wilfred said. "I don't think she was an apparition—though those were certainly some spooky sounds she conjured up."

"I touched her." Bettina murmured. "She felt solid enough."

Pamela felt a tingle at the back of her neck. It was silly, though, to imagine that they had been chatting with a ghost, and the body on the dining room floor was certainly real enough. But suddenly the room and the people in it might as well have been apparitions too, so unreal had everything come to seem. The sound of feet on the porch was welcome then.

"Police, no doubt," Wilfred declared as he strode to the door. He opened it to admit two uniformed men who Pamela recognized as the youthful Officer Anders and an older, burly officer named Officer Keenan.

"You reported a murder?" Officer Anders said, striving for authority by imposing a frown on his boyish features.

"A body, possibly a murder." Pete edged toward the dining room. "It's Chad Donahue, Tassie Hunt's boyfriend. I know it's him because I was working for him, on this house."

Officer Keenan stayed behind, perhaps to keep an eye on the rest of them, as Pete led Officer Anders through the doorway.

"We might as well sit," Bettina commented as she lowered herself onto the sofa next to the spot that had been Esme's.

Wilfred settled in next to her with Woofus on the floor at the end of the sofa, and Pamela took the chair she'd occupied earlier. Officer Keenan remained standing, seemingly at attention. Low murmurs, unintelligible, reached them from the dining room. Nobody in the living room said anything. After a bit, Pete and Officer Anders returned.

"Clayborn's coming," Officer Anders told his colleague. He nodded to Pete and said, "You can sit," then nodding to all of them, he added, "Detective Clayborn will want to interview each of you separately."

Silence descended once again. Officer Keenan was still keeping a watchful eye on them, and Officer Anders had stationed himself at the front door, presumably waiting for Detective Clayborn. Only about ten minutes had passed—though the awkwardness of the situation made it seem longer—when Officer Anders responded to a tap on the door and opened it to admit Detective Clayborn.

He was wearing his usual generic tie and nondescript sports jacket, unbuttoned to reveal a shirt that strained at the buttons in the waistline area. The expression on his homely face was nondescript as well, except for a sharpness in his glance.

"In here, sir." Officer Anders gestured toward the dining room. En route Detective Clayborn paused before the little group occupying the chairs and sofa.

"Have you gotten their names?" he inquired.

Officer Anders blinked a few times. "It's . . . they're . . . I think we know them, sir. Ms. Paterson and the Frasers, from town. And Pete Paterson. He has a key to the house because he's doing—*was* doing—some work here for the victim. It's just a coincidence that his name is Paterson too."

Detective Clayborn grunted. "Take their names anyway." His gaze shifted to Officer Keenan. "Keenan, you do it. And get their addresses and contact information too." He followed Officer Anders through the doorway, whereupon a light switched on in the dining room.

"Somebody found the light switch," Pete murmured, sounding amused.

The position of the body relative to the doorway, however, was such that it was impossible for Pamela to see either Detective Clayborn or Officer Anders once the detective had embarked on his investigation.

Providing Officer Keenan with names, addresses, and contact information provided a diversion that was almost welcome. Once he had tucked away his pen and notepad, though, there was nothing to do but wait for whatever the next step would be. More time passed, with no sound emerging from the dining room. In the living room, Officer Keenan shifted from foot to foot, and Woofus slept, curled so compactly that his tail nearly touched his nose. Pamela closed her eyes briefly, wishing she was at home in her bed. A peek at her watch showed it was nearly eleven. She stared at the carpet, wondering what actual flowers the stylized flower shapes were based on. Bettina sagged against Wilfred, and he tucked an arm around her waist to pull her closer.

A snatch of conversation drifted from the dining room, to the effect that the county crime-scene unit should be summoned. A moment later, Detective Clayborn stepped through the dining room doorway.

"I'll be interviewing people in the kitchen," he said. "Ms. Fraser," he added, and beckoned Bettina to rise. Pamela smiled to herself at his formality in requesting that Officer Keenan record Bettina's name, address, and contact information. Detective Clayborn knew perfectly well who she was because he spoke with her at least once a week in connection with her reporting for the *Advocate*!

Detective Clayborn presumably wanted privacy for his one-on-one interviews, and short of heading upstairs or using the room where Chad's body lay (and where the crime-scene people would be working), the kitchen was the only choice. It was directly off the dining room, as Pamela recalled from the day she and the ANGWY group had come upon Tassie's body. As if to spare Bettina the sight of the body—though she'd seen it already, of course—Detective Clayborn extended an arm as a sort of shield and executed a curious dance as he steered her through the dining room doorway.

Bettina emerged from the interview some time later looking drained. It had been hours since she'd refreshed her lipstick, and the wan face beneath her scarlet pouf of hair was barely recognizable. Wilfred rose to his feet as she approached, doing his best to conjure up a comforting smile, though he himself was also drooping.

Detective Clayborn had escorted Bettina through the dining room and now remained standing in the doorway. But instead of summoning his next interviewee, he gestured for Officer Keenan to join him. The two men withdrew a few steps into the dining room, but Pamela caught enough of their conversation to gather that more officers would be summoned to search the house for the possible suspect.

Pamela directed a questioning look at Bettina, and Bettina mouthed, "*I had to tell him about Esme.*"

Pamela would not see the additional officers arrive. Once he had given Officer Keenan his instructions, Detective Clayborn stepped into the living room and requested that "Ms. Paterson" accompany him to the kitchen. Again, he extended the shielding arm and executed the curious dance, guiding Pamela directly to the kitchen door as Officer Anders sat in one of the ornate chairs on the opposite side of the long mahogany table, watching over Chad's body.

Detective Clayborn gestured for Pamela to take a seat at the small wooden table she recalled from her visit with the ANGWY group. But as she crossed the worn linoleum floor, she heard a hiccupping gasp. It was coming from her, and it was followed by a voice, her voice, exclaiming, "Another one of those pies!"

Sitting on the counter between the sink and the refrigerator was a pie, obviously homemade and obviously blueberry—to judge by the purplish stains that edged the haphazard steam vents carved into the top crust.

"There was a pie just like that on the counter the last time a body was found in this house," she added, still staring at the pie.

"Ms. Fraser pointed that out." Detective Clayborn's stolid expression didn't change. "The crime-scene unit will be impounding it as evidence. Please sit down."

He took a seat too, facing her, in the table's only other chair. A pen and a small notepad were waiting, and he lost no time in seizing the pen and holding it poised over the notepad as he regarded her silently.

"What was your group doing here tonight?" he inquired after a moment.

"Bettina was chasing a story for the *Advocate*," she said. "A neighbor who's convinced this house is haunted called Bettina to report that the 'weird lights in weird places' she'd noticed earlier were back. Pete Paterson was at my house for dinner . . ."

Pamela's voice slowed. The angle of Detective Clayborn's head had shifted the tiniest bit, as if this tidbit of information demanded an altered perspective— but certainly Bettina had already told him exactly the same thing.

He didn't say anything, so she went on. "Bettina came over to tell me about the lights, and since Pete had been doing some work here for Chad, he had a key—and he thought the weird lights might be the result of a glitch in the wiring, something Chad would appreciate him checking on. So we all got in Wilfred's car and drove here."

"Dog included." Was he poking fun at the "more the merrier" aspect of the adventure? Detective Clayborn's voice gave no hint. In the same dry tone, he inquired, "And what did you discover?"

"Someone—a human someone—had taken up residence in the attic."

"And did you speak with that someone?"

"We spoke with *someone*," Pamela said. "Apparently a human someone, and apparently *that* someone, though . . ."

"Do you believe in ghosts, Ms. Paterson?" Seeming truly curious, Detective Clayborn leaned forward to stare at her.

"Of course not." Pamela felt herself draw back from the stare. "She disappeared though, just like that, after Woofus found the body. She was there, and then she wasn't."

"When you spoke with her, before Woofus—who, I presume, is the dog—found the body, what did she say?"

Bettina had told Detective Clayborn the whole story, Pamela was sure. That was why he had asked Officer Keenan to summon more officers to search the house—for Esme. She knew, though, that the police liked to verify details by hearing separately from all the people present at a crime scene.

The fact that Esme disappeared when the police were on the way certainly made her seem suspicious, but with Detective Clayborn sitting across the table from her, so serious and taking notes, Pamela had no choice but to describe Esme's devotion to Voorhees House, her musical project, and her wish that the house remain uninhabited.

When she finished, Detective Clayborn thanked her and rose, in a signal that the interview was over. "Don't leave town," he added with a wry half-smile as she rose too and he moved around the table to escort her back to the living room. But before they could step through the kitchen doorway, they nearly collided with Officer Keenan.

"The suspect is in custody, sir," he said, sounding a bit breathless—whether from excitement or because he had personally chased Esme down, Pamela wasn't sure.

CHAPTER 18

Indeed, when they entered the living room, burly Officer Keenan in the lead, Pamela next, and Detective Clayborn bringing up the rear, there was Esme. Definitely real, Pamela said to herself, not an apparition—but a more defenseless creature it would have been hard to imagine.

Tiny, pale, blond, and garbed in white, she stood between two officers Pamela didn't recognize. She'd never seen them among those tasked with such duties as monitoring traffic near the grammar school or directing drivers around road-repair crews. Esme met Pamela's gaze with a reproachful tightening of the mouth and a bleak stare. Her hands were behind her back, whether secured with handcuffs or not, Pamela couldn't tell.

"We'll question her at the station." Detective Clayborn directed the words to one of the unfamiliar officers, who took Esme's arm and moved toward the front door.

At that moment, however, the door opened, and a woman in white coveralls entered, followed by a man in the same outfit. The next several minutes were filled with activity, as Esme was escorted through the front door, presumably to a waiting police car, and the people from the county crime-scene unit were escorted into the dining room, with Detective Clayborn leading the way.

It was after midnight by the time Wilfred and Pete had had their turns with Detective Clayborn and were free to leave. Having had a long nap, Woofus was the sprightliest of the group that made its way along the creaking porch and down the rickety steps to where Wilfred's Mercedes shared curb space with two police cars and the huge silver van from the sheriff's department.

When they reached the car, Wilfred hurried to open the passenger-side door and, in his most solicitous husbandly manner, make sure that Bettina was seated and comfortable. Pamela and Pete ended up side by side in the back seat with Woofus between them.

"I hope you don't mind it back there," Bettina said, twisting around to address Pete, "with your long legs."

"Perfectly fine," Pete responded. "This car is very roomy."

"All's well that ends well, I guess," Wilfred commented from behind the steering wheel, but his voice lacked its usual buoyancy, and he added, "though we don't know how this will end." He thrust his key into the ignition, and soon they were on their way. The solid chug of the car's engine took the place of speech for a time. No one felt very conversational.

As they approached the corner of Arborville Avenue

and Orchard Street, however, Bettina spoke. In doleful tones, and as if she'd been pondering Wilfred's earlier comment, she said, "All certainly didn't end well for Esme."

When there was no response—after all, who would contradict that statement?—she went on. "She's such a tiny, fragile little person. How could she overpower a big man and smother him—or even a normal-sized woman like Tassie? And if I hadn't told Clayborn about her, she'd still be free, and safe, up in the attic, making those weird sounds to her heart's content."

"It wasn't just you," Pamela replied. "We all told him about her—at least I think we did. *I* certainly did. I had to—because he asked what we were doing there and I told him and then he asked whether we'd found an explanation for the weird lights at weird times. Esme was the explanation."

Bettina sighed, loudly. "The police went to a lot more fuss this time than when they responded to our call about Tassie—though as I recall, a sheriff's van came then too."

"It was probably because of the medical examiner's report," Pamela said. "Now they know that Tassie was murdered—smothered, which explains why there were no obvious signs of foul play in her case—and so they likely assume Chad was murdered too. And both murders happened in Voorhees House, and so they probably suspect that the same person, Esme, committed both murders."

Bettina sighed again and murmured, "I wish it hadn't turned out like this."

They were halfway down Orchard Street now, with the Frasers' house on the right and Pamela's house, where Pete's black Porsche sat waiting at the curb for its owner, on the left. Wilfred veered into Pamela's driveway, braked, and turned off the ignition. Sensing that the car's motion had ceased, Woofus leaned past Pamela to check the view from the window.

Bettina swiveled in her seat, and her voice came out of the dark. "Well, you two," she said, "I'm sorry. I thought it might be an interesting adventure—but not *that* interesting. And it's gotten terribly late, but I hope this doesn't ruin your plans for the rest of the evening . . ."

Bettina's voice trailed off, but Pamela heard herself squeak. What "plans" could Bettina possibly have in mind? Plans for an activity that she had feared she might be interrupting earlier, an activity she described only as "*you know*"?

"You're right," Pamela agreed. "It *has* gotten terribly late, and so . . ." She reached for the door handle.

Wilfred, ever the gentleman, stepped out onto the asphalt of the driveway and pulled Pamela's door open as she pushed from inside. Pete opened his own door, and he and Wilfred shared a handshake and a "Good night" while Bettina added her own farewell through a rolled-down window.

Pamela and Pete retreated to the front walk to watch Wilfred back the Mercedes out and swing around to steer it toward its customary spot in its own driveway.

"I don't know what to say," Pamela said.

"You don't have to say anything." Pete reached out and drew her to his side. "I'm glad I was there, with you. I know you don't need protecting, but I'm glad I was there anyway." He encircled her with his other arm, and then they were face-to-face, Pete a bit taller but not much, and the streetlamp offering just enough light to reveal that tenderness had replaced the melancholy in his eyes. "I'd like to continue to be there," he whispered, and Pamela was happy to raise her face to his for a kiss.

And there was another kiss, longer, after they'd climbed the steps to the porch. That was all, though she might have been glad to have him step inside after that second kiss. But he had things to consider, she suspected, before turning an enjoyable flirtation into something more serious—his children, for example—and she did too. So she watched him walk to his car, stepped over her threshold, and closed the door behind her.

Rain was threatening, but Pamela was grateful. The sun that usually set her white eyelet curtains aglow was hidden by clouds, leaving her bedroom shadowy long after her normal waking time. It had been so late when she got to bed, and then sleep hadn't come immediately. Even rising now, as ten a.m. approached, she was far from refreshed, but the extra sleep had been welcome.

The cats had slept long too, perhaps responding, as she had, to the absence of the sun. Now, seeming as groggy as she was, Catrina and Ginger straggled after her as she made her way down the stairs to the kitchen. They perked up as Pamela applied her can opener to a can of salmon paté, and Precious joined the group then, drawn by the aroma of a cat food variety that she liked too.

After setting water to boil for coffee, Pamela headed to the entry. There, she leaned close to the lace that curtained the oval window in the front door, shifting the angle of her head to get a view of the street unobscured by the curlicues that made up the lace's design. It was late to be dashing for the newspaper in her robe, but no one was about, and the foreboding clouds even seemed a kind of cover.

Back inside, she slipped a paper filter into her carafe's filter cone and ground coffee beans with a clatter that startled the cats. Once the boiling water was added and the comforting coffee-brewing process had been launched, she extracted the *Register* from its plastic sleeve and spread it out on the kitchen table.

Marcy Brewer had been busy! Several column inches on the *Register*'s front page were devoted to the Voorhees House *murders*—officially plural now. The article, by Marcy Brewer, bore the bold headline AN-OTHER DEATH AT ARBORVILLE'S VOORHEES HOUSE. Smaller print below elaborated: "MEDICAL EXAMINER CONFIRMS TASSIE HUNT WAS MURDERED; BOYFRIEND CHAD DONAHUE IS LATEST BODY. MURDER IS SUS-PECTED."

Pamela had gotten no further than the headline when she was interrupted by the doorbell's chime. Stepping to the kitchen door, she could see through the window's lace that her caller was Bettina, and she hurried to greet her friend.

Bettina entered talking. "She doesn't rest, not at all," she said, shaking her head. "Big article in the *Register* already—I don't know how she managed that, no sleep at all, I guess—but that's not enough, so she's prowling around this morning too. I just hope she didn't disturb that sweet friend of yours, Pete Paterson. And she wasn't the only one. That pest from the TV station was here too."

Pamela stared. "What . . . ? What are you talking about?"

"Reporters!" Bettina exclaimed. "Marcy Brewer,

and that pest from the TV station. They didn't come here? About seven a.m.?"

Pamela rubbed her face. "I must have been asleep," she said. "Really sound asleep. I guess they gave up."

"They woke us." Bettina twisted her lips into an annoyed knot. "Woofus, mostly, and he started barking, and then Wilfred went down and chased them away. People don't have to give interviews to the press, you know. It's not like the police."

As if suddenly realizing that she had come bearing gifts, Bettina thrust a foil-covered plate at Pamela. "Wilfred's cinnamon rolls," she explained. "We didn't eat them all. Do I smell coffee?"

"You do," Pamela said. "Two cups' worth, and I can make more." She gestured toward the kitchen doorway, and Bettina, still carrying the foil-covered plate, led the way.

The late night had left dark circles under Bettina's eyes, but her makeup was as perfect as ever, including a hint of green eye shadow that echoed the green of her crisp linen slacks and shirt. Bold hoop earrings, gold, added a jaunty touch to the ensemble, as did her scarlet hair.

As Pamela busied herself collecting cups, saucers, and plates from the cupboard that housed her wedding china, Bettina put the plate of cinnamon rolls on the table and removed the foil. Then she glanced at the *Register*.

"Did you read it yet?" she asked.

"Just the headline. Then you rang the bell."

Pamela poured two cups of coffee, delivered them to the table, and backtracked for the sugar bowl and cream pitcher. Meanwhile Bettina set out the plates, silverware, and napkins and filled the cream pitcher from the carton in the refrigerator.

"Esme was taken into custody and questioned, but she hasn't been charged," Bettina said as she sat down, "and Tassie was estranged from a rich plastic surgeon named Mervyn Fossil. Her full name is Anastasia Huntington-Fossil." She pulled the sugar bowl closer. "I only know those things from the *Register*, because Clayborn didn't have time to talk to me in person this morning."

She made a disgusted snort that resembled a cat sneezing. "Obviously he had lots of time to talk to Marcy Brewer, last night even, but me? No." In an unconvincing attempt to imitate Detective Clayborn's deep rumble, she added, "And it's too late to get anything into this week's *Advocate* anyway."

Bettina snorted again. "Or so he says."

After adding two spoonfuls of sugar to her coffee, she went on. "He *did* tell me, though, that the pie is being analyzed for poison and Chad's body is with the medical examiner, who will check for down in the nasal passages." She paused. "Take one of those cinnamon rolls."

Pamela obliged, transferring the nearest cinnamon roll to her plate. They were spirals of rich-looking pastry, dusted with cinnamon and glistening with sugary glaze—thus perhaps better eaten with a fork than with fingers. She carved a bite-sized piece from the outermost twist of the spiral and conveyed it to her mouth.

The taste didn't disappoint. The pastry was yeasty and buttery, and fragrant with the spice that gave the cinnamon rolls their name. She took a sip of black coffee next, enjoying the hot and bitter contrast.

Bettina had added cream to her coffee, then stirred it

until the pale mocha color was uniform throughout. She had also made considerable inroads into a cinnamon roll, and its spiral had untwisted, revealing inner surfaces dark with their heavier dusting of the spice.

"I can't stop thinking it's my fault Esme was arrested," Bettina said suddenly. She released her fork, and it clanked against her plate. "If I hadn't blurted out everything Esme told us about squatting in the house and her interest in it, there wouldn't have been a motive for Clayborn to latch onto. In fact, he wouldn't even have known about Esme because she disappeared before the police got there."

"She had managed to be pretty inconspicuous in general," Pamela commented. "The neighbors hadn't noticed her coming and going when the 'hauntings' were taking place because she didn't drive a car. She just rode her bike and parked it inside."

Bettina sighed and closed her eyes. Her head drooped forward until her face was hidden by her scarlet hair, whose wavy tendrils seemed as dispirited as the woman herself. "If they charge her with murder, I'll be to blame."

"We all will," Pamela said. "I'm sure we all told Detective Clayborn the same thing." She took a sip of coffee. "But maybe Esme really did do it," she added, jolted by the burst of caffeine. "Murder for the sake of one's art might not be something ordinary mortals could understand, but she did seem committed to her music—completing her magnum opus. And there was a pillow in her little nest up in the attic—a down pillow, perhaps. Forensics might be analyzing the down in it at this very minute."

Bettina's head twitched, and she reared back unexpectedly. "Don't say those things!" she exclaimed, her eyes bright with distress. "You're just making me feel worse. If Esme was really the killer, would she have been so open with us?" She picked up her fork, scooped off a large portion of cinnamon roll, and opened her mouth.

Seeking to counterbalance the argument she had just made in favor of Esme's guilt, Pamela murmured, "Of course, there's the pie."

Bettina was chewing, so she substituted a vigorous nod for words.

Pamela elaborated. "It appears that the killer used the pies as gifts to make contact with the victims and get into the house."

Bettina swallowed, nodded again, and spoke. "Both times there were bodies, there were pies."

"Esme was already in the house," Pamela said, though of course Bettina knew that too. "Detective Clayborn told you the latest pie is being analyzed for poison. The pie—both pies—were whole. Tassie was smothered. If the latest pie was meant to poison Chad, and it was still whole, and he was dead anyway . . . ?"

Pamela felt a wrinkle forming between her brows, and she reached up to massage it away. "Whatever the purpose of the pie," she observed, "it definitely looked homemade, and Esme doesn't exactly fit the profile of a home cook."

Bettina did not respond. She seemed content, for now, to set aside the disturbing topic of Esme's possible guilt and focus on the delights of Wilfred's cinnamon rolls and the remains of her coffee. Pamela had barely started on her own cinnamon roll, so for the next few minutes, the only sounds were the clicking of forks against china and the soft clunk as cups, lifted to lips, were replaced on their saucers.

Pamela, however, had not set aside the disturbing

topic of Esme's possible guilt. Esme hadn't been arrested, but were the police perhaps seeking more evidence so they *could* arrest her, rather than searching for other likely suspects?

Bettina served herself another cinnamon roll. She inspected the contents of her cup and twisted around to glance toward the counter where the carafe was sitting.

"A few inches," Pamela said, "and you can have it—or I can make more."

"Do you want more?" Bettina turned back to face Pamela.

"I'm thinking we should drive over to Voorhees House."

"Now? Why?" Bettina's carefully shaped brows contracted in a puzzled frown.

"Neighbors might have seen something yesterday." Pamela paused as Bettina adjusted her expression from puzzled to interested. "Specifically some*one*," she added. "Some*one* carrying a pie."

"So, you really don't think Esme did it!" Bettina brought her hands together in a delighted clap. She stood up, the cinnamon roll forgotten. "Let's go, then. No time like the present, as Wilfred would say. But let's not talk to Win, at least not first. She just goes on and on. Let's see who else we can find, like that Spud."

Pamela stood up too.

"You're not dressed yet!" Bettina sat back down. "So, run upstairs and get dressed. I know it won't take long because you'll just put on the same thing you were wearing yesterday. Wilfred's busy making bread, but I'll call to let him know I'll be a while."

As Pamela headed for the doorway, Bettina rose and stepped toward where the carafe, with its last dab of cold coffee, waited. She transferred it to the stove and lit the burner under it.

As Bettina had predicted, it didn't take Pamela long to dress, though she did trade the previous day's blouse for another in the casual style she preferred. But by the time she returned to the kitchen, Bettina had drunk what was left of the coffee, put the cream away, tucked the foil back over the remaining cinnamon rolls, and rinsed the dishes and silverware. She was seated in her customary chair at the kitchen table watching Ginger bat and stalk an amusing cat toy that was weighted so as to roll in an erratic path.

"Ready?" Pamela inquired, peeking in from the entry. She collected her purse, Bettina did likewise, and they proceeded out the door, down the steps, and across the grass to the driveway and Pamela's serviceable compact.

"I guess Pete took off right after we left last night?" Bettina said after she had settled into the passenger seat and fastened her seat belt. Her tone was the same one might use in commenting on the weather, but Pamela wasn't fooled.

"You've been longing to bring that up, haven't you?" She had inserted her key in the car's ignition, but she turned to face Bettina, suppressing the urge to smile.

"No . . ." The word came out like a defensive *meow*. "I was just making conversation."

"On your pet topic." Pamela laughed. "My romantic future." She turned away, gave the key a quick twist as she stepped on the gas, and backed into the street.

Apparently chastened, Bettina kept her mouth closed and her eyes on the road as Pamela steered the car up

Orchard Street, only speaking once, to point out that everyone's roses looked prettier than ever this year.

Pamela didn't answer, because she had reached the corner and a parked delivery truck was making it hard to see whether the way was clear to turn. As they approached the Co-Op, Bettina tried another conversational gambit.

"Libby Kimble has been very active on Access-Arborville lately," she said, "just rambling about this and that. Have you seen her posts?"

"Not really," Pamela murmured. "I don't look at it that often."

"I don't either, really. But I like to keep track of what people are talking about—for the *Advocate*."

They chatted on and off as Pamela continued en route to their destination.

CHAPTER 19

The strip of grass between the street and sidewalk in front of Spud Birdsall's house was piled high with . . . everything one could imagine: a bicycle with a twisted frame and missing wheel, a battered guitar, decades' worth of old magazines spilling out of tattered cardboard boxes, overstuffed garbage bags in mountainous heaps, and much much more.

Spud's car, no longer parked at the curb, was back in the driveway, which looked very clean after its scrubbing. His garage door was open and a few items stood nearby, an armchair with stuffing bursting from tears in its upholstery and two mismatched floor lamps. The brooding clouds made the day dark and the garage's interior even darker, but a figure could be dimly made out moving around in the gloom.

"It's probably him," Bettina said, and she set out over the pavers that composed the driveway's surface, walking delicately in her strappy high-heeled sandals. Pamela followed.

"Hello?" Bettina called as she approached the spot where the unfortunate armchair sat. "Hello?"

"Who's that?" a voice responded.

In a moment, Spud Birdsall emerged from the depths of the garage, clad as before in a T-shirt, and even sweatier than he had been the last time they spoke with him.

He wiped his brow with a burly forearm and blinked as if bothered by sweat dripping in his eyes. Then he peered at Bettina and said, "Bettina Fraser from the *Arborville Advocate*. What can I do for you today—as if I didn't know?"

His manner was genial enough, and he seemed happy to take a break from his labors.

"What do you think?" Bettina tilted her head flirtatiously and winked.

"I'll take a wild guess and say you're here about Chad Donahue. All the news that fits."

"You may have seen in the *Register* that the police have a suspect, a young woman who was squatting in Voorhees House?"

Spud nodded and laughed. "She might as well have been a ghost," he said. "I sure never would have guessed a live person was in residence."

"I'm wondering"—Bettina leaned close and whispered, implying that Spud might have secrets to impart—"if you noticed anyone next door yesterday, coming and going, anyone who wasn't that poor young woman."

"I wasn't here," Spud said. "I'm on shifts at the water treatment plant. Days sometimes, nights other times."

"How about your wife?" Bettina was still whispering. "Did she mention seeing or hearing anything out of the ordinary?"

Spud stepped back. "No—uh, no. Definitely not."

"Maybe she just didn't think you'd be interested in neighborhood doings, after a long shift at the water treatment plant." Bettina's soothing tone suggested that she herself would spare a tired husband inconsequential chatter.

"Umm." Spud nodded. "She was . . . I mean she is . . . thoughtful that way."

"Is she here now?" Bettina asked brightly, shifting her gaze from Spud to the house. "I'd love to talk to her. I think you mentioned that she enjoyed the *Advocate*."

"No, oh no." Spud shook his head spasmodically. "She's busy, very busy. Always out somewhere doing something." When Bettina didn't answer, he wiped his brow again. "The police came here though, first thing this morning. They asked me—*us*, I should say—the same thing you asked. But no, we certainly didn't have anything to report, no strange cars coming around or like that."

A soft rumble overhead, like an echo of a faraway explosion, interrupted the conversation, and all three of them tilted their heads to study the dark, low-hanging clouds.

"Sounds like we're going to get our rain," Spud commented.

He had no sooner spoken than a few huge drops landed on the driveway. The drops began to fall faster, releasing a moist, earthy aroma from the surrounding grass and shrubbery.

"Ladies, you're welcome to join me in the garage."

Spud edged toward the wide doorway and the sheltering space beyond.

"Thanks, but I think we'll be off." Bettina's coiffure was already beginning to wilt. She turned and hurried toward the curb, her delicate sandals splashing through the puddles already forming on the driveway.

Pamela hurried too, faster than Bettina, and was waiting behind the steering wheel with the passenger-side door open by the time Bettina reached the car.

"I don't suppose you want to see if we can talk to Win," Pamela said once Bettina had settled into her seat.

"No! I'm soaked, and my shoes are completely ruined," Bettina moaned.

Pamela was wet too, but since her outfit and toilette were less complicated, the rain's effect was less dramatic. The curls that formed Bettina's careful bouffant were now limp tendrils, and the crisp linen of her slacks-and-shirt ensemble was damp and creased.

Wilfred Fraser opened the Frasers' front door as Pamela eased her car into a spot behind Bettina's Toyota. In a moment he had stepped out onto the porch, wearing an apron and unfurling a large umbrella.

"Oh, thank goodness," Bettina sighed when she caught sight of him, "though I don't think I could get any wetter."

When Wilfred reached the car, it was decided that he would escort Pamela home under the umbrella and return for Bettina.

"Dear wife, and Pamela," he said, "you will both change into dry clothes. And then," he added with a cheer that counteracted the wet misery of their state, "we will all sit down to lunch."

Pamela crossed Orchard Street again fifteen minutes later, with dry hair, wearing dry clothes, and sheltered by her own umbrella. When Wilfred responded to the doorbell, she didn't even have to step over the threshold for proof that Wilfred's bread-baking venture had been a success. The tantalizing aroma of yeasty dough baked to crusty perfection had wafted all the way to the Frasers' front door.

"Bettina will be down shortly," Wilfred said as he escorted Pamela to the kitchen, the tantalizing aroma intensifying the closer they got.

The source of the aroma sat in splendor on the high counter that separated the cooking area of the kitchen from the eating area. Loaf-shaped, with a domed top crust burnished golden-brown from the oven, it rested on a wooden cutting board with a gleaming bread knife nearby. The scrubbed pine table had been set with Bettina's flatware and orange linen napkins, arranged on orange raffia placemats.

On the stretch of counter near the stove sat a jar of mayonnaise, a plate of lettuce leaves and tomato slices, and another plate of sliced turkey breast. A package of bacon waited near the stove, and a very large skillet occupied a front burner on the stovetop.

"Club sandwiches coming right up," Wilfred announced. "Please have a seat in the meantime."

Pamela lowered herself into one of the chairs that surrounded the pine table, and Wilfred continued on until he reached the stove. Once there, he twisted the knob that brought the flame under the skillet to life and opened the package of bacon. One by one, he lifted the long, fat-streaked strips from the slab and laid them carefully in the skillet.

Bettina arrived then, her scarlet hair restored to its customary pouf and her makeup fresh. She had traded the damp linen slacks and shirt for a fetching jumpsuit in a flattering shade of powder blue.

"Dear wife!" Wilfred turned to greet her. "Dried off and more beautiful than ever."

He did not step away from the stove, however, because the bacon had already begun to sizzle. Almost instantly, the kitchen was infused with the seductive aroma of fat pork charring on a hot griddle.

"Who wants to slice some bread?" Wilfred called from his post.

"I will!" Pamela jumped to her feet.

"Nine slices," Wilfred said, "because I'm making triple-deckers. But don't cut them too thick." He turned around as she approached the high counter. "And you might want to move the cutting board. It's awkward to slice on that counter."

Pamela rejoined Bettina at the pine table, setting the cutting board in the spot with no placemat.

She made short work of the slicing project. Wilfred's special bread knife glided smoothly through the golden-brown crust, each slice falling away to reveal its pale, fine-textured interior. Meanwhile, the aroma of the frying bacon was becoming more intense, hinting at the crispy state Wilfred was aiming for.

When nine perfect slices had been carved from the loaf and stacked next to the remaining uncut portion, Pamela delivered the cutting board and its cargo to the counter where the other sandwich components were waiting. Wilfred at this point was lifting the bacon piece by piece from the bubbling fat that had accumulated in the skillet and setting the pieces on folded paper towels.

Pamela watched as he assembled the sandwiches. First he arranged three plates from Bettina's sage-green pottery in a row on the counter. He applied mayonnaise to three slices of bread, set one on each plate, and layered on sliced turkey and bacon. Then he added a second slice of bread, with mayonnaise on both sides. On that slice, he arranged a few leaves of lettuce and a few slices of tomato. Finally he added a last slice of bread, with plenty of mayonnaise on its bottom side. After cutting each sandwich in half on the diagonal, he speared each half with a toothpick that featured a festive cellophane frill.

"Just like Hyler's, no?" He laughed. "And wait till you see what we're drinking."

Pamela had noticed a blender on the counter near the refrigerator, an appliance that she knew didn't usually come out of its cupboard unless required for a recipe. She had also noticed three tall glasses staged near the blender.

"Pamela," Wilfred said, "if you will deliver the plates to the table, I will join you and Bettina in a very few minutes."

As Pamela set out with two plates, Wilfred opened the refrigerator and then the freezer. A minute later, an intense whirring sound emanated from behind her. She set the plates down, one in front of Bettina and one at Wilfred's place, and returned for the third sandwich. She slipped past Wilfred and then watched as he lifted the blender's mixing chamber from its base and tipped it over one of the tall glasses.

A pale, chilly liquid, quite thick, surged forth and filled the glass, whose exterior instantly frosted.

"You made milkshakes!" Pamela exclaimed. "Just like Hyler's."

"We'll see," Wilfred replied, "but nothing ventured, nothing gained."

In no time at all, lunch preparations were complete, and everyone was settled in their chairs with sandwiches and milkshakes before them.

Wilfred, still in his capacious chef's apron, surveyed his creations with a satisfied smile and uttered a hearty *"Bon appétit!"*

"Better than Hyler's," Bettina declared after pulling her frosty glass close to sample her milkshake—Wilfred had even provided straws.

It *was* better, Pamela agreed, though not by much, since Hyler's also used whole milk and locally made ice cream in their shakes. The club sandwich, too, surpassed the version of that classic offered by Arborville's venerable luncheonette. Undoubtedly the homemade bread, with its tender yet substantial crumb and just-baked aroma, contributed to the sandwich's success, and the sliced turkey was enlivened by the salty bacon with its hint of char. Wilfred had sought out local tomatoes that guaranteed a fresh, acidic tang, and the crisp lettuce lent a contrasting texture. The mayonnaise, liberally applied, melded all the flavors together with its rich creaminess.

No one spoke as sandwich halves were lifted from plates and rapidly reduced to mayonnaise-streaked crusts, which were then devoured as well. Sips of milkshake served as a kind of intermission before the remaining sandwich halves were addressed. Pamela was

several bites into her second half, savoring the inter-
play of bacon and tomato against the background of
the less-assertive turkey, before her thoughts turned to
that morning's adventure.

Something had occurred to her as she'd hurried
down Spud Birdsall's driveway in the rain. Because
the side of Voorhees House, rather than the front, faced
Beech Street, anyone opening the back door of Voorhees House would have a direct view of that driveway,
the driveway Spud had been so industriously washing
the first time Pamela and Bettina called on him.

She swallowed the bite she was chewing in a huge
gulp and blurted out, "What if Spud Birdsall is the
killer?"

Bettina's mouth was full and she couldn't speak, but
she turned to Pamela, signaling disbelief and amazement with wide eyes. When she managed to swallow,
she said, "Why on earth?"

Not sure whether Bettina meant why she would think
that or why Spud would do that, Pamela frowned as she
sorted through the jumble of thoughts that had invaded
her mind once she recalled the insight she'd had while
escaping from the sudden downpour.

She decided to start with, "He was so evasive about
his wife—nervous when we asked about her. And at one
point he referred to her in the past tense, then quickly
corrected himself."

"Oh, my goodness!" Bettina lowered the remains of
her sandwich half to her plate as Wilfred, too, paused
in his eating. "I never thought of that," she breathed.
"Spud's wife could be dead." Her eyes widened again.
"He killed her right there on his driveway, and he was
power-washing the evidence away!"

"Yes." Pamela nodded enthusiastically. "That's what

I'm thinking. And remember how he slammed the trunk of his car closed when we showed up? Something was in there, something big and bulky and wrapped up tightly."

"Big enough to be a body?" Wilfred leaned toward Pamela, who was sitting opposite him at the table.

"It filled up almost the whole trunk," she said in response, then she turned to Bettina. "Picture Spud's driveway in your mind. Did you notice that the view from the back door of Voorhees House is a view of that driveway? And there's that little porch off the back door. People take out trash and garbage and recycling at night, and Tassie or Chad—or both—might have stepped out the back door quite late when Spud thought he was unobserved."

"And Tassie or Chad—or both—witnessed Spud killing his wife . . ." The remains of her sandwich forgotten, Bettina stared straight ahead, as if picturing the grisly scene.

"Or more likely, he killed her inside," Pamela cut in. "Otherwise they would have heard screaming. But he drags the body out onto the driveway and into the garage to package it up for disposal. And one or both of them see that, and he knows they know his secret, so . . ."

"Oh, my goodness," Bettina whispered. "And he seemed so nice. And she liked the *Advocate*. Such a shame."

"Seeming nice could be his cover," Pamela said. "We don't know why he might have killed his wife, but as far as killing Tassie and Chad goes, he certainly had motive and opportunity. And means? Everybody has pillows."

"He was big," Bettina added, "and he seemed quite

strong, easily able to overpower a man or a woman and smother them with a pillow. I like the idea of Spud Birdsall as the killer much better than Esme—or Edmund McClintock, for that matter. And obviously now that he himself has been killed, we can rule out Chad."

Bettina picked up a stray sliver of bacon from her plate. She tucked it between two bits of crust and transferred the result to her mouth. Only crumbs remained on her plate now, and Pamela and Wilfred had also finished off the remains of their sandwiches, though Pamela's glass still held an inch of melted milkshake. She slurped it through her straw as Bettina pulled her own nearly empty glass closer and Wilfred, dispensing with his straw, tilted his glass to his lips.

"How about refills on the milkshakes?" he inquired after setting his glass down with a pleased sigh.

"Not for me," Pamela said, "but they were delicious. I don't think I'll be hungry again for a long time."

"Dear wife?" Wilfred glanced toward Bettina.

"Well . . ." She drew the word out as her lips curved into a smile. "Maybe a half . . . ?"

"Your wish is my command." Wilfred smiled in return and hoisted himself to his feet. The sounds of the refrigerator, and then the freezer, opening and closing were followed a few moments later by the whirr of the blender.

"I hope it's Spud," Bettina said suddenly. "That all makes sense, what you figured out." The smiling anticipation of the milkshake had vanished. Bettina raised her hands to her cheeks and regarded Pamela with troubled eyes. "I feel so bad about Esme, what she's going through, and it's all my fault."

"It's not!" Bettina had lowered her hands to the table, and Pamela reached for the nearest one. "We all heard what Esme said, and I'm sure we all reported exactly the same thing to Detective Clayborn."

"I was the first one though," Bettina murmured.

Wilfred had overheard the conversation, and he weighed in as he made his way back to the table, half-full milkshake glass in hand.

"Esme isn't the killer," he said. "I'm sure of that. She doesn't seem like someone who could overpower a normal-sized woman, let alone a man." He set the glass down in front of Bettina and added, "This Spud, Spud Birdsall, is it? He sounds much more likely as a suspect."

"We'll talk to Win tomorrow." Pamela squeezed Bettina's hand. "She's so nosy she probably knows all about Spud's relationship with his wife." She thought for a moment and went on. "I'll do all the talking. Don't worry, and if she goes for the notebook, I'll point out that the article has already appeared, and so you don't need any more details about the haunting."

CHAPTER 20

By the time Pamela crossed the street to her own house, the rain had passed, but the sidewalks and asphalt were still wet. The grass sparkled with moisture in the sunlight, and the air was soft and humid. She collected her mail, sorted all but the water bill into the recycling basket, and proceeded up the stairs to her office.

An email from Penny had arrived while she was out, and anticipating a newsy update on the Guatemalan adventure, Pamela leaned back in her desk chair and opened the message. She was not disappointed. Penny described how the hundreds of plastic bottles, collected over the past year, were in the process of being filled with sand, and how a concrete slab had been poured to form the school's floor. Photos illustrated the description: volunteers from Aaron's group working side by side with the village's schoolchildren on the bottle-filling task, and Aaron giving a jaunty thumbs-up as he posed next to the completed concrete slab.

Pamela was relieved to see that Penny was apparently not keeping herself informed on current doings in Arborville, and she felt no need to reveal the medical examiner's discovery that Tassie Hunt had been murdered or the fact that there had been a second murder at Voorhees House. Her response said simply that she loved the photos, was glad things were going well, and looked forward to another update.

Work for the magazine waited, one more article to evaluate, but the sun had set the shades at her office windows aglow. A summer afternoon, fresh after a rain and before the heat of July and August took hold, couldn't be spent entirely indoors. Besides, the larder needed restocking. The pot of chili from Monday night had provided many dinners, but it was time for a change, and cheese and salad-makings were running low besides.

After rereading Penny's message, Pamela pushed back from her desk and headed downstairs. From the closet, she collected a few of the canvas grocery totes that Nell, in her crusade against paper and plastic bags, had provided long ago.

An hour later, Pamela was at home again, unpacking her groceries at her kitchen table. She stowed cat food in the cupboard and perishables in the refrigerator, including a tilapia filet, a pork chop, and a package of chicken thighs.

It was too early to sit down with her knitting, so she climbed the stairs to her office once again and opened the Word file labeled "Zero Waste." Its full title proved to be "Zero Waste: The Future of Fashion," and it profiled five designers active in the sustainable fashion movement. One goal was creating garments whose manufacturing resulted in less fabric ending up on the cutting-room floor.

Designs might use lengths of fabric—squares or rectangles—nearly as they came from the loom, or pattern pieces could be laid out in a way that resembled a jigsaw puzzle, with hardly any fabric discarded. Dyes derived from natural sources were favored, as well as fabrics whose manufacture didn't pollute or require energy derived from fossil fuels.

The article was illustrated with photographs from a fashion show for which the author had served as a consultant. Some designs had an angular Asian feel, others were almost Grecian. Colors were often muted, solid earth tones, or variegated in a way that suggested an Impressionist landscape.

Pamela closed the "Zero Waste" file, opened her "Evaluations" file, and wrote up an enthusiastic recommendation. The sky was still light behind the shades at her office windows, but darkness came late on June nights.

Two hours later, she had fed the cats, eaten her own dinner of sautéed tilapia and brown rice, and was sitting on the sofa watching a sedate British mystery as she knitted. She had finished the donkey she was working on and now a new one, pink this time, was underway.

"I feel so foolish!" Bettina exclaimed by way of a greeting the next morning. Pamela had opened her front door to reveal her friend standing on the porch.

Pamela waved Bettina in with a gesture and waited expectantly for an explanation.

"Just so foolish," she repeated as she stepped over the threshold. Feeling foolish had not prevented her from selecting an outfit suited to the bright summer day. The shoes that now stood on the parquet of Pamela's entry were dainty kitten heels in a soft shade of peach that coordinated with the peach-and-cream swirls patterning the fabric of her stylish wrap dress.

"Do you want to sit down?" Pamela asked. The time was nine a.m., and the plan had been for Bettina to pick Pamela up for their visit to Win Colley's house to ask about Spud's relationship with his wife.

"No-o-o," Bettina moaned. Catrina, lounging in the patch of sunlight on the entry's thrift-shop carpet, raised her head to stare at Bettina. "Let's just . . . go."

"You read it, I suppose," she added as they headed down Pamela's front walk. "I don't see it in your driveway."

"The *Advocate*?" Pamela asked, though she knew that was the answer. "I thought your article sounded good." She quoted, "'Voorhees House is empty again, but neighbors say, Not so fast.'"

Bettina snorted. "And meanwhile, the news has come out in the *Register* that Tassie Hunt did *not* die of fright—though *I* never believed she had—but was actually *murdered*, along with her boyfriend. But Clayborn didn't have time to talk to me, and now nobody in town is going to take the *Advocate* seriously as a news source at all."

Pamela doubted that anyone in Arborville counted on the *Advocate* for actual news, fond of it though they might be for other reasons. But she murmured a few comforting words as they crossed the street to where Bettina's faithful Toyota waited in the Frasers' driveway. Soon they were on their way.

* * *

Win Colley seemed happy to have company. Twittering her welcome, she pushed aside some of the needlepoint pillows that crowded the sofa and urged Pamela and Bettina to make themselves comfortable. She herself took a seat in the armchair that faced the window with the view of the Voorhees House porch—only to pop up again instantly.

"You'd like coffee, I'm sure!" she chirped and scurried toward the kitchen before they could answer.

In a few moments, she was back, bearing a tray that held three china mugs and a matching cream and sugar set. "I remembered," she said, focusing her alert stare first on Pamela and then on Bettina, "one of you likes cream and sugar, but I forget which one. Anyway . . ."

She lowered the tray to the coffee table. "I don't like cream and sugar in my coffee, but I could pull a chair up anyway, closer to you, instead of sitting all the way across the room." She started back toward the kitchen but turned after a few steps.

"I saw your article about the haunting. I love the *Advocate*, did I tell you that already? So happy to see it on my driveway this morning. And you described the situation so well, the lights, the sounds, and your opening line—so clever: 'Voorhees House is empty again, but neighbors say, Not so fast.'" She blinked rapidly and peered at Bettina. "You're going to do a sequel, aren't you? *The Haunting*, Part 2. That's why you came back. And I'm ready. I've been listening and watching."

From the direction of the kitchen came the hooting sound of a kettle in full boil. As Win spun away and hurried from the room, Bettina turned to Pamela with a look of despair. But by the time Win returned with a tall carafe and began to fill the mugs, she had composed herself.

"I'm sorry to say my article was a little out-of-date," Bettina said. "You may have seen yesterday's *Register* . . ."

Win had finished pouring the coffee and was now perched on a wooden chair that she had pulled up close to the coffee table. She reached for her own mug and took a sip.

"I glanced at it, yes." Her head bobbed forward in a quick nod, as if she was pecking at something.

"The lights and weird sounds seem to have been explained . . ." Bettina let her voice trail off as if waiting for a reaction. When none was forthcoming, she went on. "Someone was living in the house—unauthorized, so squatting, actually—and it wasn't ghosts that were responsible for the lights and sounds."

"And she's the killer, isn't she?"

Bettina raised a hand as if to ward off that idea and murmured, "Uh, we're not . . ."

But Win ignored her. Words, high-pitched and breathless, poured out. "Ghosts can coexist with people. The squatter doesn't rule them out—they were there long before she was because I know there have been deaths in that house before. And now, more deaths, two more, means more ghosts, new ghosts."

"Perhaps . . ." Bettina sighed and dipped a spoon into the sugar bowl.

"We were hoping . . ." Pamela spoke up quickly, aiming to steer the conversation toward the topic they'd come to discuss. "*Bettina* was hoping," she corrected herself, "that she could talk to the neighbor on the other side of Voorhees House this morning too."

"Spud is hopeless," Win declared. "Never notices anything."

Seemingly happy to let Pamela take over, Bettina focused on the important step of adding just the right amount of cream to her coffee.

"Spud's wife?"

"I haven't seen her for days."

"None of my business, of course"—Pamela raised a self-deprecating hand to her chest—"but do you think they get along?"

"Well! None of mine, either, and I try to keep myself to myself, but he's a slob, and she complained all the time about all the junk he collected. Maybe she finally just couldn't take it any longer."

"Or maybe he couldn't stand the complaining," Bettina suggested after they left Win's and were walking toward where the Toyota waited. She unlocked the passenger-side door for Pamela, but as Pamela was about to lower herself into her seat, she happened to glance past Voorhees House. The pile of trash and plastic garbage bags at Spud's curb had doubled in size since the previous day. As she watched, Spud appeared from farther up the driveway pushing a wheelbarrow overflowing with odds and ends, like flowerpots and misshapen baskets.

He caught sight of her and waved. Pamela returned the wave but stayed where she was, half in and half out of the car. Bettina, however, had noticed Spud too. She raised her arm in a friendly greeting and started toward him, calling hello.

He let go of the wheelbarrow, paused to steady its unwieldy cargo, and reached the sidewalk in a few long strides. Looking particularly cheerful, he folded his brawny arms across his chest and watched Bettina advance.

Pamela wasn't sure what her friend had in mind, but Bettina did have a nose for news, though "Voorhees House Neighbor Admits Triple Murder to *Advocate* Reporter" seemed an unlikely headline. Still, abandoning the idea of sitting, she stepped onto the grass, closing the car door behind her. A few moments later, she was standing next to Bettina, listening as Spud listed the many items that had left his garage, basement, and backyard and were now waiting for the town's trash collectors to carry them away.

"It feels good," he said, "like starting life over. You get to a point where you ask yourself, What do I need? What things do I need? What *people* do I need? How can I free myself of the unnecessary—the *burdensome*, even—to make space for the necessary?"

He bent down to make eye contact with Bettina, who was a great deal shorter than he was. "Do you know what I mean?" He repeated the words, in a more demanding tone. "*Do you know what I mean?*"

Bettina hopped back. "Of course," she said.

"My life . . ." He wiped his sweaty forehead with a huge hand. "My life had gotten out of hand." His voice coarsened. What had earlier struck Pamela as cheer now appeared more like manic energy.

Bettina seemed unable to suppress her reporterly impulses. With an attentive head-tilt that promised both interest and sympathy, she said, "Out of hand? In what way?"

"My wife." Spud's eyes enlarged, a striking effect in his sunburnt face, given that his irises were the palest of blue. "She hated my things. She hated *me*. I had to do something." He reached out as if to seize Bettina's arm, but his hand halted in midair. "It was either my wife or my stuff. One of them had to go."

He laughed, a sound that was more like a bark. "Or both."

"Oh, my!" Bettina turned to Pamela, her eyes as wide as Spud's. She raised a hand to her mouth. Turning back to Spud, she said, "We should let you get on with your work . . ." and began to edge away.

"She did have a point," Spud added, sounding calmer, "and it's nice to be able to fit my car in the garage again."

Just then, another voice joined the conversation, a female voice, floating their way from the open doorway of Spud's house. Framed by the storybook façade, with its peaked roof and half-timbered gables, was a woman, pleasant-looking, smiling, and holding a frosty glass in one hand and a towel in the other.

"Sweetie," the voice repeated, growing louder as the woman got closer. "You're working so hard I thought you'd like some lemonade."

"My wife," Spud explained, giving her a fond look. "She came back."

"Well, happy ending there, I guess," Bettina commented after they had said goodbye and were on their way down the sidewalk. "Spud's wife isn't dead, and she's returned, and he can fit his car in the garage again. I guess I could have asked her about the ghosts. Win Colley seems to think that story still has legs."

"There goes our theory about the murders though." Pamela sighed. "It made so much sense too."

They didn't talk again until they were settled back in the Toyota and cruising along Arborville Avenue. As Hyler's came into view, Bettina spoke up suddenly.

"Maybe Edmund did it!"

Pamela had been daydreaming, and it took her a moment to absorb Bettina's statement. Then she realized that, since Spud was no longer a suspect, Bettina had been reviewing other candidates.

"I know you don't think it was Esme," she said, "and neither do I. She's such a delicate little thing."

"I think it really could be Edmund." Bettina signaled her conviction by tightening her jaw and gripping the steering wheel more firmly. "He was so vocal about protecting Voorhees House from 'remuddling.' And he got so frantic when he was talking about it that day we visited him, almost like he had some alter ego that might be capable of anything." The light at the big intersection changed to red, and she stomped down on the brake.

"He did seem changeable," Pamela agreed. "Gentlemanly one minute, and then . . ." She recalled his breathless rant about the evils of modern home design, and the way he had buried his face in his hands and whimpered at its conclusion. When he'd lowered his hands once again, the look in his eyes had been alarming.

"I just thought of something!" Bettina squealed. The light turned green, and the Toyota lurched forward.

"Please, be careful . . ." Pamela reached out a soothing hand.

Bettina swerved to the curb in front of Borough Hall. She whirled to face Pamela. "Pete could be in danger if Edmund is the killer!" she exclaimed. "Edmund might not understand that he's only doing clean-up work, not 'remuddling'."

The thought of Pete being in danger caused a pang, and Bettina's alarm was catching. Pamela forgot to breathe for a moment, long enough to be aware that her pulse was ticking faster than usual. But then an image rose in her mind—Edmund in his Victorian garb squaring off against a handyman whose athletic build made it clear that he was up to the physical labor involved in his line of work.

"I'm not sure Edmund would be able to overpower Pete," she said, "especially if the weapon was a pillow. And Chad looked pretty fit as well, though I didn't really stare. A dead body isn't a sight to linger over."

"I guess you're right . . . about not needing to worry about Pete." Bettina depressed the gas pedal with the toe of her dainty shoe and eased back into the flow of traffic.

Five minutes later, the Toyota was parked in its customary spot next to Wilfred's ancient Mercedes, and Pamela and Bettina were standing at the end of the Frasers' driveway chatting. Pamela was about to set off across the street when Bettina nodded toward Richard Larkin's house.

"He's due back from Maine tomorrow, isn't he?" she said.

Pamela knew that, but she shrugged and murmured, "I don't know. Is he?" There was no telling how Bettina would interpret any sign that she had been keeping track of Richard's travel plans.

"Wilfred was out with Woofus last evening, and he talked to Sybil. She's expecting him around dinnertime."

"It's too bad Penny had to leave when she did," Pamela said. "I hope Sybil wasn't too bored, cat-sitting for a week in Arborville all by herself."

Bettina lifted her wrist to consult her pretty gold watch. "I should get going," she observed. "I'm covering a benefit luncheon for the *Advocate*. The seniors are raising money for the county's literacy program, and an author from Timberley is coming to speak."

CHAPTER 21

Pamela was standing on her porch collecting her mail from the mailbox when the faint sound of a phone ringing deep within her house reached her ears. She quickly twisted her key in the lock, pushed her door open, and hurried to the kitchen, only to discover that her caller was Bettina.

"Didn't I just see you?" she asked with a laugh.

"I thought of something, right after you left." Bettina sounded breathless. "Tassie and Chad were both married before. In fact, Tassie was technically still married. Maybe her husband, or whoever Chad was divorced from, was resentful, resentful enough to commit murder—*two* murders, actually. Tassie and Chad, or Chad and Tassie—the spouse who left and the new love, blamed for the spouse's flight."

"Certainly the police would have interviewed them," Pamela said.

"Maybe they didn't ask the right questions though, not the kind of questions they'd ask a suspect."

"Hmm. True." Pamela sensed a thoughtful wrinkle forming between her brows. "Tassie originally seemed to have died from natural causes, and right after the medical examiner revealed that she was murdered, Chad was murdered too. So the police now consider Esme their prime suspect and are presumably trying to gather evidence to bring her back in and charge her."

Bettina jumped in. "Yes! Why would they backtrack to identify and interview other possible suspects?"

"We have to see what we can find out about them," Pamela said, "and, most important, we have to discover whether they have alibis for when the killings took place."

"Her husband—still her husband because they were only 'estranged'—is a rich plastic surgeon. That was in the *Register*."

"Mervyn Fossil," Pamela added. "It's a hard name to forget. I don't think any information has appeared about Chad's ex-wife."

"Not that I know of." Bettina's tone implied a shrug. "But we have to start somewhere. Mervyn Fossil should be easy to locate."

"I think we should talk to Esme first though." Before Bettina could ask why, Pamela went on. "If we're going to be looking for alibis—or lack of alibis—we need a more specific sense of when the killings occurred. And assuming the same person killed both Tassie and Chad—"

"Probably," Bettina cut in. "The method was apparently the same. At least, just like with Tassie, there were no obvious signs of foul play, but he was most definitely dead."

Pamela took up the thought again. "Chad's death

should be easier to pinpoint because it happened after Esme had taken up squatting in the house again."

"So we talk to her about her schedule for last Wednesday." Bettina's voice carried a lilt of excitement.

"When she's not squatting in the attic of Voorhees House, she lives in a commune in Haversack. I suppose it has an address." As an afterthought, Pamela added, "Her last name is Grindale."

"I'll poke around," Bettina said. "I can get access to some police records through the *Advocate*. I'm sure Clayborn got her contact information."

"Off to Haversack at two o'clock, then?" Pamela asked. "And I'll drive."

The address, when they found it, proved to be a house dating from an era before the malls spelled the demise of downtown Haversack. Once, prosperous people would have lived in the wood-frame houses that lined Stafford Street. They would have walked or taken a short bus ride to a downtown that offered nice things: shops and offices and restaurants, even a movie theater. Now those prosperous people lived farther out, in other towns, and they got in their cars to drive to the malls, and not very many nice things were left in downtown Haversack.

The house where Esme lived was rambling and ramshackle, with a weedy yard and a sagging porch furnished with a dusty sofa. Bettina rang the doorbell, a discolored plastic button embedded in a tarnished brass plaque, and the door was opened by a young man wearing cutoff jeans and a faded T-shirt.

Behind him stretched a long hallway with a worn

wooden floor, uncarpeted. Doorways revealed shadowy rooms with curtained windows off to each side.

"We're looking for Esme Grindale," Bettina ventured. "Is she home?"

The young man stared for a moment, then he said, "Who?"

"Esme Grindale," Bettina repeated. "Does she live here?"

He shrugged and stepped away from the door, leaving it ajar.

Bettina shrugged too, and turned to Pamela. But then Esme emerged from a doorway at the end of the hallway, a wraithlike apparition in a pale, shapeless dress and bare feet.

"Hello?" she said, sounding curious but not surprised. "Something told me I had visitors."

"I'm Bettina"—Bettina summoned her most comforting tone—"and this is Pamela. We met you—"

"Wednesday night at Voorhees House." Esme completed the thought for her. "I *do* remember."

"Yes, yes." Bettina nodded, setting her earrings, pearls that dangled from little gold rings, in motion.

She paused. Was she wondering what to say next? Pamela wondered. They hadn't actually discussed what their rationale would be for quizzing Esme about her schedule that day. But Bettina was seldom at a loss for words.

"I know the police have gone over all this with you," Bettina said, again in her most comforting tone, "but as the chief reporter for the *Arborville Advocate*, I like to make sure my readers can trust me to double-check my facts."

"Oh . . . okay." Esme shrugged, as acquiescent as an obedient child.

"Maybe we could sit?" Bettina eyed the porch sofa, suspiciously. "Or go inside?"

Esme made a noncommittal gesture, headed for the sofa, and lowered herself onto its dusty upholstery as Bettina perched gingerly on the edge of a cushion. Pamela, wearing her usual jeans, was less squeamish. The view beyond the weathered porch railing was of the sidewalk and the sunbaked street. A pack of teenagers on bikes careened by, shouting to each other and doing wheelies.

"What I'm wondering," Bettina said, once the lively crowd had passed, "is what time Chad was actually killed. The body was there at about nine p.m., when we were there. But how long had it been there before that?"

Esme had turned toward Bettina, and Pamela couldn't see her face. A long moment passed. When she spoke, her childlike voice was tinged with wondering amazement.

"You mean, you don't think I'm the killer?"

"It doesn't seem likely." Bettina's kindly expression seemed intended to inspire trust. When she went on, it was to ask, "Would it be accurate to say that you weren't aware of Chad's body in the dining room until my dog alerted us?"

"Of course I wasn't aware!" Suddenly lively, Esme sat up straight and glanced from Bettina to Pamela. Focusing again on Bettina, she said, "Do you think I'd have just stayed in the house with a . . . corpse . . . and not called the police?"

"Why did you vanish then, before they came?"

"Things seemed . . . complicated. It would have been

different if I'd been the one to find him . . ." She closed her eyes and thought for a moment. "It would have been like I couldn't possibly have had anything to do with it, but now . . ."

Bettina seized one of Esme's pale hands. "How long had you been in the house before we came on Wednesday?"

"Since about noon," Esme said. "And I came in through the back door because, like I told you before, the back door doesn't actually lock very securely. So, coming in the back door, I had to pass through the dining room on the way to the attic, and at noon on Wednesday, there was no body in the dining room."

"He'd been coming around though, while you were coming around. I guess he had no idea he was sharing the house with someone else?"

"He wasn't sleeping there," Esme said. "If he came, it was usually in the evening, checking on things or dropping things off. I could see his car from the attic windows."

"What time in the evening?" Bettina asked.

Esme lifted a delicate shoulder in a shrug. "About six thirty. I suppose he came from work, whatever his work was."

"So that means . . ." Bettina shifted her gaze from Esme to Pamela, perhaps to make sure the import of what she was about to say wasn't lost on her co-sleuth. "That means Chad was killed sometime between six-thirty and nine p.m."—she looked back at Esme—"while you were in the attic."

"It's two floors up." Esme shrugged again. "I had no idea what was going on. I'm glad. I would have been creeped out."

No one said anything for a bit. A pair of chatting

women pushing strollers provided a brief distraction as they lurched aside to let a skateboarder pass. Pamela was thinking that, since they now knew Chad had been killed between six-thirty and nine, it was time to thank Esme and take their leave. But Esme spoke up again suddenly, though staring straight ahead and seemingly addressing herself.

"What will happen to Voorhees House now?"

"There must be an heir . . ." Bettina's raised eyebrow and puzzled lip-twist undermined the certainty implied by her words.

Esme seemed uninterested in following up that conversational thread. "I'll probably never be able to finish my 'Voorhees Suite,' " she murmured, without shifting her focus. "But"—her tone lightened, and she swiveled to face Bettina—"I have a new project now."

Without waiting for a response, she jumped to her feet.

"Come inside," she sang out, as cheerful now as she had been downcast moments earlier. "This one is all about the voices of the vegetable kingdom!"

Pamela glanced at Bettina, who shrugged and then nodded. Esme had already stepped into the shadowy hallway, leaving the front door wide open. Pamela and Bettina followed her over the worn wooden floor and past two doorways through which a few pieces of furniture were visible, similar in age and condition to the sofa on the porch.

"Back here," Esme called and swerved toward a third doorway at the very end of the hallway.

Pamela and Bettina continued on and found themselves in a room that was empty but for a long table, actually a battered door supported at each end by sawhorses. Laid out along the table was an assortment of vegetables and fruits. Most were curious knobby things, though Pamela recognized a few apples and a pear.

"Dragon fruit," Esme explained, pointing to a magenta oblong whose glowing surface featured random green shoots. "Fennel root, rambutan, papaya . . ."

Her hand hovered over a squat globe, pale green, sprouting stubs of clipped-off tendrils. Then it moved to a cluster of smaller globes, dark red and bristling with sharp spikes, and a large oval object, yellow and melonlike. Warty squash, leathery tubers, and a long skinny eggplant were also part of the arrangement.

A thin cable plugged into each vegetable and fruit ran to a boxlike device in their midst, matte black and studded with knobs. It featured, behind a glass panel, something that resembled the tuning dial on a radio.

"A synthesizer," Esme explained, pointing to the device. "It lets me turn the biorhythms of, say, a rutabaga into music. When I touch a vegetable or fruit, I complete an electrical circuit and trigger a sound." Her hand rested on the dragon fruit, and a quavering treble hum filled the air.

Pamela leaned forward to study the dragon fruit. "Would one of them make a sound if I touched it?" she inquired, quite fascinated by the idea of hearing the voice of even something as mundane as a potato.

"Try it," came Esme's voice from behind her.

Bettina leaned forward too and extended an experimental finger toward the eggplant. As she stroked it, the quavering treble hum was replaced by a shrill squeal. Bettina retracted her hand, and the room was silent.

"Amazing!" she exclaimed, and both turned back to Esme.

Except Esme wasn't there.

"Where did she go?" Bettina whispered.

This sudden disappearance reminded Pamela of the way Esme had vanished from the Voorhees House living room Wednesday night. The recollection of that moment, combined with the otherworldly sounds produced by the dragon fruit and the eggplant, made Pamela feel curiously dislocated, as if she was observing the scene from afar.

"Where did she go?" Bettina repeated.

Pamela blinked a few times and willed herself back to reality. "Fetching another vegetable?" she suggested.

They'd entered the room where they presently stood from the hallway, but through another door, a corner of a stove could be glimpsed.

"Maybe," Bettina agreed, but it was Pamela who ventured toward what she supposed was the kitchen.

Cracked linoleum covered the floor, a stained Formica counter surrounded a grimy sink, and the stove and refrigerator dated to the fifties at the latest. A young woman was standing at the sink running water into a saucepan, but the young woman was not Esme. She turned and asked Pamela pleasantly enough what she was looking for.

"Esme," Pamela said. "My friend and I were talking to her—she was showing us her new music project, in fact. Then she just . . . vanished."

The young woman's expression as she listened to Pamela was enigmatic: a hint of a smile, a slight crease of the brow. "Esme comes and goes," she responded when Pamela finished. "Now you see her, now you don't. Especially lately . . ."

"Does she cook?" The words came out, surprising Pamela. Not quite sure why the question would even be relevant—since Esme already had access to Voorhees House, why offer a pie to gain entry?—she nonetheless elaborated. "Baking I mean, specifically. Pies?"

The hint of a smile turned into laughter. "Esme? No. Why would she?"

CHAPTER 22

"We did get the information we wanted," Bettina commented as they walked back to where Pamela had parked her serviceable compact. "Chad probably arrived at Voorhees House about six-thirty, and by nine he was dead. So, next step, what was Mervyn Fossil doing between six-thirty and nine last Wednesday?"

No sooner had she settled into the passenger seat than Bettina took her phone from her handbag. As Pamela cruised along Stafford Street and then zigzagged east to Water Street, Bettina's fingers coaxed from her phone the location and hours of Mervyn Fossil's plastic surgery practice.

"His office closes at six," she announced.

"We'll have to find his home address," Pamela said after she negotiated the turn that would take them along the Haversack River to the bridge and the east-west route that led to Arborville.

"Looking, looking . . ." Bettina murmured, continuing to finger her phone. "If we can figure out where he lives, we can see if his neighbors noticed him around on Wednesday night."

"*Or not*," Pamela added. "In which case we'll . . . *what*?"

"First things first," Bettina said. "Rome wasn't built in a day."

By the time Pamela pulled up behind Wilfred's Mercedes in the Frasers' driveway, Bettina had discovered that Mervyn Fossil lived at 3 Elipse Crescent in Kringlekamack. The two friends parted then, but not before making plans to visit Elipse Crescent the next day.

The winding dirt road was not actually Elipse Crescent, but something that led to Elipse Crescent. Bettina was behind the wheel of the Toyota with Pamela navigating. The road was one lane wide and it meandered up a slight hill, with mailboxes the only clue that it served residences. The residences themselves were set far back, hidden from passing vehicles by dense thickets of trees displaying lush summer foliage.

"It's here!" Pamela exclaimed.

They had reached a fork, with signage indicating Elipse Crescent to the right. No sooner had Bettina veered in that direction than Pamela, reading from a weathered slab of wood nailed to a post, called out, "Three Elipse Crescent." A narrow driveway, also dirt, led into the trees off to the right, and the outlines of an impressive house could be seen, but barely. A wooden gate, however, suggested that the driveway was only to be used by the house's inhabitants.

"We're not here to talk to him," Pamela reminded Bettina, "even though he might be home, since it's Saturday. We're here to talk to neighbors."

"How do we find them?" Bettina asked. She had pulled off the road onto a kind of shoulder that sloped toward a shallow ditch. Beyond the ditch was a strip of scanty grass and then a cluster of saplings. "I didn't think it would be like this, and I didn't wear the right shoes for walking around in the woods."

Her shoes were low-heeled, but a design that featured exposed toes, as well as many many narrow straps. They were bright chartreuse, which echoed one of the shades in the colorful fabric of her wrap dress.

"Let's push on," Pamela suggested. "There might be houses along Elipse Crescent that are closer to the road."

Bettina eased the Toyota off the sloping shoulder and continued on. Soon they came upon another driveway cutting off in the same direction as the one that served Mervyn Fossil's house. A posted address indicated that a house lay within the trees, but the driveway lacked a gate. Bettina swung the steering wheel to the right, and the Toyota changed course.

"Nothing ventured, nothing gained," she remarked in response to Pamela's unspoken comment. "I'm not hiking up there and ruining a pair of good shoes for nothing. Besides, it looks steep."

It *was* steep, even for the Toyota. The rugged terrain certainly offered the homeowners privacy, though Pamela wondered how they got around in snowy conditions. After a bit, a house came into view, a grand house built of wood and shingled, as if to allude to its woodsy setting, but with dramatic angles that made it modern in feel. A three-car garage to one side featured an expansive apron of earth-colored pavers, and parked on the pavers before the one open garage bay was a sleek and gleaming sports car. A vigorous-looking gray-haired man was hovering over the car, apparently polishing it.

But instead of continuing on, Bettina braked when they were still a few hundred feet away. She leaned across Pamela toward the passenger-side window.

"Look down there," she said. "I think that's Mervyn Fossil's house."

The hill they had climbed meant they were now looking down at the property they would have accessed if they had driven up Mervyn Fossil's driveway. Bettina sat up straight again and prepared to drive on as Pamela asked herself what explanation her friend would come up with for this excursion onto a stranger's secluded property. And the stranger by now had noticed he had visitors.

As the man watched, Bettina allowed the Toyota to creep ahead, braking and turning off the ignition within several yards of where he stood. Then she pushed the car door open and hopped out, calling a cheerful, "Hello there!" She waved. "Mervyn Fossil! I love your car!"

The man advanced, polishing cloth in hand. "I'm not Mervyn Fossil," he said when he was close enough to speak at a normal volume. "This is a Jaguar. Merv's got a Lamborghini."

"Don't tell me I have the wrong address!" Bettina raised a hand to her mouth. It was obvious to Pamela that her confused amazement was feigned, but the man simply responded, "An easy mistake. Number three is next door."

"Do you think he's home now?" Bettina asked with a flirtatious tilt of the head.

"The Lamborghini is home," the man said. "I saw it drive into its garage a while ago." Noticing Bettina's puzzlement as she surveyed the thick woods surrounding his house, the man added, "One of my upstairs windows looks down on Merv's place."

Despite the polishing cloth and the grubby jeans, the man had the distinguished air and easy confidence of the financially successful.

"Would you know if he was around last Wednesday night?"

The man blinked and twitched slightly, as if not sure what he had heard. Then he said, "Why don't you ask him yourself? Like I said, he's right next door."

"Well . . ." Bettina drew the word out as if postponing a confession.

"Well . . ." the man repeated with a teasing smile as he watched her closely.

"He might not want to tell me."

"Uh-oh!" The man laughed. "I thought you were looking for him. What's Merv been up to, anyway?"

"I can't really say." Bettina leavened the comment with a wink. "But maybe you were at your upstairs window watching for the Lamborghini . . ."

"Okay, Sherlock." The man laughed again, seemingly won over by Bettina's coquettishness. "The Lamborghini was, in fact, home last Wednesday night. It had an early start that day, up and out at dawn for morning surgery, but it was back home by dinnertime."

The man resumed polishing his Jaguar then, after suggesting that Bettina pull up and turn around rather than trying to back down. Maneuvering down the steep and narrow driveway required concentration even so, but as Bettina reached the end and prepared to swing left onto Elipse Crescent, she murmured, "I wonder if

Mervyn Fossil has another car. A Lamborghini would be a pretty conspicuous vehicle, especially if you were up to no good."

"Didn't we already ask Spud and Win whether they noticed anything out of the ordinary on Wednesday?" Pamela said. "I'd think they would have noticed any car, not just a Lamborghini."

Bettina made the turn. They passed Mervyn Fossil's driveway and then veered left onto the winding dirt road that seemed the only access to the grand houses hidden in the Kringlekamack woods. Soon they were back on a paved road, heading south, and Pamela was musing on the implications of what they had learned.

"Mervyn Fossil probably didn't kill Chad," she observed, mostly to give words to the thoughts swirling in her mind. "But Chad's wife could have killed Chad."

"We have to find out more about her."

"Starting with her name," Pamela suggested. "And if it's not her, it has to be Edmund. I can't think of any other possibilities."

Pamela returned to her musing and didn't speak again until the Toyota was speeding along the stretch of County Road that bordered the nature preserve. She'd been enjoying the soothing effect of the huge trees, so fully in leaf, and the shadowy spaces between them that seemed to beckon a person into a secret world.

"What if there are two killers?" she blurted suddenly, surprising herself with the idea. "It could explain a lot, especially Mervyn Fossil's alibi for last Wednesday."

"He killed Tassie," Bettina exclaimed, "but not Chad."

"So he inherits Voorhees House," Pamela added.

"*Maybe*. We were never sure whether Tassie had a will leaving it to Chad."

"And Chad's ex-wife killed Chad."

They had reached Orchard Street, and soon Bettina was pulling into the Frasers' driveway.

"There's lots more to figure out," Pamela said. "The time frame for Tassie's murder is much wider than for Chad's, and she could have been killed in the middle of the night—while your new friend was sleeping instead of keeping tabs on the Lamborghini."

"He's not my new friend!" Bettina turned to Pamela with a smile that she tried to disguise.

"He acted like he wished he was."

"We found out what we wanted," Bettina replied demurely. "At least about Wednesday night."

The excursion to Kringlekamack had taken up the whole morning. Pamela crossed the street to her own house, collected her mail on the porch, greeted the cats, and checked her email. She made a quick cheese omelet for lunch and then, with Knit and Nibble scheduled to meet at her house the following Tuesday, she devoted the afternoon to housecleaning.

Several hours later, the house clean and dinner eaten, she was lying on the sofa with Catrina at her side. The day had been demanding—both mentally, with the visit to Kringlekamack, and physically, with the vacuuming and dusting and scrubbing. Pete was spending Father's Day weekend with his children, and it was supremely pleasant to do nothing at all.

But just as she was about to drop off to sleep, Catrina's purring was interrupted by the doorbell's chime. Pamela struggled to her feet and rounded the corner into the entry. Beyond the lace that curtained the front door's oval window, only a dim shape was visible in the gathering dusk. She switched the porch light on to reveal a tall figure, female, with light hair that cascaded past her shoulders, and she opened the door to greet Sibyl Larkin.

"There's a deer," Sibyl explained without preface. "In the back." She stepped aside as if to invite Pamela to venture over the threshold. "It's eating my dad's perennial bed, but it's really pretty."

Pamela followed Sibyl down the steps and across the lawn to the sidewalk. "This way," Sibyl whispered, "but we have to be quiet."

A slate path ran along the side of Richard Larkin's house, skirting the tall hedge that marked the boundary with Pamela's lot. Sibyl started down the path with Pamela behind, stepping carefully because the path was uneven. When Sibyl stopped, holding out an arm to signal that Pamela should stop too, Pamela looked up.

Richard Larkin stood before her, but not facing her. And she, for a few moments at least, was more interested in the vision that Sibyl had summoned her to share.

The perennial bed was in full bloom. Iris in shades of purple and blue rose from clusters of bladelike leaves, and pink peonies weighed down by ruffled petals strained their slender stems. Hosta—dark green, light green, variegated—sent up shoots sprouting belllike blossoms in white and lavender. Tucked here and there were tulips, sprays of salvia, masses of smooth leaves, velvety leaves, spotted leaves.

Browsing among this bounty was a deer, a doe

probably, given that it had no horns. It glowed golden brown against the intense green of the yard, with all colors intensified by the gathering dusk. Its delicate legs, stepping here and there among the plants, seemed barely sturdy enough to support its sleek body. It raised its head, showing its elegant muzzle in profile, and one expressive eye. Its large ears shifted forward and back, alert to any threat.

Though they were all as still and silent as they could be, the deer suddenly lifted its head and froze. With a graceful leap, it cleared the perennial bed and slipped through a leafy thicket at the back corner of the yard.

Richard Larkin turned then, clothed in a pair of worn jeans and a faded T-shirt to which his lanky body gave a kind of elegance. Seeming as surprised as the deer had been, he stared at Pamela and then whispered her name.

"The deer's gone, Dad," Sibyl said. "You don't have to whisper."

Pamela spoke up, in her normal voice, though being face-to-face with him had paused her breathing for a moment. She'd waved at him in a neighborly fashion over the past months, and even found him a kitten to adopt. His presence this close was something different, however—a physical sensation that left her nearly dazed. Grateful that, since he'd just returned from a week away, a banality wouldn't be out of place, she managed, "Welcome back. How was Maine?"

A smile came and went, leaving his angular features at rest and the gaze with which he regarded her as serious as if he was about to ask her something much less banal in return. His response, however, was a simple, "Productive. Very productive," after which he shifted his gaze to the grass at his feet.

"That's . . . that's good to hear." Pamela spoke to his bowed head, a relief from the curious experience, for her, of having to look up to meet the eyes of a conversation partner.

"And you?" He raised his head. "You've been well?" Again, the gaze was probing.

"Very well, yes."

"And Penny?"

"Having an adventure building a school in Guatemala."

Discovering that she could chat about everyday things calmed her down, and they did chat, then, with Sibyl joining in, about the deer and other things, until the dusk gave way to darkness.

Back at home, Pamela was happy to find a new email from Penny and to be able to respond with news of the deer and greetings from Richard and Sibyl.

It was Sunday morning, and the coffee was ready, so tempting with its aroma that Pamela could barely resist pouring a cup. Bettina had said to wait, though, and not to bother with toast. Thus, Pamela occupied herself setting out two rose-garlanded cups, saucers, and little plates from her wedding china, arranging napkins and silverware, and pouring a goodly splash of heavy cream into the cut-glass cream pitcher already in place beside its companion sugar bowl.

From the corner of the kitchen where the cats took their meals, Precious looked up in seeming puzzlement, as if curious about the change in routine. The other two had already finished their breakfast, and Catrina had gone off to nap in the sunny spot on the entry carpet.

But then the doorbell chimed, and a few moments later, Bettina was crossing the threshold with a white bakery box in hand.

"Crumb cake, like I promised," she announced, "because we haven't had it for a while."

Pamela accepted the box and led the way to the kitchen, past the slumbering cat.

"Wilfred went out for it first thing," Bettina continued, "even though it's Father's Day and he should be the one being pampered. But we're going to Wilfred Jr.'s later and they're doing a barbecue."

"Coffee's all ready," Pamela said as she set the box on the table and tugged at the bow that secured the string.

Bettina fetched the carafe from the stove and tipped it over one cup and then the other, monitoring the dark brew's rise against the pale porcelain. Meanwhile, Pamela folded back the top flap of the bakery box and transferred a portion of crumb cake to each plate.

"I have something to report," Bettina said en route to the table from replacing the carafe on the stove. "But first . . ." She pulled the sugar bowl and cream pitcher closer and began the process of transforming the dark and bitter contents of her cup into a sweet elixir the color of a camelhair coat.

When she was through and had taken a sip that left her smiling the smile of a contented cat, she said, "I know all about Chad's ex-wife now."

Pamela had been just about to sample her first bite of crumb cake, but she lowered her fork back onto her plate.

"Tell me more," she said. "And how did you find out what you found out?"

"The *Advocate* has been privy to more details about

Chad from the police department. Her name is Samantha Blanton, now. She went back to her birth name after the divorce. No children, so she had no need to stay in touch with him in any way."

"I don't suppose the police revealed whether they've talked to her."

Bettina had taken a large bite of crumb cake to complement the many sips of coffee that had followed the first taste, and Pamela had to wait until she swallowed.

"You're right not to suppose," she said at last. "That was not revealed."

"Maybe she's got an online presence though." The forkful of crumb cake was still waiting, but coffee seemed a more fitting accompaniment to sleuthing. Pamela lifted her cup to her lips. "Samantha Blanton isn't a very common name," she added after a moment.

"I'll get my phone." Bettina rested her fork on her plate and leaned on the table to push herself to her feet, which were shod in the chartreuse sandals she had worn the previous day. On this day, they were paired with a sleeveless jumpsuit in the same bright chartreuse. Bold jade earrings completed the look.

While Bettina was fetching her phone, Pamela transported the neglected bite of crumb cake to her mouth. The taste of Co-Op bakery crumb cake, familiar as it was, never failed to delight—rich, moist, and hinting of lemon, with a buttery crumb topic infused with sugar and cinnamon. She followed up with a long sip of pleasantly bitter black coffee.

Bettina's fingers were already busy as she appeared in the doorway holding her phone and made her way to the table. Pamela watched attentively as, once seated, she continued her online search, murmuring to herself. Bettina smiled, then frowned. Her busy fingers speeded up, then slowed down as she hummed and bent closer to the screen of the device.

"'On the Road with Sam,'" she announced, raising her head to address Pamela. "Samantha Blanton has a travel blog, and she's been exploring Spain in a van since mid-May."

"I guess we should think more about Edmund," Pamela said. "He's the only suspect we've got left— unless we want to believe Esme is the killer."

"Clayborn's still working on that angle . . . I guess." Bettina nodded, a meditative nod like a gentle, rocking motion. "Searching for the definitive *something* that will confirm her guilt. And he hinted that they believe she had an accomplice."

Silence descended then, with neither Pamela nor Bettina seeming disposed to pursue that topic or introduce a new one. The crumb cake and coffee offered comfort, not meager, but the idea of Esme being tried for murder had taken on a new reality, and it had joined them at the little table like an unwelcome guest.

CHAPTER 23

After breakfast Monday morning, Pamela had spent an hour checking over the three evaluations and the copyedited book review for Fiber Craft. She had sent them off and gotten a swift response: a thank-you and a promise of more work to come soon. But now she was standing at her kitchen counter happily rolling out dough.

Local blueberries had begun appearing at the Co-Op, and she had decided to take advantage of the bounty by serving blueberry pie to the Knit and Nibble group. A vintage pie pan waited nearby, bottom crust already in place and heaped with dark, purplish berries.

She gently shifted the dough on the pastry mat, sprinkled more flour to guard against sticking, shifted the dough back into place, and resumed rolling. When the dough had grown to a circle that would cover the heap of blueberries in the pie pan with enough overhang to crimp a pretty edge, she set the rolling pin aside. The next step was to fold the dough in half, handling it carefully, and fold it in half again.

Now she had a triangle that could easily be lifted and placed atop the berries, with its point right at the pie's center. She unfolded it then, smoothed it over the berries, and trimmed the overhang, bottom crust included, to leave an even inch remaining beyond the rim of the pie pan. She folded that surplus under neatly all the way around. Then, using the first two fingers of her left hand and the thumb of her right hand, she worked her way around the pie's perimeter, crimping the ridge of dough into a scalloped edge.

The last step was to cut steam vents in the top crust. Tidy, symmetrical steam vents raying out from the center like spokes were her preference, though not all pie-makers were so fastidious. The steam vents in the pies delivered to the Voorhees House had been disturbingly haphazard. And she'd recently seen another pie with haphazard steam vents too, somewhere. It was a shame, actually, to go to all that effort and then be in such a hurry at the end as not to finish up in a tidy way.

The light that indicated the oven was heating up had just clicked off, and she slipped the pie onto the top rack and turned away to clean up the counter. Before she had done more than tuck a measuring cup and set of measuring spoons into the dishwasher, though, the phone rang. She dried her hands and picked up the handset.

"Pam Paterson?" said a voice, vaguely familiar.

"Yes?" she replied.

"Joanie Grail," the voice went on. "At the library. We're putting together an exhibit highlighting local craftspeople, and we're wondering if you or anyone in your knitting group would like to add an item to the display."

"Oh . . . oh, sure." Pamela reached for a notepad and pen on the counter behind her. "I'm seeing the group tomorrow. I'll put the word out. Sounds like fun."

She noted Joanie Grail's contact information and returned to her cleanup job.

Pam, she mused as she worked. She'd never been *Pam*, though people called her that sometimes. And her husband had been Michael, not Mike. Pete, on the other hand, was Pete, not Peter. Penny was just Penny, though some Pennys were Penelope.

Sometimes the connections were harder to see. Tassie's given name, for example, was Anastasia, according to the article that had appeared in the *Register* after her death, and her real last name was Huntington, not Hunt. The name embroidered on the children's clothes in the secret room at Voorhees House was Elizabeth. What could a nickname for Elizabeth be? Liz, of course. Beth too.

The pie-making bowls and equipment had all been stowed in the dishwasher, and the pastry mat had been washed and draped over the drainer to dry. It was time to turn the oven temperature down and, that done, Pamela repaired to the sofa to knit, while keeping an attentive eye on the clock as the aroma of blueberries melding with sugar in a crust growing golden brown wafted from the kitchen.

Soon it was time to take the pie out. Pamela set her knitting aside, nearly finished with the first section of the new in-progress donkey. The marigold-yellow donkey was all sewn together and stuffed, ready to present to Nell tomorrow night.

In the kitchen, she opened the oven and leaned toward its warm interior to check that the pie was really done. The pie's top was pale golden brown, with the scalloped edge of crust a slightly deeper shade. The rich purple syrup produced as the blueberries baked had oozed from the steam vents, calling attention to the spokelike pattern of Pamela's careful slits.

Esme, according to her friend at the commune, barely knew how to turn the stove on, so she certainly would not have baked a pie of any kind. And Pamela was sure that Edmund, if he had baked a pie, would have done the job with the precision befitting his taste in clothes and décor. Yet the pie that had appeared on the kitchen counter in Voorhees House on the occasion of each murder had been crafted so carelessly.

Surely the pie was a clue, but in what direction did that clue point?

Pamela reached for a pair of potholders and lifted the pie to the stovetop. Then she darted into the entry and peeked through the lace that curtained the oval window in the front door to check whether either of the Frasers' cars was gone. Both were there, and she hurried across the street. Ignoring the doorbell, she tapped vigorously on the door.

It was Bettina who answered, looking startled.

"What's wrong?" she inquired as she leaned forward to study Pamela's face. "Has something happened to Penny?"

Realizing her message, though significant, wasn't as dramatic as her excitement must have implied, Pamela took a deep breath.

"It can't be Esme or Edmund," she said. "But the pies are the answer, somehow. We have to keep thinking."

Back at home, she detoured through the kitchen to admire her own very tidy pie and ascended the stairs to her office. As she had suspected, an email from her boss lurked in her inbox, complete with the stylized paperclip that indicated attachments. But she didn't feel like working again, yet, after spending an hour first thing that morning dispatching her previous *Fiber Craft* assignment.

Instead, she clicked on "Favorites" and from that list chose AccessArborville. She scanned the new messages. Gone were the conversations about Voorhees House—the murders, the hauntings, and even the house's likely value on the real estate market—that had been so lively. In their place were more mundane postings: a lost dog, a trundle bed for sale, a need for a reliable airport limo service.

Just as she was about to leave the site, however, a new post popped up.

"Are the police asking the right questions about the Voorhees House murders?" it read. "Who needs fingerprints or DNA when you have pies? Every cook has her own style, but some people, suspects even, don't cook at all." It was signed, "Bettina on Orchard Street."

"Okay." Pamela shrugged. She herself wouldn't have posted such a thing, but maybe Bettina thought Detective Clayborn needed a nudge—and that sharing the nudge with the inhabitants of Arborville, at least those who paid attention to AccessArborville, would enhance its effect.

She returned to her inbox and read the message from her boss instructing her to evaluate the attached articles. Opening a file labeled "Scarlet Letter," she found "Was the Scarlet Letter Really Scarlet? The

Dyer's Art in Early New England," written by T.C. Lambert at the University of Massachusetts. But then her stomach reminded her that the nutritive possibilities of toast and black coffee had long since been exhausted, so before setting to work, she had a quick lunch of canned lentil soup.

An hour later, the ringing telephone distracted her from Professor Lambert's argument that the scarlet letter in Hawthorne's novel couldn't have been the color recognized as "scarlet" in the twenty-first century, or the twentieth, or even the latter part of the nineteenth—because the natural dyes dyers relied upon in the era before aniline dyes were invented created much softer tones.

"Interesting, interesting," she murmured as she swiveled around to pick up the phone.

Bettina's voice reached her from the other end of the line. "I'm at Libby Kimble's," she announced, "and she suggested I invite you to join us. She said it's been a while since we all had a nice visit."

"I'm in the middle of an article for *Fiber Craft*," Pamela said, twisting her head to glance back at her computer's screen.

"All work and no play . . ." Bettina caroled. "You know the rest."

"Really, Bettina, it's not like actual work. The article is interesting."

"We're having coffee and pie"—Bettina's voice sank to a whisper—"and I think Libby is really lonely. Remember, she lost her mother not all that long ago, and she tells me her grandson's leaving when his parents get back from Europe . . ."

"Pie!" Pamela felt her body tense. "Bettina," she whispered back, "be careful. I'm coming."

She made sure to grab her phone on her way out of the house.

Zach Kimble, the wrestling-champion grandson, met her at the door, greeting her as "Ms. Paterson" and dipping his head in a slight bow.

"They're in the kitchen," he explained, stepping back as she entered, and gesturing down the hall. "Just go on in."

The hall led past the pretty living room, off to the left, with the family gallery of photos on the table by the window. As Pamela got closer to the kitchen doorway, on the right and farther down, she could make out Libby speaking in the mild voice that went with her colorless, undemanding looks.

"Such a surprise," she was saying. "I'm related to the Voorhees family, in a sense, and to think I only found that out when my mother—the woman I thought was my mother—was on her deathbed."

Pamela reached the doorway and turned the corner into the cozy kitchen with its frilly curtains at the windows. Bettina and Libby occupied two of the four wooden chairs that surrounded an old-fashioned maple table. Libby looked up and smiled.

"Yes, you were right about the pies," she said. "Here's one I just made this morning. Help yourself to a piece."

The pie, missing two slices, sat in the middle of the table. A large knife, its blade smeared with dark purple syrup from the pie's juicy filling, sat next to it. The steam vents visible in the pie's crust were haphazard slashes, leaking the dark syrup like wounds. Pamela held back, though, transfixed by Libby's voice, which was calm, almost monotonous.

"Edith Voorhees was my mother, but Jack Voorhees wasn't my father. My father lived in this house, right here on Catalpa Street. He and Edith were neighbors—this house backs right up to the side yard of Voorhees House. They became lovers, and his wife became my adoptive mother. My father and my adoptive mother never had children of their own, and she was very forgiving. It was an era when women felt they had no purpose unless they had a child to raise."

Pamela heard footsteps in the hall. She glanced toward the doorway to see Zach lurking around the corner holding a large pillow.

Libby grabbed Bettina's hand. "I know you've been nosing around about the Voorhees House murders," she said, "but you're such a sympathetic person that I'm sure you'll understand when you know why I did it."

"Did what?" Bettina asked.

Libby continued to speak but ignored that question. "Tassie inherited Voorhees House through Jack's younger brother, Joe—because Jack had no real offspring of his own. My adoptive mother had sworn never to reveal my true origins, but after Edith died, she decided I could—*should*—know the truth. When she herself was near death, she told me who I really am, Edith Voorhees's daughter. Jack forced Edith to give me up, and Edith retreated into her own world, knitting and knitting and knitting. Everyone in the neighborhood knew her as an eccentric recluse, but I didn't know she was my mother."

"You're the baby in the hand-knit christening gown," Pamela said, "in the photo in the living room."

"That photo was always on the table by the window when I was growing up. I never knew who it was until . . ." Libby's voice trailed off.

"And you're Elizabeth . . . Libby . . . Elizabeth. She knit so many clothes for you, whole wardrobes, and hid them away in a secret room. The christening gown is in there too."

Libby shifted her gaze to the doorway and nodded, whereupon Zach lunged across the threshold, still holding the pillow. His free hand held something else, a pair of plastic zip ties. He handed the pillow to Libby and, with a quick move like those that must have discomfited his opponents in the wrestling ring, stooped over Bettina and used the zip ties to anchor one wrist and then the other to the sturdy front legs of her chair.

That done, he pulled Pamela to her feet and pinned both arms behind her, while seeming to enjoy Bettina's futile squirming.

"Go on, Grandma," he urged, as calmly as if immobilizing people with zip ties was an everyday event for him. "You deserve to have your story heard."

In a quavering monotone, Libby explained that she had approached Tassie and Chad, seeking some acknowledgment of Edith's pain at the hands of the Voorhees family, but her entreaty was rebuffed. In fact, they laughed and pointed out that neither she nor Edith were related to the Voorhees family by blood, whereas Tassie's mother, Mildred, had been Joe Voorhees's daughter.

"So . . ." Libby nodded firmly and tightened her already-thin lips into an implacable line. "I decided Voorhees House would stay empty. Zach and I"—the tiniest smile softened her expression as she glanced up at him—"worked out a plan. The pies were gifts.

Who'd turn away a neighbor bearing a home-baked pie? And then, once we were inside . . . I think you know the rest."

She half-stood and extended the pillow toward her grandson. He seized it with his right hand while tightening the already-tight grip of his left hand on Pamela's arm and attempting to drag her backward. In her mind, Pamela saw herself flung to the floor or trapped against the wall, as the pillow, pressed against her face, relentlessly cut off her air supply. And Bettina would be next.

She struggled against the muscular hand that held her, so close to her attacker that she could hear him breathing. Then the breathing halted, replaced by a strained gurgle. A chair scraped against the floor. Zach gurgled again, cursed, and suddenly Pamela was free—for a moment, at least.

Bettina, still fastened to the chair, lifted a foot and aimed the slender heel of her fashionable shoe at Zach's instep, bare except for the straps of his clunky sandal. An angry spot oozing blood and a small flap of loose skin suggested she had already made contact once.

He backed away, caught his balance, and stepped forward again, heading for Pamela with the menacing pillow held securely in both hands. Pamela sprang forward and seized the knife, its blade smeared with the dark crushed-blueberry syrup, from the kitchen table. She whirled around and lunged toward Zach, raising the knife high and slashing at the pillow, again and again.

As the air filled with flying down, Zach reeled back, hopping on one foot and batting the blizzard of tiny feathers away from his eyes. Libby moaned and lowered her head to her arms, which she had crossed in front of her on the table. A few feathers landed on the remains of the pie and the empty plates, sticking fast to the sugary puddles. Pamela kept a grip on the knife, lest Zach attempt another wrestling move.

"My phone," Bettina said. "It's in my bag, right here. Tell the police to hurry—and see if you can find a pair of scissors to cut these zip ties loose."

"I brought my own phone." Pamela tugged it from her pants pocket and managed to key in 911 without letting go of the knife.

CHAPTER 24

"I don't know how you can stand to look at another blueberry pie," Bettina exclaimed. "Even one that you made yourself."

The pie in question sat on Pamela's dining room table, with a lace tablecloth under it. Arranged around the table were six small wedding-china plates, six wedding-china cups nestled onto their saucers, and six napkins, six forks, and six spoons—all in preparation for when the pie would be sliced and served with coffee and tea at eight p.m. The antique crystal chandelier cast a gentle light over the scene.

"This pie will have ice cream," Pamela said. "Of course, if you'd prefer not to have a slice . . ."

"I'll see how I feel when the time comes. Yours is much nicer though—I can see that." Bettina leaned close to inspect the pie's crust. "Libby isn't really a very good baker." She straightened up and turned her attention to Pamela. "How late did Pete stay?"

"Till about ten." Pamela moved a few cup and saucer

sets to make the arrangement more symmetrical. "I certainly appreciated Wilfred cooking dinner last night, and it was thoughtful of him to include Pete."

"Pete was part of it all, really—finding the secret room with the christening gown and all the clothes Edith knit for 'Elizabeth.'"

"Marcy Brewer tracked him down this morning, you know," Pamela said. "He called me around lunchtime."

"She'll squeeze all she can out of the story, I'm sure. I can see the headline in tomorrow's *Register*." Bettina's voice took on a dramatic quality. "'Local Handyman Held Key to Family Secret Behind Murder Plot.'"

"And there she was yesterday in the parking lot, all ready to pounce on us when we finished giving our statements at the police station." Pamela stepped toward the kitchen doorway, still talking. "Penny knows all about it now too. Her friend Lorie texted her to look at the *Register* online. I had to talk her out of coming home early."

Bettina had followed her to the kitchen, where Pamela measured coffee beans into her grinder while Bettina spooned loose tea into one of Pamela's thrift-shop teapots. The beans clattered briefly in the grinder, subsiding to a smooth whir.

"Zach Kimble will be in the *Advocate* this Friday," Bettina commented with a laugh. "Just not in the form he—or Libby—expected when I interviewed him." The conversation was interrupted by the doorbell's chime.

"I'll get it," Bettina said. As a happy hubbub of greeting reached her ears, Pamela finished preparing for the coffee service at break time.

A few minutes later, she entered the living room to see Holly and Karen on the sofa and Roland on the hassock at the far end of the hearth. Roland was already hard at work on his knitting. Bettina was perched on the hearth itself, as if poised to respond when the doorbell chimed again.

Holly looked up. She studied Pamela for a moment, smiled, and then commented, "None the worse for wear, I'm happy to see. And Bettina, of course, is as chic as ever."

Bettina extended a foot shod in a stiletto-heeled pump and glanced at Pamela. "I know you think high heels are impractical, but you have to admit they can be useful at times." The stilettos were black patent leather, and they complemented the bold black-and-white print of Bettina's summery sheath dress.

Karen shuddered. "I hate to think what would have happened if you hadn't been able to fight off that terrible man."

Holly was still studying Pamela. "You had it all figured out even before you got to Libby Kimble's house, didn't you?" she said.

"Not exactly . . ." Pamela had been replaying the episode in her own mind. What *had* she expected when she'd responded to Bettina's summons? She remembered telling Bettina to be careful, but . . . She thought for a moment. "I knew the blueberry pies found at the crime scenes were a clue, and it occurred to me yesterday morning while making my own blueberry pie that I'd seen a similar one recently somewhere—on the counter at Libby's, as I later realized. I was so excited that I ran across the street to tell Bettina the pies were the answer."

Bettina cut in, "And then I posted a message on AccessArborville suggesting that the pies were the answer."

"Not such a good idea, in retrospect," Pamela said, "because Libby saw it and realized we were on to something."

"Not such a good idea at all." Roland spoke up from his spot on the hassock. "You both put yourselves in very serious danger." His lean face was serious. "I pay taxes in this town, and I would like the town's police force to solve crimes efficiently enough that ordinary people don't have to take matters into their own hands."

Holly reared up and addressed Roland in a mock-scolding tone. "Pamela and Bettina are far from 'ordinary'!"

Roland frowned in puzzlement, then shook off his momentary confusion to say, "No, of course not, not ordinary in the least," and returned to his knitting.

"But then, in Libby's kitchen, as it was all happening, I realized things I should have realized sooner." Pamela was still standing just inside the arch between the entry and the living room. Everyone else was seated, and all eyes were on her. Feeling a bit self-conscious, she lowered herself into the extra chair she always set out when the Knit and Nibble group was due.

"The clothes in the secret room . . ." (Marcy Brewer had made sure readers of the *Register* knew all about that fascinating dimension of the story.) "The clothes in the secret room," Pamela repeated, "were a piece of the puzzle. Why had Edith Voorhees devoted her life to knitting whole wardrobes for a person who seemed . . . imaginary? But the answer to that question was right in front of me, or it should have been."

Bettina leaned forward and nearly stood up. "Libby isn't the most common nickname for Elizabeth," she said. "Yes, some of the knitted garments were personalized with the name Elizabeth, but who would see that as a link to Libby Kimble?"

"It seems obvious now that we know the whole story." Pamela nodded. "Libby's father and Edith were neighbors, so close that their houses backed right up to each other, and then they were lovers, and then Edith became pregnant, and then Jack Voorhees forced Edith to give up the child because he knew it wasn't his. And later, because the houses were so close, Libby and her grandson could easily carry out their nefarious plans without people in the neighborhood seeing them—no car needed."

"That poor woman!" Holly cried, the expression in her dark eyes echoing her tragic tone. "I wonder how soon she had to give the baby away. And then afterward, all those years, she was probably watching from her windows, catching an occasional glimpse of her daughter coming and going from the Catalpa Street house."

"Edith knit the christening gown," Pamela said, "so perhaps Jack didn't know right away that he wasn't Elizabeth's father."

"Maybe the christening gown was handed over with the baby," Holly suggested. "Both taken from Edith against her will."

"Edith kept the christening gown," Pamela explained. "It was preserved in the secret room too, on a very lifelike baby doll lying in an antique bassinette. But a photo of Elizabeth in the christening gown accompanied Elizabeth to her new home."

As she spoke those words, the image of the photo as she had seen it on the table in Libby's living room rose before her eyes. Then, next to it, rose the image of the doll in the actual gown.

Karen, at Holly's side on the sofa, was looking more and more dejected. "So sad," she murmured in her gentle voice. "So terribly, terribly sad."

In fact, gloom had descended over the entire group. Even Roland, who was still knitting—albeit more slowly—seemed affected. Everyone else's knitting bag sat untouched, so caught up had the knit and nibblers been in the conversation. Then Bettina rose from her temporary perch on the hearth and picked up her knitting bag. There was space for another person on the sofa, so she took a few steps in that direction, and then . . . she hiccupped with a quick intake of breath.

"Where's Nell?" she exclaimed. "We've been talking and talking and . . ."

"She probably walked." Holly moaned. "I offered her a ride, but you know Nell." She checked her watch. "It's quite a ways past seven now. What could have happened?"

Just then Nell peeked around the corner from the entry. "I've been here listening the whole time," she said. "The door was ajar, so I let myself in."

"Nell! Thank goodness you're okay!" Bettina, still on her feet, dashed across the carpet and wrapped an arm around Nell's waist. "Come and sit in your favorite chair." She tugged Nell toward the comfortable armchair by the hearth that was always reserved for her. "We were just having a little chat," she said. "Everyone was curious about . . . about . . ."

"It was all in the *Register*." Nell sighed. "The whole tragic tale, but at least now there's an explanation for those deaths that doesn't depend on ghosts, though it does add another chapter to the sad history of Voorhees House."

As if to set an example, she quickly took her seat,

extracted an in-progress donkey part from her knitting bag, and set to work. Holly and Karen, too, rummaged in their knitting bags and were soon bent over their busy needles.

Pamela was happy then to fetch the marigold-yellow donkey, complete even to ears and tail, from the bookshelf where it had been waiting. She presented it to Nell, amid coos of admiration from Holly and Karen, and explained that another was underway. But Bettina elicited even more coos with a project that was a surprise even to Pamela.

The royal-blue yarn had been set aside, and in its place Bettina was cradling a skein of delicate, pale-pink yarn in her lap.

"Did you finish the sweater for your son?" Holly inquired from her seat right next to Bettina.

"No . . ." Bettina drew the syllable out with a lilting tone and a teasing smile that hinted at a secret to be revealed. She paused for effect. When she was certain of everyone's attention, even Roland's, she said, "I'm getting ready to welcome my granddaughter-to-be!"

Everyone spoke at once, words of congratulation overlapping in a complicated chorus.

"Yes, yes!" Bettina was beaming. "It's true. Maxie got her test results back, and she's going to have a little girl. And this"—she held up her needles with an inch of lacy, pale-pink knitting already completed—"is going to be a little sweater. She's to be born in the fall, so she'll need sweaters."

"Awesome!" Holly smiled her dimple-embellished smile and clapped her hands.

And Karen followed up with, "I have lots and lots of cute patterns from when Lily was a baby. I'll bring some next week."

"A very fortunate little girl," Nell said, "with so much love all around her."

"I wonder if Libby was really loved," Holly said, "by her adoptive mother, I mean." Though this question was tangential to the details of the murders themselves, she nonetheless glanced at Nell to check for disapproval.

But Nell remained focused on the steady rhythm of her needles, and her expression was serene. Watching her, and thinking of the meditative state she herself enjoyed when deep into a knitting project, Pamela understood why Edith's knitting output had been so huge. The very act of knitting must have been an escape from the sorrow of her condition—and then, if she was to knit, why not fantasize that she was raising her own daughter, providing her with an ever-increasing wardrobe of lovingly crafted garments?

"I wonder"—Karen lowered her work to her lap— "how Edith could bear to give up her baby, no matter what Jack said or did. Couldn't she just leave, and raise the baby on her own?"

"It was a long time ago," Nell murmured from her chair by the hearth. She had apparently been listening attentively, albeit with a serene expression. "Women didn't have the opportunities they have now—so the choice would have been between struggling to raise her child in comparative poverty or knowing the child was well cared for."

"And apparently she was well cared for," Bettina observed. "Libby didn't seem to have any complaints about her treatment at the hands of her adoptive mother."

"Why would a woman be willing to do that though?" A troubled pucker marred Karen's pretty forehead. "Take in a child who was the result of her husband . . . being unfaithful?"

"It was a long time ago," Nell murmured again. "With so few opportunities, what would a woman do with herself if she didn't have a child to raise?"

Silence descended then, a kind of silence that hints at deep ponderings, perhaps occasioned by the Voorhees House revelations. But the pace of knitting didn't slacken. Pamela felt her breathing slow and her thoughts settle as the front leg of her in-progress donkey took shape.

Joanie Grail had called, she suddenly remembered, from the library—asking if anyone in the knitting group would like to add an item to the upcoming display of work by local craftspeople. Then she'd gotten so caught up in nicknames and pies and . . .

The donkeys could be offered, with the added benefit of highlighting Nell's work with the women's shelter, and other knitters might want to be represented as well. She'd mention it, but not yet. The silence was so welcome. But the silence was not to last.

Roland was stirring, resting his needles with their attached swath of bright turquoise on the lid of his closed briefcase. Once his hands were free, he pushed back his faultlessly starched shirt cuff to reveal the face of his impressive watch.

"Eight p.m.," he intoned. "Time to take a break."

Pamela was on her feet in an instant, hurrying to the kitchen. Soon—very soon—she had filled the kettle with water and set it atop a burner with a flame alight under it. Bettina joined her, contributing to the preparations by filling the cut-glass cream pitcher and transferring it and the sugar bowl to the dining room table. Now she watched as Pamela poured boiling water over the ground coffee in the carafe's filter cone and set more water to boil for the teapot.

"Have you decided whether you'll have some of the pie?" Pamela asked, though she suspected she knew the answer. "You could just have some ice cream plain."

Before Bettina could respond, they were interrupted by Holly, who had just stepped into the kitchen.

"They're asking what kind of pie it is," she said.

"Who's asking, specifically?" Pamela turned away from the counter, where she was monitoring the progress of the coffee. "Nell isn't the squeamish type—though she might object that the pie has too much sugar. And Roland is far too sensible to think that, because blueberry pies were connected with a murder case, a blueberry pie baked by a whole different person would be problematic. Is Karen the 'they' who is asking?"

"They're not saying they don't want to eat it," Holly explained. "And I'm part of the 'they' as well. We all remember that you've made blueberry pies in the past, and they were *amazing*, and since it's blueberry season in New Jersey . . ."

The kettle was whistling again, and Bettina handled the task of brewing the tea.

A few minutes later, all the knit and nibblers were seated around Pamela's dining room table. The small plates, all but one, held slices of blueberry pie, and the berries revealed by the slicing glistened with dark, sugary syrup. Each slice had been topped with a dollop of vanilla ice cream. The wedding-china cups had been filled with steaming coffee—or tea, in the case of Nell and Karen.

Bettina stared at her empty plate. "Don't I get a piece?" she inquired in a plaintive treble.

"You never answered when I asked if you'd decided whether to eat the pie." Pamela struggled to suppress a teasing smile.

"*This* pie is a whole different thing, I'm sure." Bettina's nod reinforced her statement.

"Well . . . in that case. Hand me your plate."

Once Bettina had been provided with her pie and ice cream, forks were raised in unison. After a chorus of *yums*, punctuated by a few groans of pleasure, the verdict was unanimous.

This blueberry pie was, indeed, a whole different thing.

KNIT

Nell's Toy Donkey

Nell Bascomb's latest knitting project is toy donkeys, destined for the children at the women's shelter where she volunteers. The donkey is a bit more complicated than some of the other KNIT projects, but it's fun to make, and it's a great gift for a favorite child.

The knitting projects in the Knit & Nibble series are not usually related to the story, but readers sometimes ask me about patterns for items the knitters are described as making. In this case, I thought it would be fun to include the pattern for Nell's donkey.

For a picture of the completed donkey as well as some in-progress photos, visit the Knit & Nibble Mysteries page at PeggyEhrhart.com. Click on the cover for *Knitmare on Beech Street* and scroll down on the page that opens. References in the directions below to photos on my website are to this page.

Use yarn identified on the label as "Medium" and/or #4, and use size 6 needles (though size 5 or 7 is fine if that's what you have). The donkey requires about 70 yards of yarn for the main color (sides and ears) and 30 yards of yarn for the secondary color (stomach and inner legs, face). You can also make the donkey all one color, in which case you will need 100 yards of yarn. You will also need two buttons for eyes and some fiberfill stuffing.

If you're not already a knitter, watching a video is a great way to master the basics of knitting. Just search the internet for "How to Knit," and you'll have your choice of tutorials that show the process clearly. The donkey is worked in the stockinette stitch, the stitch you see, for example, in a typical sweater. To create the stockinette stitch, you knit one row, then purl going back the other direction, then knit, then purl, knit, purl, back and forth. Again, it's easier to understand "purl" by viewing a video, but essentially, when you purl, you're creating the backside of "knit." To knit, you insert the right-hand needle front to back through the loop of yarn on the left-hand needle. To purl, you insert the needle back to front.

Casting on and casting off are often included in internet "How to Knit" tutorials, or you can search specifically for "Casting on" and "Casting off." The donkey uses the simple slip-knot casting on technique.

Sides

The donkey's two sides are mirror images of each other. In order to make them turn out that way, when you make the second side, you will knit every row you purled and purl every row you knit.

For the first side, cast on 5 stitches using your main color. Purl row 1. Knit row 2 increasing 1 stitch at the end of the row. You will do this by casting on an extra stitch right before you knit the last stitch. There is a photo of this step on my website. Continue to work using the stockinette stitch for 10 more rows (rows 3 to 12), increasing 1 stitch at the end of each knit row by casting on an extra stitch before the last stitch. Now you will have 11 stitches. Work using the stockinette stitch for 5 more rows, increasing 1 stitch at the end of rows 13 and 15 (purl rows), 16 (knit row), and 17 (purl row). Now you will have 15 stitches. Knit row 18. Increase 13 at the end of row 19 by casting on 13 more stitches. There is a photo of this step on my website. Now you will have 28 stitches. This is the beginning of the front leg.

Work using the stockinette stitch for 13 rows (rows 20 to 32), decreasing 1 stitch at the end of rows 20, 24, 28, and 32 (knit rows). You will decrease by knitting two stitches together. There is a photo of this technique on my website. Now you will have 24 stitches. Purl row 33. Decrease, by casting off, 10 stitches at the beginning of row 34. Now you will have 14 stitches. You have completed the front leg. Finish the row knitting.

Purl row 35. Knit row 36. Work using the stockinette stitch for 12 more rows (rows 37 to 48), decreasing 1 stitch at the end of rows 37, 41, and 45 (purl rows). Now you will have 11 stitches. Increase 10 at the end of row 49 by casting on 10 more stitches. Now you will have 21 stitches. This is the beginning of the back leg. Work using the stockinette stitch for 12 rows (rows 50 to 61). Cast off 12 at the beginning of row 62. Finish the row knitting. You have completed the back leg. Cast off the remaining stitches.

For the second side, cast on 5 stitches using your

main color. Knit row 1. Purl row 2 increasing 1 stitch at the end of the row. You will do this by casting on an extra stitch right before you purl the last stitch. There is a photo of this step on my website. Continue to work using the stockinette stitch for 10 more rows (rows 3 to 12), increasing 1 stitch at the end of each purl row by casting on an extra stitch before the last stitch. Now you will have 11 stitches. Work using the stockinette stitch for 5 more rows, increasing 1 stitch at the end of rows 13 and 15 (knit rows), 16 (purl row), and 17 (knit row). Now you will have 15 stitches. Purl row 18. Increase 13 at the end of row 19 by casting on 13 more stitches. There is a photo of this step on my website. Now you will have 28 stitches. This is the beginning of the front leg.

Work using the stockinette stitch for 13 rows (rows 20 to 32), decreasing 1 stitch at the end of rows 20, 24, 28, and 32 (purl rows). You will decrease by purling two stitches together. There is a photo of this technique on my website. Now you will have 24 stitches. Knit row 33.

Decrease, by casting off, 10 stitches at the beginning of row 34. Now you will have 14 stitches. You have completed the front leg. Finish the row purling.

Knit row 35. Purl row 36. Work using the stockinette stitch for 12 more rows (rows 37 to 48), decreasing 1 stitch at the end of rows 37, 41, and 45 (knit rows). Now you will have 11 stitches. Increase 10 at the end of row 49 by casting on 10 more stitches. Now you will have 21 stitches. This is the beginning of the back leg. Work using the stockinette stitch for 12 rows (rows 50 to 61). Cast off 12 at the beginning of row 62. You have completed the back leg. Finish the row purling. Cast off the remaining stitches.

Ears—Make 2

Using your main color, cast on 6 stitches. Knit row 1. Purl row 2, increasing 1 stitch after the first stitch in the row and 1 stitch before the last stitch in the row. Knit row 3. Purl row 4, increasing 1 stitch after the first stitch in the row and 1 stitch before the last stitch in the row. Work rows 5, 6, 7, and 8 using the stockinette stitch. Knit row 9, decreasing 1 stitch after the first stitch in the row and 1 stitch before the last stitch in the row. Purl row 10. Knit row 11. Purl row 12, decreasing 1 stitch after the first stitch in the row and 1 stitch before the last stitch in the row. Knit row 13. Purl row 14. Knit row 15, decreasing 1 stitch at the beginning of the row and 1 stitch at the end. Purl row 16. Knit row 17, decreasing 1 stitch after the first stitch in the row and 1 stitch before the last stitch in the row. Purl the last two stitches together, clip your yarn, thread the tail through the loop, and pull tight.

Stomach and Inner Legs

Using your secondary color, cast on 4 stitches. Knit row 1. Purl row 2. Knit row 3 and cast on 12 stitches at the end of the row. Purl row 4 and cast on 12 stitches at the end of the row. You will have 28 stitches. Work 11 rows using the stockinette stitch. Cast off 10 stitches at the beginning of row 16 and continue the row purling. Cast off 10 stitches at the beginning of row 17 and continue the row knitting. Work 15 rows using the stockinette stitch. Knit row 33 and cast on 10 stitches at the end of the row. Purl row 34 and cast on 10 stitches at the end of the row. Work 9 rows using the stockinette stitch. Cast off 14 stitches at the beginning of row 44 and continue the row purling. Cast off the remaining 14 stitches.

Face

Using your secondary color, cast on 2 stitches. Work 4 rows using the stockinette stitch. Knit row 5, increasing 1 stitch after the first stitch in the row and 1 stitch before the last stitch in the row, i.e., cast on 2 stitches in the middle. Work 5 rows using the stockinette stitch. Knit row 11, increasing 1 stitch after the first stitch in the row and 1 stitch before the last stitch in the row. You will have 6 stitches. Work 10 rows using the stockinette stitch. Purl row 22, decreasing 1 stitch at the beginning of the row and 1 stitch at the end of the row. Work 5 rows using the stockinette stitch. Purl row 28, decreasing 1 stitch at the beginning of the row and 1 stitch at the end of the row, i.e., purl the first 2 stitches together and purl the last 2 stitches together. You will have 2 stitches. Work 5 rows using the stockinette stitch. Purl the last two stitches together, clip your yarn, thread the tail through the loop, and pull tight.

Assembly

Assembly is complicated, and so I have posted many in-progress photos on my website.

To see the photos, visit the Knit & Nibble Mysteries page at PeggyEhrhart.com. Click on the cover for *Knitmare on Beech Street* and scroll down on the page that opens.

The first step is to sew on the buttons that you will use for eyes. It is much easier to do this now than when the donkey is all put together. Position them as you see in the photo on my website and use regular sewing thread.

Flatten one of the sides, right side down, and arrange the stomach and inner legs against it, lining up the inner legs with the outer legs, wrong sides together and with the little tab oriented toward the donkey's head. Using a yarn needle—a large needle with a large eye and a blunt tip—and the yarn that was your main color, sew all around the edges. To make a neat seam, use a whip stitch and catch only the outer loops along each side. Repeat this process with the other side.

Sew up the donkey's rear and part of its back, leaving an opening of 3 or so inches on the back to insert the fiberfill stuffing. Position the face between the two sides of the head as shown in the photo on my website and sew it into place. Sew up the donkey's front and neck.

Stuff the donkey with fiberfill stuffing, making sure to tuck the stuffing into the legs and the head all the way to the nose. Sew up the rest of the back. Position the ears as shown on my website and sew them into place. The wide end of the ears, where you cast on, goes against the head.

Cut 3 10-inch strands of yarn in the main color, and with your yarn needle, pull each strand through at the spot where the donkey's rear meets its back, leaving 5 inches on each side. Arrange the strands in 3 groups of 2 and braid them to form the tail. Secure the braid with a bit of thread.

Your donkey is now complete.

NIBBLE

Pamela's Blueberry Pie

In *Knitmare on Beech Street*, a careless blueberry pie with jagged slits in the top crust turns out to be the killer's calling card, but Pamela redeems this classic summer dessert when she bakes a nice one to serve to the Knit and Nibble group. Here is her recipe.

For a picture of the pie, as well as some in-progress photos, visit the Knit & Nibble Mysteries page at PeggyEhrhart.com. Click on the cover for *Knitmare on Beech Street* and scroll down on the page that opens. References in the directions below to photos on my website are to this page.

Ingredients
2¼ cups sifted flour
1 tsp salt
⅔ cup plus 1 tbsp shortening
½ cup cold water (approximately)
2 pints fresh blueberries
1 tbsp cider or white vinegar

¾ cup sugar, or a full cup if desired
3 tbsp flour
½ tsp cinnamon
Pinch of salt

Make the pie dough

Sift flour and salt into a medium-sized bowl. Using two knives or a pastry blender, cut in the shortening until the mixture resembles coarse or pebbly sand. Sprinkle with water while tossing with a fork until the dough comes together in large clumps. If dry spots remain, use a little more water. With floured hands, push the dough into two balls of dough, one a bit larger than the other. (The large one will be your bottom crust.) At this point, the dough can be wrapped in plastic wrap and refrigerated, but if you refrigerate it for an hour or more, it will need to soften up a bit before you can work with it.

Prepare the blueberries

Wash the blueberries and pick them over, removing any stems or squashed berries. Sprinkle them with the vinegar. Mix the sugar, flour, cinnamon, and pinch of salt in a small bowl, sprinkle it over the berries, and mix gently with a large spoon.

Assemble the pie

Liberally flour a cutting board, pastry cloth, or other surface. (I use a Kitchen Aid Silicone Bakeware Baking Mat.) Starting with the larger ball of dough, put the dough ball on the rolling surface, sprinkle it with flour, and flatten it slightly with your hands. Flour your rolling pin and roll the dough ball into a circle about an inch larger all around than your pie pan. As you work, turn the dough over frequently and sprinkle more flour on it and on your rolling surface to keep it from sticking.

When your circle is large enough, fold it in quarters and transfer it to your pie pan, arranging it so the point of the triangle is more or less in the center of the pie pan. (There is a photo of this on my website.) Unfold the triangle and pat the crust into place, curving it up and over the sides of the pie pan. Scoop the berries into the pie pan and gently spread them over the bottom crust.

Roll out the smaller ball of dough, proceeding as you did for the larger ball. When the circle is large enough to cover your pie pan with an extra half inch all around, fold it into quarters. Set it atop the berries with the point of the triangle more or less in the center, unfold it, and smooth it out.

Tuck the overhanging crust under all the way around and pat and smooth it until it's merged with the bottom crust. To make a fancy edge, place the index and middle finger of your left hand on the edge, pointing outward and with half an inch between them. Use the thumb of your right hand to push a little ridge into the dough, working your way all around the edge of the pie doing the same thing. (There is a photo of this on my website.) With a sharp knife, slice a few steam vents into the top crust, in a decorative pattern if you wish.

Bake the pie at 425 degrees for 10 minutes, then turn the oven down to 350 degrees and bake for 30 to 40 minutes longer. The pie is done when the crust is lightly browned, especially around the edges.

The pie is delicious served with ice cream, especially while it's still warm.

Visit our website at
KensingtonBooks.com
to sign up for our newsletters, read
more from your favorite authors, see
books by series, view reading group
guides, and more!

Become a Part of Our
Between the Chapters Book Club
Community and Join the Conversation

Submit your book review for a chance to win exclusive
Between the Chapters swag you can't get anywhere else!
https://www.kensingtonbooks.com/pages/review/